PRAISE FOR *OCCULT AND BATTERY*

"Family secrets, old mansions, and a growing list of murder victims—these elements and more blend together to make an intriguing as well as entertaining cozy mystery."
—*RT Book Reviews*

"It's fast-paced; [Gregory] never misses a beat. There's mystery mixed with just a small hint of romance and paranormal activity. It's the perfect blend for cozy mystery fans. I'm hoping to read more in this captivating series."
—Socrates Book Review

PRAISE FOR *DEATH AT FIRST SIGHT*

"As breezy and salty as a gust of wind off the chilly bay waters."
—Juliet Blackwell, *New York Times* bestselling author of the Witchcraft Mysteries

"An intriguing opening to a fun new series."
—E. J. Copperman, national bestselling author of the Haunted Guesthouse Mysteries

"The future shows much success for this series! Fun, vibrant characters (as well as a sexy smolder or two for good measure) give the novel just the right tone." —*RT Book Reviews*

CLAIRVOYANT AND PRESENT DANGER

LENA GREGORY

BERKLEY PRIME CRIME
New York

BERKLEY PRIME CRIME
Published by Berkley
An imprint of Penguin Random House LLC
375 Hudson Street, New York, New York 10014

ISBN: 9780425282779

First Edition: February 2018

Printed in the United States of America
3 5 7 9 10 8 6 4 2

Cover art © Griesbach and Martucci
Book design by Kelly Lipovich

Greg, Elaina, Nicky, and Logan, you are my world.
Thank you for believing in me!

ACKNOWLEDGMENTS

This book would not have been possible without the support and encouragement of my husband, Greg. We've built a wonderful life together, and I can't wait to see where our journey will lead next. I'd like to say a big thank-you to my children—Elaina, Nicky, and Logan—and to my son-in-law, Steve, for their understanding and help while I spent long nights at the computer. My husband and children are truly the loves of my life.

And a huge thank-you to Steven Fournier for answering all of my art-related questions. He is an amazing artist, and any mistakes made in writing this manuscript are completely my own.

I also have to thank my best friend, Renee, for all of her support, long conversations, and reading many rough drafts. I still wouldn't know how to use Word without her help. I'd like to thank my sister, Debby, and my dad, Tony, who are probably my biggest fans and have read every word I've ever written. To my agent, Dawn Dowdle, thank you for believing in me and for being there in the middle of the night every time I have a question. Words cannot express my gratitude to Sarah Blumenstock for her wonderful advice and assistance in polishing this manuscript. Thank you, Sarah.

1

Cass propped her elbow on the driftwood countertop and rested her cheek on her hand. Only for a minute. She couldn't afford to take a break in the middle of the day, even if the shop was empty. And she definitely couldn't bear the thought of another nightmare. She jerked upright. She had to stay awake.

She leaned a hip against the counter, staring out the big picture window at the front of Mystical Musings, the shop she loved so much, had invested so much in. Daffodils had just begun to bloom in the beds surrounding the small gravel parking lot in front of the shop. She shoved the worries aside. Spring was here, and business had already begun to pick up with the start of the tourist season. There would be plenty of time to worry about her nightmares. Later. She didn't need any more stress than she was already under. She sighed.

Beast, the giant Leonberger she'd inherited from Marge Hawkins and then again from her daughter, Ellie, barked once in agreement—or more likely because a squirrel had scampered across the railing along the front walkway.

"Come on, boy." She weaved her fingers through the thick fur on his neck, inhaled deeply, and tried to gather the energy to get ready for her next reading. It wasn't going to work. Exhaustion, borne from too little sleep over the past week, battered her. She should never have agreed to keep the shop open late for a new reading, especially at the last minute. But when the man had called earlier, he'd sounded so desperate, and she'd been busy with customers and hadn't wanted to lose the business, so she'd relented. "If I don't make coffee, I'm going to sleep through this guy's reading." That would probably not make the best impression on a new customer. "Come on, Beast."

She shoved away from the counter and headed straight for the coffeepot on the counter that ran along the sidewall with Beast trotting beside her. Cass had never been prone to nightmares, yet the past week they'd plagued her every time she had started to doze off.

She readied the coffeepot, turned it on, and pulled out the big, velvet-covered chair from the round table in the corner of the shop. The customer—whose name she couldn't recall— shouldn't be there for another fifteen minutes or so. She'd just sit for a minute or two until the coffee was ready. She folded her arms on the table and rested her head on them.

Beast settled beside her, the rhythmic sound of his chewing on a bone bringing an odd sort of comfort. He'd become her best friend over the past months. It was hard to believe there'd ever been a time when she'd thought of not keeping him. But he was a big dog, and his training had been largely ignored. She'd have to give Herb Cox a call now that the weather was warmer. Because Herb ran his training classes outside, he didn't offer any during the winter, and it was well past time for some kind of obedience training. Beast was friendly enough, and had definitely been well socialized since he was at the shop with her every day, but he didn't listen. At all.

Her eyes drifted closed, Beast's gnawing keeping her grounded. If the sound stopped, she'd have to get up and make sure he hadn't gotten into anything. Just this week, she'd lost another chair, a basket, and half a blanket to his chewing. The TV remote had also gone missing, and though she couldn't prove anything, she had her suspicions about where it had disappeared to.

Slitting one eye open, she shot the big dog a wary glance.

He stopped chewing long enough to tilt his head at her, tongue lolling innocently out the side of his mouth.

Yeah, right.

He returned to his bone, and her eye dropped closed again. It was too heavy to keep open. She'd just rest a moment until the coffeepot stopped. The aroma of coffee brewing filled the shop, soothing her raw nerves.

She'd worked hard to make Mystical Musings cozy and comfortable, to create an atmosphere that would put her clients at ease. She kept the shop meticulously clean—knickknacks free of dust, crystals displayed neatly in baskets and cases, bath salts and lotions arranged perfectly according to scent and purpose. Even the various lighthouse souvenirs stood perfectly aligned on glass shelves along one wall—her driving need for organization a leftover effect from a time when her life had spiraled out of control, a year when she'd lost both of her parents, one of her patients, and had caught her ex fooling around with her best friend. A year when too many things had been beyond her control. Well, no longer. She'd regained control of her life, even if it did bring somewhat of an obsession with order, and she had no intention of giving that up.

A small smile tugged at her. Warmth at the life she'd made for herself spread through her, easing some of her tension, relaxing the taut muscles bunching her shoulders and straining her back.

A wisp of warm air whispered along the back of her neck. *"Help me."*

She jerked upright and lurched to her feet, slamming her leg against the table. "Ouch."

Beast jumped up beside her and looked around, as if sensing her discomfort. Or had he heard the soft plea as well?

She massaged her leg and glanced around the empty shop. Had she fallen asleep? She didn't think so, but she must have, or the voice from her nightmares couldn't have reached her. Right?

The tinkle of the chimes over the front door announced the arrival of her new client. Great. He was five minutes early. She hadn't had her coffee, she was totally freaked out, she hadn't yet put on her robe, and her long blond hair still hung loosely around her shoulders, instead of tied back beneath the sash she usually wore for a reading. Oh well. No sense bothering now. At this point, she'd be lucky to pull herself together enough to do the reading at all.

Beast stood at her side, a low growl emanating from his

throat. Weird. Beast usually loved everyone; he rarely growled at anything.

"Sit."

He ignored her and crouched to spring.

She grabbed his collar before he could launch himself at her customer. "Beast." Her voice held a note of warning the big dog wasn't used to.

He paused and tilted his head to the side, staring at her, his big brown eyes wide.

She tried to infuse some authority into her command. "Sit."

He plopped back down with a pout. Hmmm . . . maybe there was something to this training stuff after all. Satisfied Beast might not knock the man over, she turned her attention to her new client. Hopefully, this would be a nice, light read.

One look at the frown marring the man's face and the lines of strain bracketing his mouth assured her it wouldn't be. She sighed. "Hello, Mr. . . . uh . . ." Ah jeez, she'd forgotten to look up his name.

"Becker." He met her halfway across the store and extended an extremely large hand. "Artie Becker. Thank you for seeing me on such short notice," he said, his voice the deep, harsh rasp of a longtime, two-pack-a-day smoker.

"No problem." She gripped his proffered hand. A vision slammed through her. A young woman in jeans and a dark sweater, her features obscured by her long brown hair whipping across her face. Cass's stomach heaved, and she ripped her hand away with a gasp.

Artie's frown deepened. "Is everything all right?"

Battling the nausea, she summoned a smile. "Yeah . . . I . . . uh . . ." No way was she going to tell him she was losing her mind. She massaged her temples. "Sorry, bit of a head-ache. Would you like some coffee?" She silently prayed he'd accept, desperately needing a moment to herself.

His stare lingered a moment longer, but then he shrugged. "Sure." He swiped a hand over his mouth, smoothing his full salt-and-pepper beard. "Thanks."

"Have a seat." She gestured toward the large, round, cloth-covered table in the far corner of the room.

Artie eyed Beast suspiciously as he crossed the shop and pulled out a chair.

Beast popped his head up and shot Cass a hopeful look. Her glare stopped him in his tracks, and he moaned, rested his chin on his paws, and returned to sulking.

Fairly confident Beast would behave, at least as long as it suited him, she turned to pouring the coffee. Her hands shook as she set out two foam cups, then lifted the pot from the burner.

Cass didn't consider herself psychic in any traditional sense, but her strong intuition combined with her psychiatric training and years of experience reading patients afforded her the skills necessary to "read" people with a fair amount of accuracy. Billing herself as a medium allowed her to bring an extra measure of comfort to her clients.

Recent events had her questioning that assessment. It seemed since she came back to Bay Island she was a little more intuitive than she'd originally thought. A shiver ran up her spine.

She shook off thoughts better left unexamined. She'd get through the reading then go home and take a warm bath, maybe make a small pot of herbal tea and relax. The image of the woman from her nightmares returned unbidden. On the other hand, maybe she'd see if Bee and Stephanie wanted to go to the diner and grab a late dinner . . . and coffee . . . maybe dessert.

She added milk to her cup and placed it on a tray with Artie's coffee, a small creamer, a sugar bowl, and a few stirrers, then set the tray on the table beside Artie. Pulling herself together, she lifted her cup and took a seat across the table from him. "So, how can I help you?" It felt weird to start a reading wearing yoga pants and a long sweater.

Leaving his coffee untouched, Artie pulled a small tape recorder from his shirt pocket. "Do you mind if I tape this?"

Used to the request, since people often recorded their sessions to share with friends and family or refresh their memories about the things she told them, she gestured for him to go ahead.

He placed the recorder in the center of the table between them and pushed the record button, then leaned forward, folding his bulky arms on the table. "I've been told you're a medium as well as a psychic. Is that true?"

Sort of. "If you tell me what you're looking for, I'll know better if I can help you."

The intensity in his gaze as it held hers sent goose bumps running over her. His dark eyes seemed to bore straight through to her very soul. "My daughter, Kelly, is missing."

Panic gripped her throat. If his daughter was missing, and he was in her shop having a reading instead of at the police station, well . . . it certainly explained some of the desperation she'd felt on the phone with him earlier. "Do you have reason to believe she's . . . uh . . . no longer with us?"

He lifted his hands to the sides and shrugged. "Quite

frankly, I don't know what to think. I've been to the police, but they can't help."

An image of the woman she'd seen when she first gripped his hand shimmered into view behind him. Cass bit back a groan at her seemingly new ability to catch glimpses of ghosts—or something—and squinted, trying to make the woman's features clear, but it was no use. The image was hazy, too cloudy to offer any real detail. "Have you tried a private detective?"

He slapped his hands against the table and surged to his feet, sloshing coffee over the rim of her cup. "Look, if you don't want to help me—"

Beast growled again, but thankfully remained where he was. The last thing she needed was him chasing another man out of the shop.

"No, no." Cass stood and held up her hands. "I didn't mean I wouldn't try to help you. I just meant in addition to what you've already been doing, you might try a private detective." She grabbed a handful of paper towels, then mopped up the spill and set her cup on the counter. Best to just get this done and over with.

His clenched jaw worked back and forth a few times before he settled back in the chair and folded his arms across his chest. "Detectives cost money. A lot more than psychics."

Letting the matter drop, she tossed the paper towels in the garbage, grabbed a stack of white paper and a basket of colored pencils from a shelf beneath the counter, and returned to the table. "Do you have a picture of your daughter?"

"Not a recent one." He dug out his wallet then slid what appeared to be a standard school photograph across the table.

A young girl, around twelve or thirteen, stared back at Cass with a tight smile that didn't reach her muddy brown eyes. Her dark blond bob hung limply tucked behind her ears. A crease ran through one corner of the photo, as if it had been folded over, and the image had started to fade. "How long ago was this taken?"

"Ten or twelve years, I suppose." He met her gaze and held it. "Give or take a few."

Years of experience in her psychiatric practice helped her keep her expression neutral. "So your daughter is in her early twenties?"

"Twenty-five."

She massaged her right eye to keep her brow from arching up on its own—and to cover the twitch she could feel developing. "Okay. How long has she been missing?"

"I ain't seen her in about six or seven years." His expression hardened, as if daring her to pass judgment. "But I sort of kept tabs on her. Seems she went missing sometime between six months and a week ago."

Cass frowned. No wonder the police couldn't help this guy. "Can you narrow it down any?"

"Nope." He lifted a wooden stirrer from the tray and stuck it between his teeth. He clenched his jaw, keeping his gaze on her the whole time.

It was past time to get this guy out of her shop. It didn't take any kind of psychic powers to feel the negative energy pouring off him in waves. "Okay, then. Why don't we get started?" She lit a white candle and pushed it to the side of the table, then set the paper and pencils in front of her.

Color readings tended to be calming, and her clients usually left with a sense of peace. Hopefully, it would soothe what she perceived as an undercurrent of violence in the big man. Maybe that's why Beast took such an instant dislike to him. Couldn't dogs sense stuff like that?

Without looking, she grabbed a handful of pencils from the basket and placed them beside her. She rolled her hand back and forth over them, coaxing them into a straight line.

"If your daughter is still alive, and you have no idea where she could be, I'm not sure how much I'll be able to do for you." Holding her breath, she waited for another outburst. When none came, she lifted a pencil and pressed it to the paper. Black. Hmmm . . .

She'd never started a reading with the color black before, and she had to wonder if it was her own opinion of the man guiding her choice of color. She always tried to let her subconscious—or whatever—guide her hand, but this time she couldn't be sure. Perhaps she was transferring her intense dislike and lack of trust for him to the reading. She shook off the concern and tried to focus.

Black was a color of mystery. While it didn't always have a negative connotation—it could also represent power and strength, which this man obviously possessed—more often than not, it did.

She began to scribble, just a random blotch of color toward the top of the page. Black could also symbolize death. Was that the message she was supposed to pass on? That his daughter had died? No way could she tell him that, even if she was certain of it, which she wasn't. Actually, she was getting surprisingly few impressions from this man, other than an overwhelming sense of anger.

She continued to scribble, the rhythmic scratch, scratch, scratch of the pencil against the paper the only sound as her blob of black began to take on a definite shape. She frowned. That had never happened before. Her color readings usually left her with a random palette of colors that could tell her something about her client. This was different, surreal.

A faceless silhouette began to form . . . Blackness lifted off the page, surrounded her, embraced her in shadow. The shape of a woman emerged from the darkness, the same woman who'd haunted her every nightmare for over a week now, robbing her of the sleep she so desperately needed. Was it Kelly? The age difference between the woman and the picture Artie had provided made it impossible to tell.

"She needs help." The words shot out before she could censor them.

"Who? Kelly?"

"No . . . I'm sorry . . ." Her thoughts drifted away with the image of the woman, her high collar, pearl buttons done up to her chin, hair pulled severely back, all giving the appearance of someone from another time, someone who'd lived and passed over a long time ago, and yet, something about her youth tugged at Cass. Something she couldn't quite put her finger on.

Artie cleared his throat, dragging her back to reality with a jolt, and she tossed the pencil into the basket.

"Uh . . ." How long had she been silent, gripped by the vision of death? "I'm sorry. I . . . umm . . ." She couldn't tell him what she'd seen, she wasn't even sure it had anything to do with his daughter. She inhaled deeply. "Black is a color of mystery. It could be the mystery surrounding your daughter's disappearance . . ." *Or it could be something more, some secret he's keeping.* She kept that to herself.

"Let's see." She rolled the pencils back and forth beneath

her hand, searching for calm, then lifted a red one from the middle of the line. "Red. Another color of power." That was true enough. But it was also the color of blood—a warning of danger or violence. "You need to be careful." She shook her head as she continued to add red in a halo around the large area of shadow she'd already created. "But I'm not sure why yet."

She returned the red to the line and picked up a gold pencil, a color that could be associated with wealth and extravagance. While Artie's flannel shirt, thick build, and ruddy complexion screamed lumberjack more than luxury, you never could tell. Yet she was suddenly very sure she'd chosen gold to symbolize achievement. "You are going to accomplish something you've set out to do." Or maybe he already had. But did that success have anything to do with his missing daughter?

2

Cass pulled the door shut behind her, turned the key in the lock of Mystical Musings, and tightened her hold on Beast's leash. When she'd walked along the beach to work that morning, she hadn't expected to be at the shop so late. She should have left earlier, but once she'd gotten rid of Artie, she'd lit several candles and scrubbed the shop clean. Her need for organization wouldn't allow her to leave a mess, even under normal circumstances, but having Artie there had left a sense of foreboding hanging over everything, and the need for cleansing had overwhelmed her.

She shivered at the thought that Artie could still be lurking somewhere in the cloudy, moonless night, and glanced around the deserted boardwalk. On a Friday night during the summer, in the height of tourist season, there would still be shops open and people milling around, couples would still be walking on the beach, and groups of teenagers would have a bonfire going, but on a cool, rainy spring night, not so much. No way was she leaving out the back door of the shop and walking home down the beach in the pitch black. "Come on, boy. We'll walk down the boardwalk." It would take her a little longer to get home, but at least the boardwalk and road were well lit.

Cool drizzle dampened her long blond hair, sticking strands to the sides of her face. A perfect night to go home and curl up with a cup of tea and a good book . . . if not for the risk of falling asleep.

She pulled her cell phone from her jacket pocket and dialed Bee's number, then switched the call to her Bluetooth. If Beast decided to run after anything, she might well need both hands to restrain him. She'd already lost one phone that way.

"Hello, dear."

Cass smiled. "Are you at the shop yet?" Bee's dress shop, Dreamweaver Designs, which was only a few doors down from Mystical Musings, appeared dark, but that didn't mean anything. Bee hated interruptions when he was working on a design— "in the zone," as he called it—so he often worked in the back room of the shop through the night.

"Nah, not yet. I was just thinking about getting dinner and heading in. Why, what's up?"

"Oh, that's great." She continued on her way past Dreamweaver. "Want to meet at the diner?"

"Sure. Did you call Stephanie?"

"Not yet. I'm walking home, and I was passing the shop, so I figured I'd give you a try in case you were already there."

"Oh, so you were going to interrupt my work?"

"Uh . . ."

Bee laughed. "No worries. I'll call her and meet you at the diner in about a half hour."

"Okay, I just have to—"

An image of the woman from her dreams appeared in the new art gallery window, stopping Cass dead in her tracks.

Her heart pounded wildly as she turned to face the large display window. The vision of the woman's head and shoulders hovered dead center. Blackness surrounded her.

"Cass?"

"I . . . uhh . . ." She pressed her palm against the cool glass.

"Are you all right?"

"Yeah." She shook her head and squeezed her eyes closed, trying to dispel the vision. Nothing like this had ever happened to her before. When she opened her eyes, the woman was still there. "I gotta go, though. See you in a few." She disconnected the call.

An easel stood in the center of the display with a painting of the woman exactly as she'd been appearing in Cass's dreams. No frame surrounded the vision. It just appeared to be a canvas with the woman's head and shoulders surrounded by black. A lamp above the painting created an aura of light around the woman.

Cass used her sleeve to wipe streaks of rain from the window. Cupping her hand above her eyes, she leaned closer and strained to see into the shop.

Paintings were carefully displayed throughout the window, mostly portraits, but an occasional landscape or beach scene as well. And, of course, the obligatory lighthouse paintings, many with angry seas. Powerful, yet a little dark for a display window—or maybe that was just Cass's mood.

A black backdrop kept her from seeing any farther into the shop.

She returned her gaze to the woman in the painting. The severely pulled-back hair tightened her expression, a stark contrast to the pouty full lips. Cass tilted her head. It seemed to her the woman's mouth should be pressed into a firm line . . . but why? She couldn't remember the woman's mouth from her dreams. The same or different? She squinted—

A peal of thunder rattled the window.

Cass jumped back.

Beast yelped.

Heavy, cold raindrops pelted her, dripping down the back of her jacket, returning her to the reality that she was standing with her back to a deserted street. Pulling her hood up, she briefly considered running back to the shop and calling Stephanie to pick her up, but she was already pretty creeped out and didn't feel like hanging around the boardwalk any longer. She turned and started briskly toward home.

Beast trotted happily at her side. Rain never seemed to bother him. Who knew? With all that thick hair, it probably felt nice and cool.

She moved closer to Beast, the giant dog making her feel safer as she splashed through the growing puddles with visions of the two women—Artie's daughter and the woman from her dreams—battling for a place in her mind. She had to figure out if there was a connection. There didn't seem to be, and yet . . .

Even with Beast at her side, she breathed a sigh of relief when she rounded the last curve in the road, and her lit yard finally came into view. Ignoring the urge to get inside as quickly as possible, she took the time to open the gate and follow the driveway around to the back door. If she brought him in the front door and he shook himself off as he bolted for the kitchen, she'd spend the next hour cleaning up the mess.

She unlocked the door and braced herself. "Okay, Beast. I won't leave you out in the rain, but please don't shake before I can get to a towel." She pushed the door open and ran for the laundry room off the kitchen.

Beast almost plowed her over as he ran in beside her, his wet paws slipping and sliding on the tile floor.

She fumbled but reached the laundry room without going down and grabbed a towel from the dryer.

The jangle of Beast's collar told her she was too late.

With a sigh, and the acceptance of the knowledge that she was going to be delayed meeting Bee, she toweled Beast off and wiped up the mess from the cabinets, the wall, the door, and the floor. When she finished, she grabbed her keys from the hook by the back door and slung her big bag over her shoulder. Then she turned to Beast. "Okay. Here's the deal. You don't eat the kitchen while I'm gone, and I'll bring you a hamburger when I come back."

He licked his chops, and she took that for agreement.

"Good enough."

The bright lights washed over the car as Cass pulled into a spot close to the diner, hoping to avoid another drenching. She turned off the car but sat watching the sheets of rain run down the front window. Thirty percent chance of rain, huh? What difference would it make, anyway? Since she hadn't had time to change, she was still damp from her walk home. She sighed then jumped out and ran for the diner door.

When she reached the door, her best friend, Bee, pushed it open for her. "It's about time." He cocked an eyebrow and eyed her up and down.

"Yeah. Long day." She tried to comb her fingers through her hair but gave up quickly. The wet tangled mess wasn't going to be smoothed without a good brushing. "Is Stephanie here yet?"

Bee hooked a thumb toward the back room of the diner. "She's in back looking at pictures of Shelly's new baby."

"Shelly's back from maternity leave?"

"Today's her first day back, but she's only working part-time," Bee said.

"I don't know how she works at all. How many kids does that make now?"

Shrugging, Bee gestured for Cass to precede him to the table. "I don't know, like four or five I think."

"Just the two of you tonight?" The hostess, Gabby, grabbed two big, plastic menus.

"Nah, Stephanie's in back," Bee said.

She shot Bee a knowing look and picked up a third menu. "Got caught up with baby pictures, huh?"

"Stephanie loves that stuff." Bee shrugged off his brown leather jacket, hung it on a post behind the table, and slid into the booth.

Cass hung her dripping coat beside Bee's and sat down across from him.

Gabby left the menus on the table and ran to ring up a customer waiting by the register.

"Beast in the car?" Bee asked.

"No, I brought him home then had to clean the kitchen."

Amusement flickered in his big brown eyes. "Did you call Herb Cox?"

Cass scowled and lifted the menu in front of her face. She already knew she had to call the trainer.

"Yeah, that's what I figured."

"Ugh . . ." She didn't want to talk about her failure as a pet owner, or her recurring nightmare.

"Cass?"

"Oh, uh . . . sorry." She dropped the menu onto the table.

Bee frowned. "Is everything all right?"

"Yes. I just wanted to . . . um . . ." Now she felt bad. He was only trying to help. He loved Beast just as much as she did and didn't want him to get hurt. "I just wanted to know if you'd like to come to dinner Sunday," she blurted. "I'm going to cook."

Bee's tone turned serious. "You're dying."

"What!" Cass stared at him briefly before massaging her temples between her thumb and forefinger. After the past week, she had little patience for Bee's flare for drama. "I'm not dying."

He scoffed. "Someone else is dying?"

"Knock it off, Bee. I just want to cook dinner for you guys. No one is dying."

"Not yet, anyway." Humor flooded his voice.

Unfortunately, Cass was in no mood for Bee's teasing, and she couldn't curb the crankiness in her voice. "Do you want to come or not, Bee?"

"Uh-oh . . . someone sure is snippy. Again."

Now he had a pout plastered on his face. Great. The last thing she needed right now was Bee in full diva mode. She sighed. "Look, I'm just tired."

"Fine."

"Would you like to come to dinner Sunday?"

"Wouldn't miss it for the world." His laughter assured her all was forgiven. "If I remember correctly, last time you tried to cook, the fire department showed up and hauled your stove right out of the kitchen onto the back deck." He harrumphed, lifted his chin, and tossed his scarf over his shoulder. "And I had to hear about it in the deli the next morning." The last statement held a bit of reproach. Bee liked to get anything gossipworthy firsthand.

She bit back a growl, the memory of her last attempt at eating something healthy—something that didn't come from a can, a frozen tray, or a drive-through—taunting her. "For the last time, that was not my fault. I forgot I turned on the rice and went to do my taxes." And doing her taxes had led to ideas of how to increase her income through the winter months, and then she'd totally lost track of time.

"You set the house on fire, Cass."

"Watch it, buddy. Besides, it was only a small fire . . . and I didn't need that dish towel anyway."

Bee laughed long and hard, melting some of Cass's stress away.

She finally grinned.

"Well, this time I'm not missing it." He sobered. "Just do me one favor?"

"What's that?"

"Cook early enough so we can hit McDonald's if things

don't work out. I've already had fourthmeal at Taco Bell three times this week."

"Smart aleck." Ignoring Bee, she opened her menu and studied her options—not that she didn't already know the menu by heart, but the idea of a salad or a wrap, her usual choices, didn't really appeal. A chill rattled her, probably from being cold and wet, but she still stole a suspicious glance around the diner, half-expecting the vision of a woman to assail her. She needed comfort food.

"Hey." Stephanie offered a half smile as she slid into the booth beside Cass. "Why so late?"

She shrugged and closed the menu on the table. "I had a late reading." The negative energy surrounding Artie Becker was still affecting Cass's frame of mind. Or maybe she was just exhausted.

"Oh, right. The new guy. How'd it go?" Deep lines furrowed Stephanie's brow.

Cass sat up a little straighter and studied her friend. "Are you okay?"

"Fine." Stephanie, who could also recite the menu forward and backward, opened her menu and flipped through the plastic-coated pages.

Hmmm . . . weird.

"Well, aren't we all perky tonight?" Bee glanced pointedly at Stephanie's bent head and cocked an eyebrow at Cass.

With no idea what the problem was, she shrugged and shook her head. Obviously, something was bothering Stephanie, but if she didn't want to talk about it—

"Okay, guys, what'll it be?" Elaina Stevens stood beside the table, pen poised over a small pad.

Cass plastered on a smile. "I'll have two bacon cheese-burgers, fries, coleslaw, and a chocolate shake."

Elaina just stared at her.

Cass frowned. "What?"

"Uh . . . oh, nothing." Small patches of red blossomed on Elaina's cheeks as she quickly scribbled the order and shifted her attention to Bee. "What'll you have, Bee?"

Bee and Stephanie simply sat, staring at Cass, Bee's mouth slightly agape.

"Okay, what's the problem?" Cass shrugged. "So I'm hungry."

Bee cleared his throat, holding her gaze.

"Oh, fine. One of them's for Beast." She held up her hands in a gesture of surrender. "I know, I know, Doc said to stop feeding him so much table food." She thought of Beast roaming freely through her house. Hopefully, he was either sleeping or lying in the kitchen, chewing one of the million toys she had stashed, not doing any serious damage. "But I promised him a hamburger if he didn't eat the kitchen while I was gone."

Bee burst out laughing, then shook his head and placed his order.

Stephanie only ordered coffee. "I ate earlier with Tank."

"I'll be right back with this." Elaina hurried off to place the order.

"Is he working tonight?" Bee asked. Even with the truce he and Tank had sort of achieved, Bee was still leery whenever Stephanie's husband was around. The fact that he was a detective only added to Bee's unease.

"He's sleeping now, but he has to go in at midnight." She pinned Cass with a stare. "So, what's up?"

Cass folded the corner of the paper place mat. Then, she

folded it again in the opposite direction and smoothed the crease. How could she explain what was happening to her when she didn't even understand it herself?

"Last time you ate that amount of food in one sitting was . . ." Bee made a production of scratching his head. "Hmmm . . . you've never eaten that amount of food." He rested his clasped hands on the table. "Spill it, girl."

Cass laughed, but sobered quickly and massaged her temples. Bee and Stephanie were her best friends. They'd stand by her side no matter what. Who knew? Maybe they could help her make sense of . . . whatever was going on. "I haven't had a decent night's sleep in more than a week."

Bee frowned and patted her hand. "Are you feeling all right?"

Leaning against the seat back, Cass slid lower. "I've been having nightmares." She paused. If she were to be honest, they weren't exactly nightmares, they just felt like nightmares. If she wanted their help, she had to try to be as accurate as possible. "Okay, not exactly nightmares, but really weird dreams about a woman."

Bee waggled his thick, bushy eyebrows and grinned. "Really?"

She kicked his shin under the table. "Knock it off, Bee." But some of the tension drained away. She sighed. "At least I think I'm dreaming. I keep dreaming that I open my eyes, and there's a woman beside the bed."

Stephanie leaned forward. "What does she do?"

"That's just it. She doesn't really do anything. I can't tell if she's standing or sitting. I can only see her head and neck and a little bit of the front of her blouse. She stares at me for a while, then speaks."

A tremor ran through Bee. "What does she say?"

"Help me."

"Okay, that's creepy."

Eagerness lit Stephanie's eyes, whatever was bothering her earlier obviously forgotten. "Are you sure it's a dream? Maybe it's a—"

"That's it." Bee held a finger up in warning. "If this conversation starts heading down the heebie-jeebie path, I'm outta here."

Stephanie shot him a glare. "Well, how would you explain it then?"

"I have no idea, but I don't want to hear anything more about . . . whatever it is you're thinking." He turned to Cass. "Now. What does this woman look like? Could it be someone you know?"

"I . . . uhh . . ." She started to tell them about the painting in the art gallery window, but she hesitated, afraid if they went back there it wouldn't be the woman from her dreams at all. Had it just been a hallucination? "I don't think I've ever seen her before. And it's odd, but it seems as if she lived in the past. Her hair is pulled back tight against her head, and she's got on one of those old-fashioned blouses with the collars that button up all the way to your chin."

"Can you see the whole blouse?"

"Actually, no. Just the collar and a bit of the chest. I assumed it was a blouse, but I suppose it could be a dress or something."

Bee frowned. "Hmmm, I haven't—"

"Here you go, guys." Elaina sorted out the food, placing each of their orders in front of them, and handed Cass a foam box. "That's for Beast."

"Thanks, Elaina."

"Do you need anything else?"

"We're good, thank you."

Cass studied her cheeseburger, which was loaded with cheese, bacon, lettuce, tomato, pickles, and two huge onion rings, then doused it all with ketchup and squashed the bun down on top.

"I cannot even believe you're going to eat that." Stephanie frowned. "No wonder you're having nightmares."

"Oh, knock it off," Bee said around a mouthful of cheese-burger. "You can't live on salads and tacos."

"And McDonald's. Don't forget she eats cheeseburgers from McDonald's." Stephanie laughed.

Bee waved her off. "Those cheeseburgers don't even count. They're like . . . what . . . a quarter of the size of these?" He bit into his burger again.

"Once in a while she eats a Big Mac, I've—"

"What did you start to say before, Bee?" Cass interrupted before their argument could escalate any further. The scent of fried food made her mouth water, and she took a bite while she waited for Bee to finish chewing and answer.

"Oh, right." He dabbed his mouth daintily with a napkin. "Keep in mind, just because the clothing appeared to be old-fashioned, doesn't necessarily mean it's from the past." He shifted a bit to face her and hooked his elbow over the back of the booth seat, warming up to a discussion of fashion—or more likely just happy to have moved past the mention of ghosts. For a man who didn't believe in anything otherworldly, Bee avoided the subject like the plague.

But fashion was Bee's thing. If anyone knew about wom-en's clothing, it was Bee. "It could be someone you saw in a movie that was set in the past, someone you noticed but don't necessarily remember."

She thought again of the painting in the window. Maybe it had been there all along and she just didn't remember seeing it, but somehow it had stuck in her subconscious. Then again, maybe it was just her mind playing tricks on her, and it wasn't the same woman at all. There had definitely been something different about the mouth, if she could just—

Bee intruded on her thoughts. "Or it could be a costume of some sort. Or, it could be thrift shop clothing. There have been several times throughout the years when those high collars were popular, some not that long ago." He grinned, mischief dancing in his eyes. "Or could be she just has terrible taste in clothes."

Cass laughed, feeling considerably better since she joined her friends.

"What? Some people do, you know." He returned to his cheeseburger.

Stephanie squirted a pile of ketchup onto the side of Cass's dish, snatched a fry from Cass's heaping pile, and swirled it through the ketchup. "Is the dream always the same?" She popped the fry into her mouth.

"Yes." There was no background she could ascertain, just blackness with a woman's head and shoulders floating. A chill gripped her. "But that's not the only weird thing. The man that came in for the reading tonight?" She grabbed a fry before Stephanie could finish off the pile. "His adult daughter is missing."

Stephanie's hand stopped midway to her mouth. "Do you think it's the same woman?"

Tossing the fry she'd been about to eat back onto the

plate, Cass sat back. "I have no idea. When he came in . . ." She wasn't ready to share the vision of the woman who'd accompanied Artie into the shop. It didn't really prove anything. It had been so hazy, and she couldn't tell if it was the same woman. Heck, she couldn't even be sure it was real. Maybe she was losing her mind. "I didn't care much for him, and neither did Beast."

Bee frowned. "Beast likes everyone."

"I know, right? But he didn't like this guy. For a minute I thought it was going to be a repeat of when he chased Jay Callahan out of the shop."

"That bad?" Bee finished off the last of his burger.

"The man's not coming back again, is he?" Stephanie gave up on the fries and sipped her coffee.

Cass shrugged. "He didn't schedule another reading, but I have no idea."

"Maybe you should go to the police," Stephanie suggested.

Bee's eyes widened. "And tell them what? She had a dream about a woman?"

"You know . . ." Stephanie sat up straighter. ". . . like those psychics that work with the cops to find missing people. Maybe the woman is still alive and—"

"Think about that for a minute." Bee lowered his voice and leaned across the table toward Stephanie. "Cass is supposed to be a medium. If your theory is correct, which borders on absurd, the woman is obviously not still alive if Cass is seeing her."

"Hmmm . . ." Stephanie pouted. "You could be right. All the more reason to talk to the police."

"We'll see." Cass had no intention of going to the police.

For what? To tell them she'd had a bad dream? Besides, Artie said he'd already been to the police, and he seemed frustrated enough with their lack of results that she believed him. But she didn't feel like arguing. Easier to just change the subject. "Do either of you know anything about the new art gallery?"

"Oh, don't they have the loveliest paintings?" Bee clapped his hands together. "I was thinking of stopping in there one of these days and taking a look at one of the beach scenes for Dreamweaver. There's one in particular, at sunset, and the colors would complement my beach wedding line perfectly."

He gushed for a little while, but Cass tuned it out. She'd have to go by there again, and if the woman in the painting actually was the woman from her dreams, maybe the owner could help make some sense of what was happening.

3

"*H*elp me." The voice, on the softest breath, caressed the back of Cass's neck.

She jerked awake. She must have fallen asleep curled in the living room chair. Trying to stretch the kink in her neck, she opened her eyes—or at least she thought she did.

A woman's head, surrounded by blackness, floated a few feet in front of her. "*Help me!*" The woman's lips didn't move; they remained firmly pressed together in a thin line. The voice slid into Cass's mind, more insistent this time.

Squeezing her eyes tightly shut, Cass pressed her head as far back against the chair as she could and counted to ten while she tried to coax the crazy staccato of her heart back into some sort of rhythm. She willed the vision to evaporate, to go back to whatever crazy corner of her subconscious had fabricated it.

Ice-cold tendrils of air curled around her neck.

Cass's eyes shot open, and she gasped as she jerked upright in the chair.

The woman's face had come closer, hovering only a few inches in front of her, their noses almost touching, her brows drawn together in a frown. *"Help me."*

Cass opened her mouth to scream, but no sound emerged. Instead, a whoosh of air exploded from her lungs. She sucked in a ragged breath and tried again. "Wha . . ." The whisper of sound was all she could manage past the fear clogging her throat.

The woman's head spun abruptly away, moving toward the opposite side of the room at about the right height for a woman who was a bit shorter than Cass's five-seven.

Without waiting for her to turn back around, Cass leaped from the chair, vaulted the new leather couch, and ran toward her bedroom. *What am I, crazy?* Changing course in the hallway, she slid on the area rug but managed to regain her footing. She headed toward the kitchen. When she slammed through the door, Beast shot to his feet.

"Come on, boy. We're outta here." Barely slowing her pace, she grabbed the leash and keys from the hooks beside the back door, yanked the door open, and ran out with Beast on her heels.

He seemed to think it was some sort of game, though, because he danced around in the mud then jumped up, propping his big paws on Cass's shoulders. Mud splattered her face and neck, and a big glob ran down the inside of her shirt and got caught in her cleavage.

"Beast, no!"

He licked her cheek.

"Down, boy." She pushed against his chest, which had

somehow also gotten caked with mud, and he dropped to the ground, rolled onto his back, and squirmed back and forth in his very own mud bath.

Ugh . . . really?

She eyed the back door and swallowed hard, the taste of mud clogging the back of her throat, then glanced at the new Dodge Dart she'd bought with the insurance check from the Jetta she'd wrecked a few months ago.

Beast jumped to his feet and shook himself off, spraying mud everywhere.

That solved that. She wasn't going anywhere covered in mud. And no way was Beast getting into her new car like that. Well, actually, the car was used, but it was new to her, and she didn't want mud all over the clean interior.

She tried to wipe the mud from her clothes as she walked toward the back door, but she only succeeded in smearing it more. Ghost or no ghost, she needed a shower. She glanced down at Beast.

He'd stopped short beside her, staring at the door. He whined and moved closer to Cass, pressing his side against her leg.

Never mind. Mud probably wouldn't stain the black fabric seats anyway. She bolted for the car, cringed as Beast climbed into the backseat, and hopped in. No way was she going back into the house alone. Five after seven. She could call Luke, but it wasn't like he'd be much help from the mainland. Besides, what was she going to tell him? Their long-distance relationship was proving hard enough without making him think she was crazy.

Stephanie was probably still sleeping, but Bee might not have gone to bed yet. Since he worked on his designs all night, he usually didn't go to bed until seven or eight. Definitely a better option than running into Tank and having to explain why she was so frazzled. She headed for Bee's house.

He would not be happy to find her on his doorstep, covered in mud, at just past seven in the morning, but what else could she do? She hadn't grabbed her bag or her cell phone in her hurry to flee the house . . . uh-oh. She lifted her foot off the gas and slowed. What was she going to tell him? If he knew a . . . *something* had spooked her, he'd never agree to come over.

The drive over was not comfortable. The mud had started to dry and was tightening her skin, and the damp clothes were bringing a chill, but it was better than being alone at home. Of course, nothing was stopping the woman from materializing in the car. She started to look at the—hopefully empty—passenger seat, but thought better of it and kept her eyes firmly on the road until she reached Bee's driveway and parked. What she didn't know couldn't hurt her. Probably.

"Come on, Beast." She hooked the leash to his collar, stepped out of the car, and started toward the door.

Before she even reached the porch, Bee had opened the door and was doubled over laughing, gasping for air.

"Not funny, mister." She strode toward him.

He bit back the laughter—sort of—when his gaze landed on Beast. His eyes widened, sending his bushy brown eyebrows straight up beneath his bleached blond bangs. "Oh, no. Stay right there, missy. Don't you dare come any closer with that animal."

She kept walking toward him without slowing her pace.

"Did you hear me, Cass? I'm not kidding. You are not coming up here with that dog." He squinted and eyed Beast more closely. "What on earth happened to you two?"

Cass finally stopped. "I need you to come home with me."

He lifted a brow, and a smirk played at the corner of his mouth. "That is so not happening, honey."

Cass held the leash in the air, keeping a firm enough grip so that Beast couldn't escape—unless he really wanted to.

Beast wagged furiously, spraying mud everywhere.

She cocked a hip and propped her free, mud-covered hand on it. "Either you come home with me, or I'll let him go."

Bee's mouth fell open. He snapped it shut and narrowed his eyes, pinning her with a glare. "You wouldn't dare."

She loosened her hold, letting the leash slip just a little.

Beast crouched, practically vibrating with the need to escape, barely able to restrain himself.

"Okay. You win." Bee held up his hands in defeat. "But I'm following you in my own car."

"Fine."

Keeping one eye glued to the rearview mirror to make sure Bee stayed true to his word, Cass drove home. When she got there, she left Beast in the car with the windows cracked, and left the car running—you never could tell when you might need to make a quick getaway. She climbed out and wiped her now-sweaty palms on her filthy yoga pants.

Bee parked behind her, turned off his car, and got out. Muting the rumble of the black Trans Am Bee called his baby left a deafening silence as he strode toward her. "So what's going on?"

"Uh . . . weeell . . ." She squinted and scratched her head, unsure of how to break the news that she had a ghost following her without making him run screaming in the other direction.

Bee firmed his mouth into a tight line, propped a hand on his cocked hip, and tossed the end of his multicolored scarf over his shoulder. "Spill it, girl. Now."

"Oh fine." She threw up her arms, exasperated with his drama. "I fell asleep on the chair and when I woke up I thought I saw . . ." She pressed a hand to her neck where what had felt like ice-cold fingers had wrapped— "Hey. Where are you going?"

Bee stalked toward his car, keys in hand.

"You can't leave, Bee. Please." She hated the pleading note in her voice. "Please, Bee. Just long enough for me to shower and get dressed." Ah jeez, now she was just plain whining.

He shook his head and kept walking. He rounded the front of his car and kept going.

A small glimmer of hope flared. Maybe he'd go in with her after all.

He disappeared into her small shed. She really had to remember to get a lock for that thing, but she only kept some gardening equipment and a push mower that had seen better days in there.

When he emerged a moment later, rake in one hand, metal bucket in the other, hysteria borne of exhaustion took hold.

Bee was a sight to behold on any occasion, but this was more than she could take. A head over six feet tall even without the platform shoes he usually wore, dressed in leather with a multicolored print scarf draped just so around his thick neck, he held his makeshift sword and shield at the ready.

She clutched her stomach, bent at the waist, tears pouring down her face, and laughed until she could barely breathe.

He glared at her and lifted a brow. "Something funny?"

She clamped her teeth together, desperately trying to control herself, and shook her head.

"I didn't think so." He strode past her. When he reached the back door, he started to juggle the rake and bucket to turn the knob, then stopped and shot her a dirty look. "A little help here?"

Tamping down the last of her hysteria, she sighed and met him at the door. She peeked in the window. Even though the kitchen appeared empty, she turned the knob, pushed the door, and stepped back.

Bee poked the door open with the rake.

Together, they stood in the open doorway, poised to run, and studied the empty kitchen.

"Sooo?" Bee kept his gaze firmly locked on the closed doorway to the living room. "Where'd you see . . . whatever it was that spooked you?"

"In the living room."

"Great." He started tentatively across the kitchen.

Cass clung to his side. This was ridiculous. But no matter how hard she tried, she couldn't dismiss fears she knew were irrational. Though she did believe there was something past death, and could even accept she might somehow be tapping into that energy, she didn't believe a ghost could just drop in for a visit. Of course, the alternative—that she was losing her mind completely—wasn't that much more appealing.

Bee stopped a couple of feet back from the door, took a

deep breath, waited for her to turn the knob, then shoved the door open with the rake handle.

Empty. No head floating across the room. No ghostly apparition whispering in her ear. Nothing.

Heat crept into her cheeks.

Bee flopped onto the couch and propped his feet on the coffee table. He set the bucket on the cushion beside him and leaned the rake against the couch within easy reach. "You okay?"

She shrugged and swiped tears from her cheeks. "I have no idea."

"What happened?"

She sighed and sat on the chair across from him, then pulled her knees up to her chest and wrapped her arms around them. "I guess I fell asleep in the chair sometime during the night. When I opened my eyes this morning, I thought I saw the same woman from my dreams."

Bee dropped his feet onto the floor, leaned forward, and propped his elbows on his knees. He contemplated her for a few minutes without saying anything.

She shifted, uncomfortable under his close scrutiny. "What?"

"Look, Cass." He paused.

This time, she waited him out. He obviously had something on his mind. Eventually, he'd get to sharing it. In the meantime, she scanned the room, hoping not to find anything otherworldly.

"You know how I feel about any kind of psychic nonsense, and I'll probably regret asking, but you never talk much about how you do what you do." He pursed his lips and stared at her. "Are you . . . you know . . . really psychic? Can you really hear . . ." He cast a suspicious glance around the empty room and lowered his voice to a whisper. "Ghosts?"

Cass had never given it much thought. Stuff came to her, and she said it. Could the information she'd been relaying have come from spirits? Possibly, she supposed, but even if it did, it wasn't as simple as that. "It's not like that. I don't just hear voices or anything like that. And I definitely never saw a ghost as clear as day."

Except for the man's image she—along with a roomful of other people—thought she saw during the first séance in the Madison Estate. Of course, she still clung tightly to the possibility of mass hysteria.

Bee stared a moment longer then waved his hand, dismissing whatever he'd been about to say.

Cass didn't press. The last thing she needed was any further evaluation of her mental state. "I need a shower."

"Go ahead. I'll call the groomer and see if they can take Beast. Will you be all right?"

"Thanks, Bee." Relief flooded her, at both the offer of help and the fact that he let everything else drop. She wasn't sure which she was more grateful for. She resisted the urge to beg him to sit outside the bathroom door. "I'll be fine." A chill touched the base of her neck. *Probably.*

4

Cass slid into the passenger seat of Stephanie's car. "Thanks for following me to drop the car off and for giving me a ride, Steph."

"No problem. Will you need a ride back to Emmett's later?"

"No, thank you. Emmett will detail the car then drop it off at the shop when he comes to work on the upstairs. Then I'll go pick Beast up from the groomer."

"You're going to put him in your clean car?"

Cass shrugged. "How dirty could he get going from the groomer to the car?"

Stephanie pinned her with a stare and raised a skeptical brow. "This is Beast we're talking about."

She couldn't really argue that. One time last winter when she took him to the groomer, he walked out the door and dove straight into a filthy pile of plowed snow in the parking lot between the front door and her car.

Stephanie remained unusually quiet as she drove, her gaze firmly riveted on the road ahead of her.

"Are you okay, Steph? You seem quiet lately, like something's bothering you."

Stephanie offered a weak smile, but tears shimmered in her eyes. "Yeah, I'm okay. Thanks."

"You know I'm always here if you need help or if you need someone to talk to, right?" She forced a grin, hoping to elicit some sort of reaction from Stephanie. "I've been told I'm a good listener."

The tiniest bit of laughter slipped out. "You're a great listener, Cass, and a great friend, and I appreciate that you want to help, but there's really nothing to talk about, just a lot on my mind." She reached over and squeezed Cass's hand. "I'm fine. Really. But if I ever do want to talk to someone, you're at the top of my list. Promise."

Cass let the matter drop. Stephanie didn't usually get moody—that was Bee's department—but everyone was entitled to be down once in a while. She'd just let her be and keep an eye on her. For now, at least.

Stephanie flipped on the radio and soft rock blared from the speakers. She seemed lost in the music as she drove, and Cass's mind began to wander.

She had no interest in thinking about ghosts or anything else that was stressful, so each time her mind started down that path, she shoved the thoughts aside.

Emmett had been moonlighting for her as a handyman, working on expanding the shop by finishing off a large room upstairs so she could increase attendance at her group readings.

The decision to expand hadn't been easy. Money was

tight as it was, but she could no longer fit everyone who regularly attended her group readings comfortably in the shop. It was either expand, or put a limit on the number of guests she could invite. Her head still swam a little every time she second-guessed herself, but Emmett had given her a good price. In addition to owning the only garage on Bay Island and doing odd jobs to generate extra income to support his son, Joey, Emmett was also a good friend.

Maybe she'd invite him and Sara Ryan, his new . . . hmmm . . . she didn't know what exactly Sara was. Girlfriend didn't seem quite right. Anyway, maybe she'd invite them for dinner tomorrow with Bee and Stephanie.

"You guys are still coming for dinner tomorrow, right?"

"Yes. Will Luke be there?"

Cass shrugged. Luke, her sort-of boyfriend—at least, he might be if they ever got a chance to talk to each other, never mind see each other—was getting to be a bit of a sore subject. With him living on the mainland and her living on Bay Island, they didn't get to spend much time together. Or any time at all lately. "I don't know. I left him a message, but he hasn't called back yet."

Artie Becker emerged from the new art gallery, his face red, his mouth set in a firm line. The man looked like he was about ready to boil over.

"Hey." She grabbed Stephanie's arm and snapped the radio off. "That's him."

"That's who?" Stephanie lifted her foot from the accelerator, and the car started to slow.

"No, no. Keep going." Cass slid low in the seat. She tried to avert her features so Artie wouldn't recognize her, but she still kept an eye on him in her peripheral vision.

He stalked toward the parking lot, hands fisted at his sides. She wouldn't be surprised if smoke started pouring out of his ears.

"Do you mind telling me what's going on?" Stephanie asked.

"That's Artie Becker. The guy with the missing daughter."

"Where?" Stephanie scanned the semicrowded board-walk. The sun had finally come out, and it was nearing seventy degrees. People ventured outdoors on one of the first nice Saturdays of the season.

"The guy with the black T-shirt." She gestured toward him.

Artie rounded a corner and headed toward the beach.

"Wait." Cass swiveled around in her seat but lost sight of him in a group of rowdy teenagers. "Darn. I lost him."

"If you wanted him, why did you tell me not to slow down?"

"I didn't want him, but I would like to know what he was doing in the art gallery."

"Do you want me to try to find him?"

Did she? She really didn't want to risk running into him just to satisfy her curiosity. Besides, she could always stop in the art gallery later and snoop around. "Nah. I have to get the shop open. I should have been there already."

Stephanie swung into the small parking lot in front of Mystical Musings. "Will you be okay by yourself?"

She shrugged, recalling the incident at the house that morning. "I'll be okay."

"I'll tell you what. Let me pick Bee up, and we'll bring lunch."

"I only dropped him off a little while ago, so he will not

be happy if you wake him." She couldn't help but grin. "Whatever you do, don't forget caffeine."

"Do I ever forget caffeine?" Stephanie laughed as Cass got out of the car and strolled up the boardwalk to the shop, then waited for her to unlock the door before pulling out.

She let the door fall shut behind her, turned the sign from CLOSED to OPEN, then crossed to the back of the store and unlocked the door that led to the beach. After propping it open, she walked out onto the wraparound porch and rested her hands on the railing.

Boats already dotted the bay, people walked along the beach, kids ran and played. A seagull dove and snatched a piece of food someone had left lying on a blanket. The Bay Pointe Lighthouse stood sentinel over it all. She inhaled deeply, the briny scent bringing memories of childhood, of a more peaceful time.

The tinkle of wind chimes announced her first customer of the day, and she reluctantly left serenity behind and went to work.

When she walked into the shop and saw Cayden and his wife, Sophie, two customers who'd been with her since she'd opened, her spirits soared. Cayden's ruddy cheeks turned even redder than usual as he lifted an infant seat and grinned.

"Oh, my gosh! You had the baby. Congratulations!" The light blue blanket spilling over the sides made her smile.

"A boy. Just like you said it would be." He shook his head, amusement dancing in his blue eyes.

Cass pulled down the blanket, careful not to wake the baby. "He's adorable, and look at all that dark hair. Just like his mama. What's his name?"

"Cayden Junior." Sophie looked down at little Cayden so lovingly it almost brought tears to Cass's eyes.

She was definitely on an emotional roller coaster. If she didn't get some sleep soon, she was going to lose it.

Cayden gripped her hand. "I'm sorry we weren't able to get out here sooner to offer more support, but I'm glad to hear everything worked out with that trouble you were having. You know we would have come back if you needed us." He squeezed her hand and moved aside for Sophie to give her a hug.

When she released her, Cass nodded and stepped back, trying to get a grip on herself.

Cayden and Sophie lived in the city, where Cayden worked as an ironworker. Out of desperation, when his rheumatoid arthritis almost cost him the job he loved, he'd come to Cass. He and Sophie were now regular customers, crediting the assortment of healing crystals Cass had given him for his recovery.

"So . . . did you guys just stop in to visit?"

"Actually, we're looking for a gift." Cayden gestured toward Sophie.

Her expression sobered. "My mother hasn't been feeling well lately." She shook her head. "She's suffered from depression ever since losing my father ten years ago."

"I'm sorry."

She sniffed. "She's been bad lately. We thought the baby might help, but she's not even interested in him. Most days she just sits in my father's chair and stares out the window." She threw her hands up in frustration. "She refuses to take the medication the doctor ordered, and I don't know what else to do. Do you have anything that might help?"

The plea for understanding, as well as the desperation in her eyes, tugged at Cass. Cayden and Sophie always came in for crystals, candles, and bath salts, but neither of them had ever had a reading, and Cass wasn't sure about their feelings on the subject. "Do you think she'll come in for a reading?"

Sophie blew out a relieved breath. "What is that, exactly?"

"Well, there are several ways I can do readings, but mostly we just sit and talk."

"Mom doesn't go out of her way to talk to people, but she will sit and talk to anyone who comes to visit, especially about Dad." She bit her lip and waited.

Cass loved Cayden and Sophie, but she really didn't feel like going into the city. Manhattan held too many bad memories for her, and she tended to avoid it like the plague. "Um . . . where does your mom live?"

"She lives in Manhattan, but we rented a house over in Southampton for next weekend, and we talked her into coming out with us and spending some time at the beach with Cayden Junior."

Taking the ferry to the North Shore and then driving over to Southampton wouldn't take that long. Besides, she absolutely loved the quaint little town on the South Shore of Long Island. But Saturday and Sunday were her busiest days in the shop. There was no way she could afford to close over the weekend. "When will you be there?"

"We'll arrive Thursday afternoon, and we're leaving on Monday night."

She could close the shop on a Monday that week instead of her usual Wednesday, since this was for work, not pleasure. Or she could close early on Friday and still have a few hours to walk through town and visit some of her favorite shops. This time of year, she didn't get much business before the weekend, anyway. Plus, Southampton wouldn't be as mobbed as it sometimes got on the weekends. "Okay. I'll tell you what. I can either come Friday afternoon or Monday morning, if that works."

"Oh, that would be perfect. Thank you so much!"

"Great. I'll call you and let you know which day as soon as I figure out my schedule." Maybe she'd see if Luke had time to meet up for a little while. If not, she could always ask Bee or Stephanie to come with her, then she'd have someone to hang out with afterward.

"If it's okay, I'll just pay you now. I'm willing to pay extra since you're coming to us." Cayden pulled out his wallet. "How much will it be?"

Cass quoted him her regular price. She needed some time away anyway, and it would feel good to spend the day relaxing with friends. The reading gave her the perfect excuse to take the time she so rarely indulged in for herself.

He handed her a stack of bills and held her hand in his. "Thank you, Cass. I don't know if it will work, but I can't tell you how much we appreciate you coming."

"You're very welcome. I hope I can help." She was pretty confident she could help some, as long as Sophie's mother believed in any sort of afterlife.

After saying good-bye to Cayden and Sophie, and having one last peek at their little guy, she put the money from Cayden—her fee plus an extra hundred dollars—into the register and set about her morning routine. The shop seemed empty without Beast, and she was surprised to find herself a little lonely.

She pulled her cell phone out of her bag, intent on calling

Luke to see if he was free on Friday or Monday, and found a missed call from him. Disappointment surged. They'd missed each other again. She hit the message button, and Luke's smooth southern drawl eased out. "Hey, beautiful. Sorry I missed you, and I'm sorry I can't make it for dinner tomorrow. Things have been crazy lately. Give me a call when you have time. Miss you."

Yeah. Miss you, too. With little hope of catching him, she dialed his number. As expected, his voice mail picked up. "Hi, Luke. I'm disappointed you can't make it tomorrow, but I understand. I have to go to Southampton next weekend, and I thought maybe we could get together. Let me know if you're free Friday or Monday. Miss you, too." She hesitated a moment, unsure of what else to say, her insecurities brimming over, but then she hung up and set the phone aside.

A cool breeze wafted through the shop, tinkling both sets of chimes she'd hung over the doors.

Cass froze and braced herself for the inevitable vision.

A shadow drifted across the shop, bathing everything in darkness, then allowing the light to return with even more intensity.

A premonition of death? Or just a cloud passing over? She had no way to know, but she was the only one in the shop at the moment. A portent of her own death? She shivered.

The chimes tinkled again, and she practically jumped out of her skin.

"Hey. What's the matter with you? You look like you saw a ghost." Bee stopped dead in his tracks and paled. "You didn't, did you?"

Stephanie almost plowed into his broad back. "Hey, watch it, buddy."

The look of horror on his face released the grip fear had on Cass. She laughed. "Nope. No ghosts," She waggled her eyebrows playfully. "Not today anyway."

"Better watch yourself there, honey, or no caffeine for you." He held up a cup holder with three large foam cups from Tony's bakery.

"Okay, sorry. I'll be nice." She smiled and fluttered her lashes.

"Smart aleck." He crossed the shop and put the cup holder on the table. Apparently, she was forgiven.

Stephanie dropped two large bags in the center of the table, slid out a chair, and sat. "Busy morning?"

Cass's phone beeped with a text, and she quickly read Luke's message. He had to work Friday and Monday. Pretty much what she'd expected. "Nah, not really. Cayden and Sophie came in, though. She had the baby."

"A boy, I presume?" Stephanie grinned.

"Of course."

"I'm sorry I missed him." She lowered her gaze to the table and muttered under her breath, "Probably better, anyway."

Cass let it go. She wasn't sure what was bothering Stephanie lately, but she never wanted to talk about it, no matter how many times Cass offered, so Cass would respect her privacy. For now. "By the way, they asked me to do a reading for Sophie's mother, but they want me to do it at a house in Southampton they rented next weekend. Either of you want to come and walk around town after?"

"You're going to close the shop on a weekend?" Stephanie frowned.

"Nah, either Friday afternoon or Monday morning. I can close all day Monday." If it was nice, they could go to the beach for a while, too. As much as she loved the Bay Island beaches, there was nothing like the sheer enormity and power of the ocean. Sitting on the cool sand, staring out at the endless expanse of water, knowing you were sitting on the edge of thousands of miles of ocean, made everyday problems seem somehow less significant.

"I have an appointment with a client on Friday, but I'll go Monday if you want." Bee grabbed a stack of napkins and a few forks and set the table.

Cass sat next to Stephanie. "Ooh, fancy today. I guess we're not eating McDonald's again?"

"Bite your tongue. I needed a real lunch, so we stopped at the diner."

Stephanie handed her a coffee cup. "I can't go either day. One of my clients completely screwed up his taxes, and now I'm trying to straighten it all out. I'll be in meetings both days."

"Why didn't he just have you do his taxes?"

"Exactly."

Ahh . . . Cass knew when to leave well enough alone. Maybe that explained the state Stephanie seemed to be in. "All right. I'll tell them Monday." Cass sipped her coffee. Mmm . . . No one made coffee like Tony and his wife, Gina.

Bee slid a breakfast skillet in front of her. Shredded breakfast potatoes, bacon, sausage, peppers, onions, tomatoes, scrambled eggs, and cheese. Her mouth watered.

"So, any new gossip at Tony's or the diner?" She tried to sound casual.

Bee's stare suggested she might have failed. "You mean, like, any talk of a woman's body turning up?" He tilted his head and lifted a brow.

"Now who's the smart aleck?"

"Maybe, but am I right?"

Cass shrugged, uncomfortable under his intense scrutiny. "It wasn't bothering me as much before Artie Becker showed up. And I can't imagine what he was doing coming out of the art gallery where a portrait of the woman from my visions is prominently displayed."

"Wait a minute." Bee held up a hand. "What portrait?"

Shoot. She'd forgotten she hadn't shared the art gallery image with them. "I uh . . ."

"Cass." Bee's tone was firm, a sure indication he wouldn't accept anything less than the truth.

"Oh, all right. Fine." She dropped her fork down onto her napkin. "When I was leaving the shop last night, I didn't want to walk on the beach, so I walked down the boardwalk. When I was passing the art gallery, I saw a portrait of a woman. It seemed like it might be the same woman I was seeing in my dreams, but I wasn't sure. I wanted to look at it again this morning on the way by, but then I saw Artie coming out of the gallery, and I forgot." She'd have to remember to get a closer look on her way home tonight.

"Well, I still say you should go to the police," Stephanie said.

Bee started laughing.

Stephanie scowled at him. "What's so funny?"

The two of them bickering was the last thing Cass needed. She shot Bee a *shut up* look.

He ignored it. No surprise there. "Don't you get it? That's where the dreams came from."

"What are you talking about, Bee?" Cass was fast losing patience.

"You probably noticed the portrait in the window, and

something about it stuck in your subconscious. Then you started having these weird, woo-woo dreams, and they scared you so badly you forgot where you actually saw the woman."

Stephanie's expression turned skeptical, but she remained silent.

Bee offered a knowing look, as if he'd solved the problem.

A cold draft prickled Cass's neck, ruffling the back of her hair. If only the solution could be that easy, but somehow, she didn't think it was. She lifted her fork and started to eat.

The tinkle of the wind chimes stopped her mid-bite, but when she turned, the shop was still empty.

5

"Come on, Beast." Cass hefted the bucket Bee had left behind the previous day, then lifted the leash from the hook by the door. She didn't bother to hook it to Beast's collar. He could run along the beach from her house to Mystical Musings without it, but she'd have to leash him before heading up to the boardwalk.

By the time Emmett had shown up with her car last night, she'd only had a few minutes to get to the groomer to pick Beast up, so she hadn't gotten to check out the art gallery window. No big deal. She'd just take a walk by this morning. At least no one should be around. She could take all the time she needed to examine the portrait. With a plan in mind, she pulled open the back door.

Beast bounded out into the yard and jumped off the deck.

Cass laughed, surprising herself, as she pulled the door shut behind her and locked up. After spending another night tossing and turning, she figured today she'd be downright somber, but the promise of a beautiful spring day on Bay Island, followed by a nice dinner with friends, cheered her up considerably. Besides, insomnia had its perks. She'd already put the roast in the Crock-Pot and cut up the vegetables and still had plenty of time before she had to open the shop. She could definitely get used to the more casually paced mornings. Most mornings had her running around like a lunatic trying to get out the door. Half the time she was late, anyway.

The sun had just begun to rise over the bay as Cass headed down the beach toward Mystical Musings with Beast trotting happily beside her. The soft breeze lifted her hair, carrying with it the scent of the sea. Waves lapped gently at the shore, leaving a soft, bubbling foam in their wake. Seagulls screamed and dove.

Returning to Bay Island had been the best decision Cass had ever made. Home brought a sense of peace she'd never quite captured while living in the city.

Beast ran ahead, leaping and jumping through the beach grass covering the dunes. If he kept it up, he'd need another bath before she even made it to the shop. She whistled for him. "Come on, boy. You're going to get ticks."

He crouched and jumped toward her, then returned to whatever game he was playing. She'd just have to brush him out and check him good later. She hated pulling ticks off him. Finding them in his long, thick coat was a nightmare. Hopefully the flea and tick repellent Doc had given her would do its job.

She dug up a piece of brown beach glass the tide had half-buried in the sand. Running her fingers over the smooth, rounded edges, she wondered briefly what it had once been, then dropped it into the bucket. The soft clink echoed in the quiet morning.

With plenty of time before she had to open the shop, she strolled along, taking her time, gathering anything that caught her eye. Beach grass, stones, seashells, driftwood, twigs, and small, oddly shaped branches. When she got to the shop, she'd fill a few mason jars with shells, rocks, and glass, then arrange the twigs, branches, and beach grass sticking out the top. They'd make great centerpieces for tonight's dinner. Hmm . . . maybe she'd make up a few extras to display in the shop. Even if they didn't sell, they'd make a great backdrop for the display of lighthouse replicas.

Beast's furious digging in the dunes intruded on her peace. Sand flew everywhere. It had to be catching in his long, shaggy coat again. Great. He was going to need another bath.

"Beast." She tried to inject some authority into the command. Apparently it didn't work, because his head didn't even pop up from behind the dune. "Beast!"

Nothing.

Giving up on trying to get his attention, she started toward him. "Beast. Come here, boy."

He lurched back, toppled over the top of the dune, landed on his back end in the sand, then rolled over and gained his footing. He charged toward her with whatever he had gripped between his teeth hanging out the sides of his mouth.

Ugh . . . What did he get into now? As he got closer, she backpedaled. "Down, boy. No, don't—"

His front paws landed hard against her chest, knocking her over. At least the sand cushioned her landing.

Beast dropped next to her and lowered his head.

Cass sat up and brushed sand from her arms and back. There wasn't much she could do about what had already gone down the back of her shirt and gotten into her hair, and she was already more than halfway to the shop, so no way was she going back home to change. She scratched her head. Great. Now she'd be itchy all day. "Thanks, Beast."

He shot her his best *I'm sorry* look from beneath his lashes.

"Yeah, yeah." She petted his head, then stood and brushed the remainder of the sand from her leggings. "I know. It's no one's fault but my own, and get him trained, and blah, blah, blah . . ."

Beast nudged her leg, offering what looked like a stick clamped between his teeth.

"What do you have there, boy? A present?" She reached for the stick. "Is that for my centerpie—"

As her fingers closed over the stick, a vision of the woman from her dreams slammed through her, knocking the wind from her lungs and driving her to her knees.

The woman called to her through a hazy veil. She reached out, her icy fingertips brushing the back of Cass's hand.

Beast nudged her side and whimpered, and Cass dropped the stick.

Although the vision released its hypnotic hold, the woman remained, hovering in front of her.

Cass held onto Beast's back and struggled to her feet, leaving the bucket's contents spilled on the sand.

The woman turned and started to float back toward the dunes where Beast had been digging.

Every instinct Cass possessed begged her to flee.

The woman stopped and glanced over her shoulder, making direct eye contact with Cass.

Cass expected to find fear through the murky haze. Instead, she found only sadness in the woman's eyes.

With a deep sigh, Cass ignored the urge to run away and started after the woman.

Apparently content that she was following, the woman continued her trek toward the dunes.

Beast barked and backed away.

Why on earth would Cass follow a specter that had been tormenting her for over a week? What was wrong with her? She must be out of her mind. *Well, I guess this is one way to find out. If there's nothing there, I'm crazy. If there is . . .* She might be better off just admitting she was crazy and moving on.

She climbed the gently sloping dune, the beach grass swaying in the breeze, tickling her ankles, sending a chill through her. At least she tried to convince herself that's what was causing the chill, because the temperature was noticeably cooler the farther she moved into the small mounds of sand. Funny, she'd never noticed that before. When she'd played on these same dunes as a child, hung out in them as a teenager, and walked them in search of shells, grass, and sticks as an adult, the temperature had always seemed consistent with what it had been on the beach.

She hugged herself tighter.

The wind whipped her hair across her face.

She pushed it behind her ears.

Beast crept warily beside her, tail tucked between his legs. A soft whimper escaped, and he glanced up at her, his eyes pleading.

She laid a shaky hand on his head. "I don't like it any more than you do, boy."

The woman stopped, hovered for a moment, then disappeared behind a dune.

Cass paused and petted Beast's head. "I guess this is it, Beast. We either check out whatever my imagination is trying to show us, or we walk away and pretend none of this ever happened."

Bee's voice screamed in her head, *"Walk away, walk away. Never mind that. Run!"*

I wish I could, Bee. But her need to help and comfort people, the same need that drove her to do what she did every day, wouldn't allow it.

She stopped in front of the dune the woman had disappeared behind and heaved in a deep, shaky breath. "Wait here, Beast." No sense making him any more uncomfortable than he already was.

He plopped down on the sand. Of course, he'd choose that moment to obey a command. Figures.

Leaving him standing guard, Cass scrambled over the dune and down into a small depression. Wet sand had been churned up and mixed with the dry top layer. Several sticks poked through the sand, probably exposed by Beast's furious digging.

She dropped to her knees and moved closer. Tendrils of ice wrapped around her. She braced herself for another vision as she closed her fingers around one of the sticks. Nothing happened. She applied a bit of pressure, gently tugging on the stick. Still nothing.

The stick didn't budge.

Giving up on trying to pull it out, she released the stick

and brushed some of the sand aside. She uncovered some sort of netting that had entangled the sticks. She shoved more sand aside, clearing a small area as best she could, then lifted aside some of the netting.

An empty eye socket stared out at her.

She screamed and jumped back, then half-scrambled, half-crab-walked backward up the dune. No way was she going back down there. She fumbled her phone from her pocket and dialed 911.

"Nine-one-one. What is your emergency?"

A sense of déjà vu assaulted her. She started to hyper-ventilate.

"Hello?"

Beast's frantic barking intruded on her panic attack.

"I'm at the beach."

"Are you hurt?"

"No. I found . . . um . . . something." What exactly did she find? She wasn't even sure. Maybe she should just hang up and forget it. Of course, the police would probably have to check the call out anyway, and she'd made it from her cell phone. Surely they had caller ID. "I think it might be a skeleton."

"Can you tell me where you are?"

"Um . . ." Cass looked around. The beach was so familiar. She'd played on it since she was a child. She walked back and forth to Mystical Musings on a regular basis. She knew every dip, curve, and indent in the shoreline. But she had no clue how to tell this woman where she was. "Uh . . ."

"Is there anyone else around?" It could be Cass's imagi-nation, or her heightened sense of fear, but it seemed to her a bit of impatience had begun to creep into the woman's neutral tone.

Okay. She was going to have to get a grip on herself. She was definitely closer to the shop than the house, so it made more sense for them to start there. "If you start at Mystical Musings and head north along the beach, I'm just past the cove."

"Where is the skeleton?"

"It's tangled up in some kind of net in the dunes."

"Do you see anyone else?"

Realization dawned. She hadn't asked if anyone was around because she wanted to talk to someone else, she'd asked out of fear for Cass's safety. "No. I don't see anyone."

"Okay. Just wait there. I've already dispatched a car." Her tone softened. "They should be there soon. Do you want me to stay on the phone with you?"

Cass thought about it for a minute. While it would be nice to have the company of another human being, she had no clue what she'd talk to this woman about for however long it took the officers to reach Mystical Musings and then walk down to the beach and meet her. "Thank you, but I'll be okay."

She disconnected the call and walked toward the water. She could call Luke, but even if he did agree to come, it would take him hours to get there. Stephanie would come in a heartbeat, but she seemed to be dealing with enough of her own problems at the moment. When she reached the edge, she stopped and sat beside Beast. "You okay, boy?"

He propped his head in her lap, and she weaved her fingers into his thick mane, then dialed Bee's number.

It took four rings before his groggy voice came over the line. "This had better be good."

"What are you doing?"

"Well, I *was* sleeping."

"I . . . um . . . I thought you might still be at the shop."

"No. I finished up around four, stopped for a donut, then came home and went to bed." He sighed, apparently accepting that he wasn't going back to sleep just yet. "What are you doing up so early, and why are you calling from your cell phone? If you woke me up because you saw another ghost, I'm not going to—"

"Actually, I did see another ghost."

"That's it. I'm hanging up now."

"This time it led me to a skeleton."

Silence.

No way would he hang up after hearing that. If he had to get gossip like that at the deli, he'd never forgive himself. She outwaited him.

"Where are you?"

"On the beach. Almost to the shop. I was walking to work when Beast dug up a skeleton. Well, at least, I think it's a skeleton. I'm pretty sure the sticks are bones, and I don't know what else could look so much like a skull. But it's all wrapped up in a net, and I'm all alone on the beach with Beast, but the police are coming. I hope it's Tank and not one of those other clowns that—"

"All right. Enough. Stop babbling. You just woke me up, and it's taking my brain too long to process all of this. Are you okay?"

"Yeah. I'm okay."

"I'm already half-dressed. I'm on my way out the door."

Bee didn't get up early for too many people. "Thanks, Bee."

At the sound of a motor, she tucked her phone into her pocket and watched a white SUV fly toward her, lights flashing. She didn't know why she assumed they'd walk down the beach just because four-wheeling wasn't allowed on Bay Island beaches. Obviously, in an emergency, the police would be allowed to have vehicles.

Tank hopped out of the driver's side and strode toward her, his pace brisk, his jaw set in a firm line.

She checked the urge to run to him.

His partner, Harry Gunther, emerged from the passenger seat. He hiked up his pants and strolled toward her as if he had all day. He was only a couple of weeks away from retirement, and his mind had already beat him to it.

"Please tell me it wasn't you who called it in." Tank stood staring at her, hands propped firmly on his hips.

She shrugged. "Sorry."

"Where?"

She pointed toward the dunes.

"Wait here." He walked away muttering something about her being a magnet for trouble.

Cass bristled. It wasn't her fault. Besides, this time trouble had found her. She couldn't control it if a spirit wanted to lead her somewhere. All she could do was follow. Well, technically, that wasn't true. She could have walked away and left well enough alone. She could have continued to believe she wasn't psychic, just intuitive. Now . . . well, now she had no idea what to think, but trying to figure it out was beginning to give her a headache.

She lost sight of Tank as he crouched behind the dunes.

Harry stared at her, a pen poised over a beat-up notebook. "So, what happened?"

Okay. This was the tricky part. Did she admit to seeing an . . . apparition?

Harry continued to stare at her, pen held ready to record any brilliant insights she might share. Harry was one of those guys who looked like a basset hound, jowls sagging, eyes drooping, frown etched firmly and permanently in place. He was also a real sweetheart.

"Beast dug up something I think might be a skeleton." She would have to remind Tank to talk to Artie Becker. The thought that the bones might belong to his daughter made her stomach lurch. Luckily, she hadn't eaten breakfast.

6

Tank emerged from the dunes a little while later and headed toward the shore, where Cass stood barefoot in the gently lapping waves.

Beast frolicked happily in the surf, despite her command—as well as some seriously intense begging and, she was ashamed to admit, whining—for him to stay out of the water.

Harry had already given up on trying to get answers and started directing arriving personnel toward the suspected crime scene. He'd made no attempt to join Tank. Even though Harry was a nice guy, he wasn't exactly the picture of ambition.

"Want to tell me what happened?" Tank asked when he reached her side.

"We were walking down the beach toward Mystical Musings when Beast dug up what I suspect are bones." She drew circles in the wet sand with her big toe, then watched the gentle waves come in and erase the lines as if they'd never even been there.

"Is that all?"

She shrugged. No way was she sharing anything more with Tank. He was her best friend's husband. He was already a little leery of her getting Stephanie into trouble. Best to leave well enough alone. Besides, nothing she'd seen could help their investigation in any way.

She was saved from having to answer when Bee charged down the beach toward them. "Cass," he yelled.

All eyes turned in his direction. Even Beast stopped and stared.

Bee was a sight to behold on a good day, even without the platform shoes he was plowing through the sand in. Now, with his bleached blond hair completely disheveled and sticking up everywhere, wrinkled clothes, shirt buttons askew, and if she wasn't mistaken, two different shoes, he was jaw-dropping.

Beast surged out of the water. Cass realized his intentions a moment too late to grab him.

"Beast, no!" She started after him.

Water poured from his thick coat as he sprinted toward Bee.

"Whoa! You stop right there, Beast." Bee held his hands up and backed up frantically. "No, boy. Down."

Beast lunged, planting his paws firmly on Bee's chest and bowling him over.

Bee landed sprawled in the sand on his back, a soaking-wet Beast straddling his chest. "Get. Him. Off," he managed between clenched teeth.

Several officers rushed to his side, reaching him a few seconds before Cass.

When they finally rolled a confused Beast off him, the big dog toppled over in the sand and rolled onto his back. Then he squirmed around a bit before he scrambled to his feet and shook water and sand off his massive body, managing to spray everyone in the vicinity.

"Beast. No." Cass grabbed his collar and pulled him away, then looked up into half a dozen angry glares. "Um . . . sorry."

Tank and another officer reached Bee and helped him to his feet.

He brushed himself off, shot Cass a dirty look, then tried to compose himself.

Tank was the first to laugh. To his credit, it seemed as if he tried to control it, and he did manage to keep it reined in, at first, but not for long. A deep belly laugh blurted out.

Some of the sand-covered officers tentatively joined in while trying to brush the mess of sand and water from their uniforms.

Cass turned away. No way in the world she'd let Bee catch her laughing at his expense, and yet, she couldn't help but find humor in the situation. Maybe because it hadn't been her lying spread-eagle in the sand with more than a hundred pounds of wet dog on her chest.

"Don't think you're getting off that easy, Cass." Tank's voice in her ear startled her. "If there's something more going on here, I will find out."

Cass just nodded, resisting the urge to swallow the guilt threatening to choke her. She wasn't exactly lying, but Tank was a friend, and she was definitely withholding information. Just not relevant information. She hoped.

He hovered quietly by her side for another moment, then let the matter drop. "Do you need a ride?"

She looked down at Beast. "No, thanks. I'll walk back to the house and call the groomer." Hopefully they could get him in and she could drop him off on her way to the shop. So much for being early.

"Okay, then I'll talk to you later." He turned and started back up the beach. When he caught sight of Bee, he just sighed and shook his head.

"Wait. Tank?"

He stopped and turned back.

She pitched her voice low. "Was I right? Is it a skeleton?"

He pursed his lips, and she didn't expect him to answer. But then he gave a brisk nod.

A million questions beat at her. Knowing she had only seconds before Tank would walk away, she blurted out the one most prominent in her mind. "Can you tell if it was a woman? And how long she's been there?"

He held her gaze. "Are you sure you don't want to tell me anything?"

She sighed. No way she'd tell him she saw a ghost, but she could mention Artie's visit. "I don't know if it has anything to do with this or not, but a man came into the shop for a reading Friday night. His adult daughter is missing, and he wanted to see if I could contact her or offer any information."

Tank pulled out a notebook and pen. "Name?"

"Artie Becker." She struggled to keep from offering her personal opinion of Artie.

"How long has she been missing?"

"He said he wasn't sure. He hadn't seen her in years, but

he thought maybe she disappeared sometime in the past six months. He said he'd already reported it to the police." She pressed a hand to her stomach, hoping to quell some of the queasiness.

"All right. I'll check it out." He flipped the book closed and dropped it into his pocket. "I'm going to ask one favor, Cass. Stay out of it. If Mr. Becker returns, find an excuse to stall him and let me know."

She nodded, a small niggle of fear rushing up her spine.

Tank's expression softened, and he smoothed a hand over his closely shaved crew cut, then looked around and leaned closer to her. "If it makes you feel any better, I doubt this is Mr. Becker's daughter if she's only been missing a few months. I can't say for sure, and I'll still check it out, but a body doesn't . . . um . . . deteriorate . . . that quickly, especially when it's been buried in sand."

Relief rushed through her, and she offered a small smile. "Thanks, Tank."

"Sure." He squeezed her arm and returned to the crime scene.

Bee stood a little ways away, looking sort of dazed. Fully expecting him to read her the riot act, she trudged toward him, intent on apologizing.

Beast trotted contritely beside her.

"Look, Bee, I—"

"Save it, Cass. I already know, you're sorry. Let's move on."

Grateful he was willing to let it go, she hugged him.

He stepped back, brushed his hand over hers, and frowned. "What happened to your hand? What are these red marks running across the back? They look almost like . . ." He lifted her hand closer to his face. "There's no blood, but the marks look like scratches, like someone raked their nails over your hand."

The memory of the woman's cold fingers grazing that same hand assailed her. She pulled her hand away and tucked it behind her. "I don't know. Beast knocked me over before, maybe I got scratched." *Sorry, Beast.* The half truth sat like a rock in her gut, but Bee definitely wouldn't want to hear that a ghost had raked her hand, and she most definitely wasn't ready to admit it.

"Well, you'd better put something on it, so it doesn't get infected."

She snatched the bucket she'd been carrying but didn't bother to fill it back up. She could pick up some stuff near the shop if it was slow later. Right now she just wanted to go home, get cleaned up, and get the shop open at a halfway decent hour.

Thankfully, Bee dropped his interrogation and fell into step beside her as they headed toward her house, only giving Beast one wary stare.

"So, are you still coming for dinner tonight?"

"Are you still up to cooking?"

"Actually, yes. I'd really like the company." The admission brought a rush of heat to her cheeks.

"Then I wouldn't miss it."

She slid her hand into his and leaned her head against his arm. "Thanks, Bee."

Leaving the chaos of the crime scene behind, they walked together in the quiet of the morning.

Bee didn't stay silent long. "So, tell me what happened." He held up his free hand. "At a reasonable pace, please."

She laughed. "Sorry about that. I was a little . . . uh . . ."

"You weren't a little anything, Cass. You were freaking out completely."

"All right. I guess that could be true." She grinned and filled him in, leaving out the hand-grazing incident. "But Tank said he doesn't think it's Artie Becker's daughter. He thinks the bones have probably been there too long."

By the time she was done talking, they'd reached her house. She dug her keys out of her pocket and opened the door.

Bee leaned against the deck railing.

"Aren't you coming in?"

"Nah. I'll wait here."

She held his gaze, trying to judge if he was too scared of her ghost to go inside.

He offered his best innocent look. "What?"

"You are going to have to come in at some point, Bee."

He shrugged. "I'm coming for dinner later, aren't I? I just want to stand out in the sun a few minutes and let my shirt dry."

"Hmm . . ." She let it drop. He was right, he was coming for dinner later, and if he wanted to eat, he'd have to come in.

Leaving Beast to run around the yard and Bee leaning against the railing to dry off, Cass ran in and grabbed the phone. She strode toward the bathroom while she dialed the groomer. She didn't have time for a shower, but she could change her clothes.

"Already? What'd he get into now, Cass?"

Shocked, she yanked the phone from her ear and stared at it for a moment, then remembered caller ID and laughed. "We went to the beach."

"I hate to tell you this, but I can't get him in until tomorrow. I'm totally swamped all day."

She sighed. It would have to be good enough. "I'll take it, but could you call the shop if you get a cancellation?"

"You bet."

"Thanks." After making the appointment and hanging up, Cass quickly stripped down, sprinkled herself with baby powder, and brushed most of the sand off with a towel. She pulled on a clean pair of yoga pants and a long, loose-fitting top. Unable to avoid the inevitable any longer, she took a deep breath, braced herself, and looked down at her hand.

Bee was right. Four red lines marred her left hand from her wrist to her knuckles, the exact path the woman's fingers had followed. Had she been trying to take her hand? To lead her into the dunes? Cass looked in the mirror. Dark circles ringed her eyes. Exhaustion was definitely getting the better of her.

A hazy image shimmered into view, its reflection hovering over her shoulder.

She jumped and spun around.

The woman from her dreams backed away but remained visible.

"Help me." The words echoed in Cass's mind as if they'd been spoken aloud, but the woman's mouth remained closed, lips pressed tightly together, strain lines bracketing her mouth.

All right. Enough was enough. She couldn't keep cowering in fear each time the apparition materialized. "I thought I did."

"No."

"I followed you on the beach. I found the skeleton you've been trying to show me."

"No."

"Then what is it you want?" Frustration and lack of sleep shortened her temper.

"Help me."

"I'm trying! I can't help you unless I understand what you want."

The woman spun and surged toward the door.

A stack of magazines on the side of the garden tub ruffled as she passed.

The apparition jerked to a stop and stared wide-eyed at the magazines. Then she disappeared, simply winked out of existence as if she'd never been there. Who knew? Maybe she hadn't.

Cass splashed a few handfuls of cold water onto her face, then grabbed a couple of ibuprofen from the medicine cabinet and swallowed them with a handful of water from the faucet. She grabbed her makeup bag and strode toward the kitchen.

Apparently finding the body wasn't enough—she was going to have to try to figure out who the woman was and what she could possibly want. She dropped her makeup bag into her oversize purse, tossed Beast's brush on top of it, and locked up.

Bee still stood in the same spot she'd left him, eyes closed, face turned up to the sun. For a minute she thought he'd fallen asleep that way. Then he slit open one eye. "So, anyone in there?"

"Uh . . ."

"Never mind. I don't really want to know." He pushed away from the railing and started toward the steps. "My car is parked at your shop, so you'll have to drive. We can drop

Beast off at the groomer on the way, but then I want coffee . . . and breakfast."

"Actually, they couldn't get him in. Apparently Sunday is one of their busier days. After I get the shop open, I'll just take him out back onto the porch and give him a good brushing."

"Fine. I'll pick up my car at the shop and go to the deli while you take this monster out and brush him." His mood seemed to improve. "I'll let you know what's being said about the skeleton when I get back."

"Thanks, Bee. You're the best." And if the skeleton wasn't the latest gossip fodder when he got there, it most certainly would be by the time he left. She grinned and gestured to Bee's misbuttoned shirt. "But you might want to fix yourself before you go into the deli."

He looked down, appalled.

"You might also want to stop home for a matching shoe." She laughed, some of her stress melting away. But as she crossed the back lawn, a chill prickled her spine, and she paused, certain a shadow would pass. The sun continued to beat down, cocooning her in its warm embrace.

7

The chimes tinkled, and Cass looked up from the inventory sheet she was working on.

A girl Cass didn't recognize walked in and looked around. She couldn't be more than fourteen or fifteen years old, and Cass glanced out the window to see if anyone else was on their way in. A red ten-speed bicycle was propped against the side of the boardwalk steps.

"Hi." Cass skirted the counter to greet her.

"Hi." Her cheeks reddened, making her abundance of freckles more prominent.

"I'm Cass." She extended a hand, which the girl took. "It's nice to meet you."

"Nice to meet you, too." She seemed to relax a little. "I'm Ava."

"Are you looking for anything special, or just looking around?"

"Actually . . ." She twisted her hands together, her expression somber. "I need a good luck charm or something."

"Is everything okay?" Cass didn't get a negative feel from her, but she wanted to make sure the girl wasn't in any kind of trouble. "It helps if I know what you need the charm for."

Ava brushed a lock of red hair that had fallen out of her ponytail off her face. "I have to take my first New York State Regents exams soon, and I'm a nervous wreck. I talked to my parents about it, and they said to just do my best, but I can't sleep because I'm so worried about failing, and I'm so tired I can't even concentrate to study." Her shoulders slumped with the admission, as if relieved to finally have it off her chest.

Cass bit back a smile, not wanting Ava to think she wasn't taking her problem seriously. She could certainly relate to this child's exhaustion, and she could still remember a time when passing exams had been her major concern. "I think I have just the thing to help you."

Her entire face brightened. "Really?"

"Yup. Come with me." She led Ava to a shelf on the other side of the shop, then pulled down a wooden box and handed it to her.

Ava studied the box, turning it over in her hands. When her gaze fell on the twenty-five-dollar price tag on the bottom, she held the box back out to Cass. "Do you have anything a little less expensive? I only have fifteen dollars."

Cass pushed the box back toward her. "Just so happens it's on sale this week. Open it."

"Thank you." Ava opened the box and stared at the row of small, handcrafted dolls, each about an inch long. "What are they?"

"They're worry dolls. They are made in Guatemala, each

one handcrafted from pieces of wood." Cass lifted one out of the box and handed it to her. "The artisans then use scraps of woven fabric and yarn to make traditional Mayan costumes."

"They're beautiful, but how do they help?"

"According to legend, you tell the dolls your worries at night, then place them under your pillow. The dolls worry for you while you sleep." Cass shrugged. "Supposedly, you wake up feeling well rested and worry free."

Ava looked skeptical. "Have you ever tried them?"

"I haven't . . ." *Yet.* Although, if things kept going the way they were, she might just have to take a box home with her. "But I do know people who have, and they swear they work."

"Okay, you've talked me into it." A huge grin spread across her face, and Cass could see through the slightly awkward but adorable teenager to the beautiful woman she would one day become. "Even if it doesn't help, it can't hurt, right?"

"That's very true." Cass took the box to the counter and rang it up, then placed the box in a shopping bag with handles so Ava would be able to carry it while riding her bike. "Good luck. Make sure you stop back in and let me know how they work out."

"You bet I will. Thank you." She slid the handles over her wrist and waved as she bounced out the door, looking much happier than when she'd come in.

That was the part of her job Cass loved most. The ability to help people. Now, if only she could figure out how to help the woman who'd sought her out in her dreams. If she was real, of course. There was always the possibility she'd been nothing more than a nightmare. But no matter how hard she tried, she couldn't shake the image of the woman, or the certainty that she was somehow in trouble. She sighed and marked the ten-dollar discount in her ledger so Stephanie would see it when she did the books.

She wished Bee would hurry back with her coffee. She needed a distraction from her overactive imagination as much as she needed the caffeine to keep her awake.

All right. Enough was enough. Unable to focus on anything, Cass gave up and decided to take a walk. She took a quick look around before locking the door to Mystical Musings. The few people meandering along the boardwalk didn't seem interested in shopping. Besides, it would only take a few minutes to peek in the art gallery window. Once she saw for herself that the woman in the portrait wasn't the same woman haunting her dreams—and now her reality—she could get back to work. Hopefully.

A squirrel scampered across the porch railing, and Beast launched himself at it. Cass tightened her hold on the leash, and it caught, stopping him from running off but nearly jerking her arm out of the socket.

She sighed. She'd call Herb as soon as she got back to the shop.

She walked quickly toward the gallery, keeping an eye out for Artie Becker. If he was still in town, and he'd visited the diner, the deli, or the bakery any time after this morning, he should already have heard about the skeleton they'd dug up. She had no idea if rumor had it that she'd been the one to make the discovery yet, but once it did, she expected Artie might return. And despite Tank's warning to stay out of this, she really wanted to know what Artie had been doing in the art gallery.

She started past Dreamweaver Designs, but the new display in the window stopped her short. Bee had outdone himself this time. A few pieces of his trial lingerie line were prominently displayed beside one of his most popular beach wedding dresses, and they were stunning. The filmy blue fabric left just the right amount to the imagination. Bee was right, lingerie could be done tastefully.

Beast nudged her leg, apparently impatient to move on.

"In a hurry to get somewhere, boy, or do you just want to walk?" She resumed her trek toward the gallery.

Beast barked once and took his place at her side.

The boardwalk was surprisingly empty for such a beautiful spring day, especially after the rough winter they'd had. Snowstorm after snowstorm had barreled up the coast, burying them for most of February and March.

She stopped in front of the art gallery and stared at the portrait in the center of the window. A young boy in a field playing with his dog. A quick scan of the rest of the window yielded the same results. The woman's portrait was gone. Had it ever even been there in the first place? A dull throbbing began at her temples. Maybe she really was losing it. She studied the new painting again, so different from what she'd seen the other night, or at least what she thought she had seen. Only one way to find out.

Cass pulled the door open and poked her head in.

A woman looked up from where she sat in front of a canvas. "Hi. Can I help you?"

"Ummm . . ." What if the portrait had never been there? What if she'd imagined the whole thing? What if it had been a vision? "I wanted to ask you about a portrait. Is it okay to bring my dog in?"

The woman eyed Beast a little warily. "As long as he'll behave."

Cass looked down at Beast, his eyes wide, tongue hanging out, innocence written all over his expression while his body quivered in anticipation of running around somewhere new. "Maybe you'd better come out here."

"Sure, no problem." She set her paintbrush aside and wiped her hands on her paint-splattered smock.

Cass let the door fall shut and returned to the window. Any change? Nope. Her portrait was still gone, and in its place, boy and dog still frolicked endlessly.

The door squeaked open, and the woman emerged, her long, blond hair tied in a messy knot atop her head. She extended a hand. "Hi. I'm Leighton Mills."

Beast started wiggling frantically, then crouched to jump.

"Beast, no." She tightened her already white-knuckled grip on his leash and shook Leighton's hand. "Cass Donovan. I own Mystical Musings down the boardwalk." She gestured over her shoulder toward her shop, then fished a toy out of her bag and dropped it in front of Beast.

Thankfully, he slid down in the shade of the awning and started to chew.

"Nice to meet you, Cass. How can I help you?"

"Actually, I walked by here the other night, and I thought there was a different painting displayed in the window. A portrait of a woman?" She held her breath, heart thundering, while she waited patiently for confirmation of her insanity.

Leighton shifted from one foot to the other, her gaze darting nervously around the boardwalk. "Oh, uh . . . That's not for sale."

"Do you still have it?"

She hesitated. "I do, but like I said, it's not for sale."

"Can you tell me anything about the woman in the portrait?"

Her perfectly arched eyebrows drew together when she frowned. "I'm sorry. I don't really know anything." With that, she clamped her lips firmly together. She obviously wasn't going to offer up anything more.

Cass glanced down at Beast, who was happily munching his bone. She tried to order her thoughts. Now that she knew the portrait actually existed, what else did she want to know? Obviously, Leighton wasn't going to hand over any information, so Cass would just have to figure out the right questions to ask. Maybe if she could figure out who the artist was, she could track the woman through the artist.

Leighton twisted a gold ring with what appeared to be a nice-size marquise-cut diamond around her left ring finger while she waited.

Cass gestured toward the window. "Did you paint all of these?"

A warm smile emerged, and her posture relaxed. "I paint everything in the display window, but I also carry paintings from other local artists inside, if you'd like to see?"

Bingo. Since the painting was displayed in the window, Leighton must have painted it. "I'd love to one day when I can come in without Beast."

Leighton looked down at him. "Oh, you can bring him in. I love dogs, I was just worried he'd damage something, but look how well behaved he is."

Cass laughed. "Maybe right at this moment, but trust me, it goes downhill fast."

"He seems like such a sweetheart. Can I pet him?"

"Sure."

She tucked her long skirt behind her legs as she squatted, then ruffled the fur on Beast's head. "What a good boy you are."

Beast tilted his head into her hand.

She had to figure out a way to get into the shop and find the painting. Without Beast. "I love your work. My friend Bee owns Dreamweaver Designs, and he mentioned wanting to stop in and look at some of your beach paintings for his shop."

"Thank you." Leighton stood and brushed sand from Beast's fur off her hands. "I'd be happy to show him some."

The shop that now housed the art gallery had stood empty, its windows boarded, all winter long. She hadn't noticed any work going on in there, then suddenly the gallory openod with no fanfare, no grand opening announce ment, no advertising. "How long have you been open?"

"I opened a couple of weeks ago, but my official grand opening will be Memorial Day weekend." Leighton crossed her arms and leaned against the white window trim. "I'm trying to put the finishing touches on a few more paintings before then."

"Are you from Bay Island?"

She shook her head. "Nah, I grew up on Long Island, but I used to come here every summer when I was younger. I fell in love with the island and always dreamed of having an art gallery on the boardwalk."

"Well, congratulations on your unofficial opening."

Leighton laughed. "Thank you."

A car horn beeped and Cass looked over her shoulder. Bee waved as he passed.

Stephanie craned her neck from the passenger seat to see past him.

Cass waved to them and turned back to Leighton. "It was nice meeting you, but I have to run."

"Nice to meet you, too. Stop in any time, even just to say hello."

She would definitely be back to find out more about that portrait and what Artie Becker had been doing there, just as soon as she could figure out a tactful way to get the information she wanted. "I will, thanks. Feel free to drop in at Mystical Musings, too."

They said their good-byes, and Leighton patted Beast's head before going inside.

Cass headed back toward the shop, relieved to know she hadn't imagined the painting, but with more questions than answers about who the woman was and why Leighton was so reluctant to discuss her.

Bee and Stephanie met her at the door, and Bee didn't even wait for her to unlock it before letting loose the inevitable barrage of questions. "What were you doing at the gallery? Was it something to do with Artie Becker? Did she say anything?"

Stephanie just rolled her eyes behind his back.

Cass grinned. "Maybe I just went for a walk and ran into the new gallery owner."

Bee's exaggerated eye roll put Stephanie's to shame. He grinned. "Look, Cass, if you don't want to tell us what happened, that's fine, but don't insult my intelligence by feigning innocence. I know you too well to fall for that, honey."

She laughed and held the door open for them to enter. "Okay, okay. I went to see what I could find out."

"That's better." He handed her a coffee cup on his way past.

Letting the door fall shut, she flipped the sign to OPEN and followed them toward the back of the shop. She unlocked the back door before joining them at the table. "So, what'd you hear at the deli?"

Stephanie fished a wrapped sandwich out of a brown paper bag and slid it across the table to her. She held another out to Bee.

"Uh-uh." Bee wagged a finger at her, took the sandwich from Stephanie, then waggled his bushy, dark brown eyebrows. "I'll only show you mine if you show me yours first."

She laughed, but sobered quickly, and then flopped into the chair, leaving her sandwich untouched on the table in front of her. "I actually didn't find out much, just that she has the painting I saw in the window . . ." Well, that actually was an important piece of information. At least, it proved her sanity. Sort of. "And that it's not for sale. Other than that, I couldn't get anything out of her."

"Hmm . . . weird." He unwrapped his breakfast, then gestured toward Cass's sandwich. "I got you bacon, egg, and cheese on a roll. I hope that's all right."

"It's fine. Thanks, Bee."

She didn't bother to mention that Leighton's behavior had seemed off when Cass had asked about the portrait. That could very well have been her overactive imagination.

Bee held up a strip of bacon and ordered Beast to sit.

Beast plopped his bottom down on the floor, his whole back end wagging wildly, energy vibrating through him, but he remained firmly planted where he was.

Bee tossed him the bacon strip.

"Hey. How'd you do that?"

Intent on quelling the smug look Bee was currently sporting, she unwrapped her sandwich and took off a piece of bacon, then strode toward Beast and held up the treat. "Beast, sit."

He launched himself through the air and snatched the bacon from her hand, then hit the floor, scrambled for purchase on the polished wood, flopped onto his side, and slid into a chair, knocking it over with a loud clatter, eliciting a burst of hysterical laughter from Bee. Beast munched down the bacon without losing so much as a crumb.

She glared at Bee. "Ha-ha."

Stephanie laughed and shook her head, but refrained from encouraging him, for which Cass was grateful.

He wiped the tears from his face and held up a business card. "Here."

Still pouting, she plucked the card from his hand. "What's this?"

"Guess who I ran into at the deli?"

Ignoring him, she read what turned out to be an appointment card. *Wednesday, 11:00 A.M.* was printed boldly in the center beneath the name *Herb Cox*.

"No excuses this time, Cass. Mystical Musings is closed on Wednesdays, so there's no reason you can't make it."

She stuffed the card into her purse and mumbled, "Thanks." It wasn't that he was wrong. Beast needed to be trained before he ended up hurting someone, but he didn't have to be so superior about it.

"Quit sulking, Cass, or I won't tell you what I found out." He took a big bite of his sandwich.

Cass shot a questioning gaze at Stephanie.

She held up a hand. "Don't look at me. He picked me up after and refused to tell me a thing."

Cass picked at her sandwich but finally relented, the need to hear the latest gossip outweighing the need to keep from satisfying Bee. "Fine. What'd you hear?"

"I thought so." He put his sandwich down on the paper wrapper, brushed the crumbs off his hands, and leaned his forearms on the table. Bee had dirt. "Well, it seems your friend Artie Becker has been making the rounds looking for his daughter. Rumor has it, he's been to the deli, Tony's, and the diner. But . . ." He held up a finger. "He's not the only one."

Cass sat up straighter, her interest piqued. "What do you mean?"

"Apparently, there's another man asking around about her." He frowned. "Well, actually, no one seems to be sure he's looking for the same woman. Everyone just assumed so, because, hey, let's face it, how many women turn up missing on Bay Island?"

"Are you sure it's a second guy?"

He shrugged. "A young guy. Slim, glasses, shaggy hair?"

"That's definitely not Artie Becker."

He waved her off. "I'll know more later, anyway."

"Why?"

"Well, when I was getting ready to leave, an order came in for coffee. Seems they are sending someone from the deli out to the beach with coffee and buttered rolls and bagels for the crime scene techs."

"Do you know who they sent?"

He grinned. "Emma Nicholls."

Cass laughed. "Yup, with Emma out there, we'll get all the dirt for sure."

"Why do you think they sent her?"

Bee was right. As soon as word spread that Emma had been anywhere near the crime scene and had contact with some of the responding officers, business in the deli would be booming for sure.

"Anything else?"

Bee shifted in his seat.

Uh-oh.

"Well, you're probably not going to like it."

"Spit it out." She braced herself for the worst.

"Rumor has it, Artie was in here talking to you before you found the body on the beach. Everyone thinks his daughter's ghost led you to her body."

"Hmm . . ." What else could she say? That might actually be pretty close to the truth.

8

The first thing to hit Cass when she walked into the kitchen was the scent of pot roast, which brought back a rush of childhood memories. Playing on the beach or riding bikes throughout the neighborhood with her friends, then coming home to the house filled with the aromas of dinner cooking or something baking in the oven. Her mom had loved to cook. The ache of losing her parents never fully went away, but sometimes, when a particularly strong reminder surfaced, the pain was nearly unbearable.

She sighed and hung Beast's leash on a hook beside the door, then filled one of his bowls with water and dumped a scoop of dry dog food into the other. Preparing the rest of dinner would be a lot easier if he was already fed.

She thought again of the woman who'd been haunting her. Was she really a ghost of someone who'd lived before? Or just a figment of Cass's imagination trying to tell her something she already knew, something she might have repressed? It was possible her subconscious was trying to relay a message. But what could she possibly know about the woman?

Frustrated, she set aside the line of thought. If there was anything, hopefully it would come to her eventually. For now, she wanted to forget about everything and enjoy a nice dinner with friends. With no talk of death.

As soon as Beast finished inhaling his food, she opened the back door, checked the gate was closed, and let him out. Leaving the door open so he could come back in when he was ready, she turned her attention to dinner. She didn't cook often, but when she did she enjoyed it.

She checked the roast, then gathered what she'd need for the salad and put it on the cutting board. She pulled out a large salad bowl, set it on the counter beside the sink, and started washing the lettuce and breaking it up in the bowl.

"Hello," Stephanie called as she came in the front door.

"Hey." Cass glanced out the window over the sink to make sure Beast was okay. "I'm in the kitchen."

Stephanie came in a moment later. Alone.

Cass frowned. "Where's Bee?"

"Either at the deli, the bakery, or the diner." She grinned. "Take your pick."

"What?"

"After we left Mystical Musings earlier, he dropped me off and went to make the rounds."

Cass couldn't help but laugh. Bee lived for gossip. "Yeah, well, he'd better still be hungry when he gets here."

"Seriously?" Stephanie shot her a pointed look. "When is Bee not hungry?"

"Okay, that's true."

Beast surged through the door, skidding when he hit the floor, but managed to regain his footing before falling or knocking anything—or anyone—over. Of course, he left a trail of mud in his wake.

Stephanie petted his head in greeting. "So, he starts training Wednesday, huh?"

"Yup. Looks like it." Cass just sighed and started cleaning up the mess. What in the world had he gotten into this time? She'd have to go check after dinner.

"That oughta be fun, no?"

Cass didn't really think it would be, but she kept the opinion to herself. She had no idea why she was so resistant to training. She wanted Beast to listen, and she definitely didn't want to see him get hurt or hurt anyone else, but the thought of going to classes to teach him how to behave just seemed weird. Of course, she'd never owned a dog before, not even as a child, so the thought of being corralled in a pen with a bunch of other dogs intimidated her just a little. Okay, actually, it scared her a lot.

"It'll be fine, Cass." Stephanie laid a hand on her shoulder. "Now, what can I do to help?"

"Do you want to set the table?" Cass indicated the stuff she'd already piled on the counter that morning. Another advantage lack of sleep had allowed.

Stephanie washed her hands, then grabbed the stack of dishes and started setting them out on the table. They worked together in silence for a few minutes, Cass readying the salad and Stephanie setting the table. When Cass had the salad finished, she glanced over her shoulder. Stephanie had been too quiet lately. It was obvious something was bothering her. If the circles under her eyes were any indication, she wasn't getting much more sleep than Cass.

Cass put the salad in the center of the table. With everything that had gone on that day, she never had gotten the centerpieces together. Maybe tomorrow. She laid a hand on Stephanie's shoulder and asked quietly, "Are you okay, Steph?"

Stephanie offered a sad smile and patted Cass's hand. "I'm okay. Thanks."

"You know if there's ever anything you want to talk about, I'm here, right?"

Stephanie nodded. "I know. It's just . . ." She looked out the back door and shook her head. "Have you ever thought about having kids?"

The question caught Cass off guard. "I don't know. I guess. There was a time when I thought about having them, but Donald wasn't ready. Then, after the divorce, I never thought about it again."

She'd have to learn to trust a man again before she could even consider having children, though she couldn't deny the fact that a little boy or girl with Luke's thick, dark hair and big blue eyes did tug at something deep within her. Of course, it would help if they could ever find a moment to spend together. Maybe when things calmed down Stephanie or Bee would babysit Beast for a night so she could visit him on the mainland. "Why, are you and Tank thinking of having kids?"

A car door slamming announced Bee's arrival. Dang his timing.

Stephanie wiped a tear that had trickled down her face, turned to Cass, and smiled. "I'm okay, hon. I promise. It's really just foolish." She waved away whatever was on her mind. "Come on. Everything smells so good, let's eat."

Bee poked his head through the open door and knocked on the doorjamb, then spotted Cass. "Hey, honey. I'm home. And lookie what I brought." He held up a Tony's Bakery box. "Gina was just putting a fresh Black Forest cake in the case when I walked in."

Saliva pooled instantly beneath Cass's tongue. Tony's Black Forest cakes were amazing. "Thank you, Bee."

When she reached to take the box from him and put it on the counter, he held on for a moment, then kissed the top of her head and released the box. His gaze slid to Stephanie. "I don't like seeing my girls so unhappy."

"We're okay." This time, Stephanie offered a genuine smile. "At least we are now that you brought cake."

Bee gave a wary glance around the kitchen. "Is there anything in there I should know about?"

Cass laughed. "Just come in, Bee. It's safe. Nothing otherworldly."

"Oh yeah? Where's Beast?"

Cass looked around the kitchen. Good question. Where was Beast? "He was here a minute ago."

"The gate was closed when I came in, and I closed it behind me, but I didn't see him out there." Bee frowned and turned back toward the yard.

Cass pushed the door between the kitchen and living room open and stuck her head in. No Beast. And no mess to indicate Beast had been there. "Beast!"

"Is he in there?" Stephanie poked her head into the open doorway beside Cass.

"No." She turned away and let the door fall shut.

"Cass?" Bee yelled from the yard.

Cass ran through the door with Stephanie on her heels.

Bee stood at the back fence, hands on his hips, scanning the beach beyond Cass's yard. A giant hole gaped open at his feet, a hole that tunneled beneath the fence, allowing Beast an escape route. He cupped his hands to his mouth and yelled, "Beast!"

Cass held her breath. Nothing.

"Which way do you think he'd go?" Stephanie looked around the yard, but there was really no point. The yard was small, and there was no way Bee would have gotten in unscathed if Beast had been there.

"I don't know."

Bee grabbed Beast's leash from the hook by the door and yelled over his shoulder as he strode toward the gate. "I'll search the beach. That's the way you usually go when you walk with him, so it makes the most sense he'd take the familiar route."

"Come on." Stephanie grabbed her arm. "We'll take my car and search the neighborhood."

They climbed into the car, and Stephanie drove slowly up and down the narrow residential streets.

Cass sat in the passenger seat, window open, yelling Beast's name. She had to find him. What if something happened to him? She'd never forgive herself. She wiped the tears streaking down her face, and Stephanie handed her a napkin.

"Thanks."

"Don't worry. We'll find him."

She just nodded.

"We live on an island, Cass, how far could he go?"

She smiled a little. That was true.

"Plus, everyone knows him from the shop or around town, and he wears a tag." She squeezed Cass's arm. "Someone will find him and call you."

Dusk was just falling, and deepening shadows made it difficult to see. She yelled his name again, then listened for any kind of response. "Slow down."

Stephanie let her foot off the accelerator. "Do you see him?"

"No, nothing. I just don't want him to hear me calling him and run out in front of the car."

Stephanie nodded and continued at an even slower crawl than she'd been going.

Small, well-manicured lawns dotted the streets. Lights had just begun to come on in a few downstairs windows and on several porches.

"Hakuna Matata" blared from Stephanie's cell phone. She fished it out of the cup holder between the seats, glanced at the caller ID, and answered as she pulled to the side of the road and stopped. "Hey, Bee. Did you find him?"

She nodded at Cass. "Yeah. Okay, we'll be right there."

Stephanie dropped the phone back into the cup holder, hit her turn signal, and made a U-turn on the empty street. "He found him."

Relief washed over her. "Is he okay? Where was he?"

"He went back to the crime scene. One of the detectives recognized him and already had him when Bee got there."

Cass took a deep breath. "He's okay?"

"He's fine. Even had a donut."

Cass flopped back against the seat, tension seeping from her rigid muscles. For the first time, she was actually happy

Bee had made the appointment with Herb. If she wasn't going to train Beast properly, it was time to give him up. No way was that happening. "The detectives were still out there? Isn't it kind of late?"

"Yeah. I haven't heard from Tank all day."

"That's weird. Doesn't he usually call you several times a day?"

"Not so much lately." Stephanie shrugged it off, but her grip on the wheel tightened. "He's been busy."

Uh-oh. Maybe things were worse between them than Cass realized. Stephanie and Tank had always had the closest relationship. Aside from being married, they were best friends. Maybe Tank didn't share Stephanie's apparent desire to start a family. "Is everything all right?"

"Yeah, it's fine. It's me. I don't know what's wrong with me lately, but I'm so cranky . . ."

An idea struck, and she blurted it out without thinking. "Are you pregnant?"

"No. No, I'm definitely not pregnant." She waved it off as she rounded the corner onto Cass's street. "Hey, who's that?"

"Who?"

"Someone just got into that white car in front of your house."

Cass shrugged, not really paying attention. "I invited Emmett and Sara, but they already had plans. Maybe they changed their minds. Are you sure it was in front of my—"

The screech of tires cut her short as the white car rocketed away from the curb. By the time Stephanie reached the front of the house the car was gone. "Do you want me to try to follow it?"

Bee ripped open the front door and stormed out onto the porch, Beast beside him barking furiously.

Cass hesitated. As much as her curiosity was piqued, seeing Beast safe was more important. "I can't right now. I have to make sure Beast is okay first."

Cass shoved the door open and ran. When she reached Beast, she dropped to her knees and threw her arms around him. "Oh, boy, I'm so glad you're okay." She gripped the fur at the sides of his neck and set him back a little. "What were you thinking? You can't take off like that. You could have gotten hurt."

He tilted his head and licked her cheek. Okay, so much for disciplining him.

"Did you see who pulled away just before you pulled up?" Bee had his cell phone in hand and was dialing.

Cass stood. "No, why? Is something wrong?"

"Look at your window." He pressed the phone to his ear and gestured over his shoulder.

In her relief to see Beast, alive and unharmed, she hadn't even noticed the shattered front window of her house. "What the . . ."

Bee handed her a brick. "Hey, Tank, it's Bee. I'm at Cass's house, and everyone is all right, but someone just threw a brick through her front window." He pointed to the word *liar* painted in black on the long side of the brick. "Uh-huh." He turned the brick over in her hand, and painted on the other side, in bold black brush strokes, was the word *fraud*. "No, we'll be here. Thanks."

The whole scene felt like something out of *The Twilight Zone*, and Cass struggled to make sense of what was happening through a fog of confusion. "What's going on here, Bee?"

"I don't know. I came in from the beach, so we went through the back door right after I called Stephanie. A second or two after we walked in, there was a loud crash. I ran into the living room and found the front window shattered and the brick lying in the middle of the mess. Beast went ballistic, so I couldn't hear anything . . ." He dropped a hand on the big dog's head. "By the time I made it out here, whoever it was had already left."

Stephanie pointed in the direction the vandal had fled. "He took off that way."

"He?" Bee asked. "Could you tell who it was?"

"No. I'm not even a hundred percent sure it was a man. I just saw a shadow getting into a car from down the street. The driver's-side door swung shut, and the car took off." She shrugged. "It was white, that's about all I can tell you."

The three of them stood there, staring off in the direction Stephanie had indicated. There wasn't much sense in trying to go after whoever it was. They were probably long gone.

Beast nudged Cass's side and whimpered.

"I have to get the glass cleaned up before Beast steps on any of it and gets hurt."

"I'll put him in the kitchen, then we'll help you clean up." Stephanie started toward the house.

"With the pot roast? Are you crazy?" Bee asked.

Stephanie laughed. "I doubt he can get the cover off the Crock-Pot."

The three of them stared at Beast, who licked his chops.

"Fine. I'll put him in Cass's room for now." She stared pointedly at Bee. "Then we'll help her clean up."

Bee huffed out a breath. "Fine. But if he's in the bedroom, we should probably leave everything like it is until Tank gets here. He said he wouldn't be long."

"Hmm . . . true." Stephanie peered through the window. "I doubt there's anything in there for him to see, but I guess we could leave it until after dinner. Is that all right, Cass?"

But her mind had already wandered away. Who would call her a liar and a fraud, and what did it mean? And more importantly, did it have anything to do with the body she had discovered on the beach or the rumors Bee had heard earlier?

9

"The display window looks gorgeous, Bee." Cass dropped her fork onto her napkin. No way could she eat another bite.

"Thank you." He beamed.

"I love the lingerie line."

"I told you you'd be good at lingerie," Stephanie added.

He laughed. Bee had been hesitant about designing lingerie, but Stephanie had been . . . persistent. Actually, she'd annoyed him to death until he gave it a try. "I can't believe how much I enjoyed doing it. And I've been talking to a buyer in the city who's been looking at my beach wedding line. He's been interested for a while now, but with the addition of the lingerie, I think it's pretty much wrapped up."

"That's great, Bee. Congratulations." Cass eyed the mess across the table. Even though exhaustion beat at her, she was grateful for the distraction. At least she wouldn't have to think about going to bed for a while. "I'm stuffed."

"I hope you saved room for cake." Bee grinned.

Hmm . . . she pressed a hand to her stomach. "Of course, I have room for cake."

The peal of the doorbell saved her from having to try.

"I'll get it. It's probably Tank." Stephanie stood and tossed her napkin onto the table.

Bee started clearing the dishes. Never comfortable around the police, Bee had recently developed a tentative truce with Tank, more for Stephanie's sake than anything else. The fact that he'd called him showed how nervous the brick-thrower must have made him.

Tank strode through the door and dropped a kiss on Cass's head. "Hey there." He nodded toward Bee. "Bee."

"Tank." Bee held out a hand, which Tank took. Hmm . . . maybe the two of them were actually heading toward being friends? Bee frowned. "Where's Stephanie?"

"Uh . . ." Tank looked over his shoulder toward the front of the house. "She wanted to get some fresh air. Said she'd be right in."

Weird. Cass had no idea what to make of the situation between the two of them, but she didn't like it. Things between Stephanie and Tank were never strained.

"This is the brick that came through the window." Bee held the brick out to him. "Stephanie put it in a Ziploc bag, but not until after Cass and I both handled it." Twin crimson patches stained his cheeks.

Tank took the brick from Bee and stared at it for a moment, then turned it over. "I'll see if we can get any fingerprints, but you'll both have to come down to the station and be finger-printed for comparison."

A shiver shook Bee. Going into a police station would be torture for him. "My prints are already on file."

Tank glanced up at him.

"They were part of the background check and stuff they did so I could work with the kids at the theater."

"Mine are on file, too," Cass added. She didn't have to remind Tank why.

He just nodded and continued to study the brick. "Any idea who would have done this, Cass?"

She'd already racked her brain a million times. "No clue."

"Do you think it could have something to do with everyone thinking Cass led you to a murder victim?" Bee asked.

Tank glared at him. "What are you talking about, Bee? Why would anyone think that?"

"Well, rumor has it Artie Becker came into Cass's shop for a reading, and his daughter's ghost led Cass to her body."

"Really?"

Bee nodded. "I heard versions of it at the deli, the diner, and the bakery."

"Busy boy today, huh?" Tank's grip on the brick tight-ened. "You didn't have anything to do with those rumors spreading, did you?"

Bee bristled. "Of course not. I listen, but I don't engage in spreading idle gossip."

Uh-oh, so much for a truce.

Tank just lifted a brow.

Cass waited as the two stared at each other for a tense moment.

Then Bee laughed and waved his hand dramatically. "Oh, fine. Even I can't pull that one off with a straight face."

Cass relaxed. There was enough tension between Tank and Stephanie; she didn't need Bee and Tank going at it, too.

"But as much as I enjoy gossiping, I never spread rumors about my friends." He held Tank's gaze. "And I would never say anything to put Cass in danger."

Tank nodded and his posture relaxed. "Yeah, I know that. Just do me a favor, and try not to discuss this situation at all. Okay?"

Bee nodded, looking a little dejected.

Tank glanced at Cass, then rolled his eyes. "But if you hear anything good, be sure to let me know."

"Sure thing." Bee's smile relieved any remaining tension. "Are you hungry? Cass made a delicious pot roast, and there's plenty left over."

Stephanie walked back in just then, seeming perfectly normal but for the deeper-than-usual lines around her mouth and her puffy eyes. A look passed between her and Tank that Cass couldn't interpret.

All she could think was that Tank looked concerned, and it worried her.

Stephanie smiled at him, but it didn't relieve the strain in her eyes, nor did it alleviate Tank's worry lines. "Go ahead and sit down, Tank. I'll get you a plate."

"Okay, thanks." Tank shook off whatever seemed to be bothering him, pulled out a chair, and sat. "Sit for a minute, Cass. I need to talk to you."

Uh-oh. What did I do now? "Sure." She dropped onto the chair across from him.

"Have you heard anything more from Artie Becker?"

"No, why?"

"I want you to promise me you'll stay away from him." He stared at her hard, his *I'm not playing games* face firmly in place.

She shrugged. She had no interest in talking to Artie Becker again anyway. Oh, wait. That wasn't exactly true. She really did want to know what he'd been doing at the art gallery. "Okay. Any special reason?"

He held her gaze another moment, maybe trying to figure out if she was telling the truth? She was confident he wouldn't, though. Even she wasn't sure if she'd talk to him again.

Apparently appeased by whatever he saw, or didn't see, in her expression, he leaned back in the chair. "I had someone research him while I was out at the beach. It seems his first wife disappeared under . . . unusual . . . circumstances as well."

Bee's breath shot out. "Are you kidding?"

"I'm not saying anything happened to her—I'll have to look into it more when I get back to the station—I just want Cass to be careful until I have time to figure out what's going on." Tank pinned him with a look. "And I better not hear about this when I stop for my morning coffee."

"Hmm . . ." Bee started.

Before the tension between them could escalate—again—Stephanie slid a full plate in front of Tank and sat down next to him.

"What do you mean, disappeared?" Cass asked.

"Sorry, that's all you're getting until I have a chance to sort it all out." Tank lifted his knife and fork and started to eat, apparently done discussing the case. He popped a piece of gravy-soaked meat into his mouth. "Mmm . . . this is great, Cass."

"Thanks." She smiled and stood, then tilted her head from side to side and rolled her shoulders, determined to relax and enjoy the company of her friends.

"By the way, I've already called someone to fix the window. They'll be here tomorrow. Emmett's coming over with some plywood later to board it up until then."

"Thanks, Tank." At least that was one less thing she had to worry about. After everyone left and she got cleaned up, she'd have to go out and fill the hole Beast had dug beneath the fence so he couldn't escape again.

She opened the bakery box, took the Black Forest cake out, and slid it onto a glass cake dish. Her mouth watered at the overwhelming scent of chocolate. After placing it in the center of the table, she grabbed mugs and set them on the table, too, then lifted the coffeepot and started to fill them. The ringtone and her phone vibrating on the counter startled her. She jerked back, sloshing coffee onto the table. Okay, maybe her nerves hadn't settled quite as much as she'd hoped.

"Go ahead, I've got it." Stephanie grabbed a handful of napkins and started mopping up the mess.

Cass glanced at the name on the screen. Luke Morgan. She excused herself and answered as she started cleaning up. "Hello, stranger."

"Hello yourself, beautiful."

Heat flushed her cheeks. She'd been . . . seeing him? Talking to him? Heck, she had no idea what she was doing with Luke, but even after knowing him for six months, that smooth, thick drawl he laid on still sent her stomach fluttering. "How's everything?"

"Crazy." He laughed. "How's everything there?"

She lowered a stack of dishes into the sink, then turned to lean back against the counter. "Not bad." No way would she get into all the weird dreams she'd been having, or the utter exhaustion now plaguing her. With Luke living on the mainland, and Cass living on Bay Island, they had little enough time together as it was. She wasn't about to waste any of it complaining. But she did have to tell him what happened at the beach. He'd just hear it from Tank later, anyway. "Beast found a bone on the beach today."

"Oh?"

Cass wrapped her free arm around her waist. "Unfortunately, it had a bunch of other bones with it."

Silence.

"Are you still there?"

A rush of breath came through the line. "What kind of bones?"

"Well, one of them looked to me like a skull, so I'm assuming human." A tremor shook her voice, despite her best efforts to steady it, and a tear leaked out and ran down her cheek.

"Are you all right?"

She smiled through the tears. Silly, since he couldn't see her. "Yeah, I'm okay."

"Did you call the police?"

"Yes. Tank's here now."

"About the bones?"

"Oh. Actually, no. He came about the brick someone sent flying through my window, but right now he's having dinner."

"Brick?"

"Oh, right. I forgot to mention that. Someone threw a brick through my front window."

"At the shop?"

"No, at home."

"Are you okay? Why didn't you mention that sooner?"

"I'm fine. I wasn't even here when it happened. Do you want to talk to Tank?" Luke and Tank had become fast friends. Maybe because they were both cops. Or maybe because of their mutual frustration with Cass. Who knew? Either way, they seemed to have bonded.

"That's all right. I'll call him in a little while. I only had a quick minute, but I wanted to let you know I could get away this weekend. If you'd like, we could go out to dinner or something."

Since Cass couldn't leave Beast, that meant Luke would be coming to Bay Island. "Sure. Are you going to stay the whole weekend?"

"I can take the ferry over Saturday morning and stay until early Monday morning."

"You know what? That's perfect. I have to go to Southampton to do that reading on Monday, so I'll take the ferry back with you." This night was definitely looking up.

"Great. You're sure you're okay?"

The ringing of a cell phone startled her. She looked toward the table. "I'm fine."

"I'm looking forward to seeing you."

"Me too." The long-distance relationship was proving harder than Cass had expected. Not that they lived that far from each other, but neither of them could ever get away. How was she supposed to get to know someone she never even got to see?

"What second body?" Tank's voice intruded on her thoughts and thundered over whatever Luke was saying. "Where?"

"Cass?" Concern filled Luke's voice.

"Um, yeah. Sorry. I'm here."

Tank shoved his chair back and dropped his napkin onto his still-half-full plate. "I'm on my way."

"Everything all right?" *Oh, right. Luke.*

"Yes, but I have to run. I'm sorry. I'll see you this weekend."

"Is something going on there, Cass?"

"Uh, something's up with Tank, but I'm not sure what."

Her gaze met Tank's, and he rubbed a hand over his crew cut. "Who's on the phone?"

"Luke."

"Yeah?" Luke asked.

"No, not you." She blew out a breath, frustrated with this whole conversation. "Tank asked who I was on the phone with."

"What's wrong?"

"Tell Luke I'll call him later. Right now, I have to run. Thanks for dinner, Cass." He kissed Stephanie, then squeezed Cass's arm. "Keep your doors locked, and don't open them for anyone. Understand?"

She nodded, and he turned to leave, but she grabbed his sleeve. "Wait. What did you mean, 'a second body'?"

He huffed out a breath. "They just found a second body buried on the beach."

Cass gasped.

He stared hard at her. "I don't know what your involvement in this is, but you stay out of anything to do with any of this until we figure out what's going on. Okay?"

Ice-cold fear gripped her. Her teeth started to chatter as she nodded and watched Tank walk away. An image hovered, just out of reach . . .

"Cass? Cass!" Luke's voice ripped her from the edge of the vision.

"Yeah. Um . . . I'm here."

"What is going on there?" A bit of anger crept into his tone. Or maybe fear. Either way that oh-so-sexy southern drawl was noticeably absent.

"I'm sorry, Luke. Tank had to leave. He said he'd call you later, but they just found a second body on the beach."

He let out a low whistle. "Boy, Tank wasn't kidding. You really are a magnet for trouble."

10

Against her better judgment, after dropping Beast off at the groomer as soon as they opened Monday morning, Cass stopped at the deli for coffee. It was packed. The worried expressions and snippets of conversation she caught were enough to tell her Tank hadn't managed to keep news of the second body quiet. Hushed whispers and the term *serial killer* battered her from more than one direction.

She scoffed. What were the chances of a serial killer on Bay Island? Slim to none—she shivered—probably. But with the start of tourist season approaching, she could certainly understand why people would be concerned. Many of the smaller businesses on the island, especially those along the boardwalk and beaches, brought in the bulk of their income during the summer months. If tourists were afraid to come to the tiny island, they'd spend their summer vacation money elsewhere, and more than one business would go under. Including Mystical Musings.

Cass squeezed into the three-deep crowd at the coffee counter where Emma Nicholls was changing the coffee filters and starting a row of fresh pots. She was also rambling a mile a minute.

She nodded toward Cass without missing a beat in her narration. "And Billy Hayes—the rookie cop with the dreamy blue eyes?—was working security, trying to keep the press out. Can you believe there were reporters from all the big stations out there? They must have come in on the first ferry this morning." She dumped a potful of water into the last machine and stepped back. "There. Should be ready in a few minutes. Sorry, we got behind with bringing coffee out to the crime scene." She puffed herself up importantly.

Cass resisted the urge to roll her eyes—barely.

Then Emma set her sights on Cass. "Hey, Cass. Rumor has it you were the one to find the first body. What did you see out there?"

All heads turned to her.

"Uh . . ." Caught off guard, Cass struggled to think coherently. What had Tank told her not to discuss? She couldn't remember. Better not to say anything. Wishing fervently that she could melt back into the crowd and disappear, Cass tried to come up with something safe to tell the mass of people now staring expectantly at her. "I don't really know. Um . . . Beast found something and brought it to me. It looked like a bone, so I called nine-one-one."

"And?" Emma prodded.

She shrugged as if finding a skeleton on the beach was

no big deal. "And nothing. That's it. After the police got there, I answered what questions I could, which were very few, and then I left."

"Hmm . . ." Emma started to say something more, but Rick, the owner, called her back behind the counter. "All right, people, coffee's almost ready, but I can start ringing some of you up now, then you can fill your cups on the way out." She herded the mob into a line and guided them toward the register.

"Hey."

Cass jumped, startled by the voice in her ear. She spun around and came face to face with Leighton Mills.

Leighton laughed. "Sorry. I didn't mean to scare you." She looked around. "Seems everyone's a little spooked this morning, huh?"

"Seems like it." Cass joined the line by the register with Leighton right behind her. At the rate Rick and Emma were filling orders and ringing up customers, all of whom, it seemed, wanted to linger and chat, she'd be there forever. There was definitely a nervous undercurrent in the room that you couldn't miss. Even without being psychic. Which Cass definitely was not. At least, that's what she reminded herself at every opportunity. She turned to face Leighton.

Leighton took it as an invitation to continue the conversation. "Well, I can't blame them for being nervous. A serial killer on such a small island is pretty scary to think about." The offhand manner in which she'd made the comment didn't match the serious expression haunting her eyes.

"I doubt it's a serial killer." At least, she didn't want to believe it was possible. But Leighton's shop did sit between the beach and the boardwalk. If she'd already been in this morning, she might have spoken to one of the officers. Maybe Emma's Officer Dreamy Eyes; he seemed to have an awful lot to say. "Where did you hear that?"

"At the dry cleaner. And the gas station. And I believe it was being discussed when I first walked in the door here." She laughed a little, her gaze darting this way and that, then lowered her voice. "Do they have any idea who the victims or the killer are?"

Cass looked around to see if anyone was listening. The last thing she needed was the killer—or worse, Tank—overhearing her discussing the case. "I have no idea."

"No?" Lifting a brow, Leighton waited.

"How would I know anything?"

She held Cass's gaze for another few seconds, then shrugged. "I don't know. Everyone's been talking about you finding the body." She lowered her voice even more and leaned close to Cass's ear. "They say a woman's ghost led you to it."

A high-pitched, nervous laugh burst out before Cass could stop it. "That's ridiculous. Where on earth did you hear something like that?"

"The diner. While I was waiting in line to pay for my dinner last night, pretty much everyone in the place was talking about it."

Great. There was probably no one left on Bay Island who hadn't heard the rumors. A dull throbbing started at her temples.

"They were also wondering if you could tell who killed her."

That brought Cass's attention back. She waved it off, even though a bead of sweat trickled down the middle of her back.

"Of course, I don't know who killed anyone. I don't even know if anyone was killed, just that they *might have* found human remains on the beach. As far as I know, that's all that happened." She raised her voice so anyone within hearing distance wouldn't miss what she was saying. "Beast found a bone on the beach, and I called the police. That's it. Nothing more sinister happened." She turned to move up in the line.

Her way was blocked by a thin guy she'd never seen before. He pushed his glasses higher on his nose. "So, are you working with the police?"

"Excuse me?"

"Are you a psychic consultant for the sheriff's department on this investigation? Is that why you can't divulge any details of the case?"

Conversation around her died.

"No. I have nothing to do with this case, nor am I working as a consultant with the police. I'm not even—" *psychic, for crying out loud.* Thankfully, she bit back the words before they escaped. That's all she needed to say. She wouldn't have to worry about a serial killer destroying her business. She weaved her fingers through her hair and squeezed, the headache raging full force. She should have just skipped the coffee and been content to let Bee deliver the gossip to her later in the day when he woke.

She was saved from any more grilling about her involvement in the case when Rick called, "Next."

The man in front of her stared a moment longer, then turned and moved to the counter to place his order.

Relieved to be off the hook, Cass took a couple of deep breaths. Hopefully everyone who'd witnessed the exchange would pass the word that Cass had nothing to do with the case. Somehow, she doubted it.

"Hey, beautiful." Bee's arm came around her shoulders and he kissed her cheek. "How's it going?"

"What in the world are you doing up already? It's barely ten o'clock. In the morning."

"Ha-ha." He waved her away dismissively. "Really, Cass. I do occasionally get up early."

"When?"

He laughed. "When there's dirt like this going around."

"Yeah, well, in your travels, please pass on that I did not follow a ghost to any bodies."

"Are you sure?" His eyes twinkled with mischief, and he winked. "I bet business would pick up dramatically if you had."

Hmm . . . she hadn't thought of that.

"Next."

Cass moved forward.

Bee leaned close. "Get me a bacon, egg, and cheese."

"Hey, Cass." Emma rested her elbows on the counter and leaned forward. "I understand if you don't want everyone to know what's going on, but you can tell me, you know."

Yeah, right. And five minutes later it would be all over town. "There's really nothing to tell."

Rick cleared his throat, and Emma straightened up, saving Cass from the uncomfortable conversation.

"What can I get you?"

"Three bacon, egg, and cheeses, on rolls, salt and pepper."

Bee nudged his way beside her and lifted a finger. "And ketchup on one." He started to back away, then stopped. "Oh, and a large order of home fries."

Cass glared at him. "Are you done?"

"You're right. I forgot the coffee." He smiled at Emma. "And two large coffees, to go."

"Three coffees." Cass stared at him a bit longer to make sure he was done.

"What? I'm starved." His grin widened. "All this gossip makes me hungry. Who's the third coffee for?"

"Stephanie is meeting me at the shop to go over the books." Cass turned back to Emma as Bee moved away. She paid for their breakfasts and moved aside to wait for her order while Leighton stepped up to the register. Thankfully, the guy who'd been harassing her in the line was deeply involved in a conversation with a woman Cass had never seen before. At least he'd leave her alone now. She hoped.

"Wade." Rick held a bag high, and the man stepped forward to retrieve it without any disruption in his conversation. Whatever the two of them were talking about, he didn't seem happy. He gestured wildly, flinging his bag around with each motion, but he kept his voice too low for Cass to hear any of the conversation. When he moved to the coffee counter, Cass gave up trying to hear anything else.

Leighton moved to stand beside her. "Are you headed into the shop?"

Cass nodded. "Yeah. I was hoping to get an early start, but I didn't expect it to be so crowded in here."

"I know, me neither. I probably wouldn't have stopped if I'd known."

"Tell me about it." If Cass had known what to expect, she'd definitely have skipped the deli stop. She looked around, wondering if it was a good time to ask Leighton about the painting again. She really wanted to know who the woman was. And now that a second body had been discovered, the need to know seemed even more urgent.

"Cass," Rick called and held up a paper bag.

She stepped forward and took the bag from Rick. "Thanks."

He nodded and moved on to the next customer in line, banging out one order after another in an effort to keep up with the unusually high volume of breakfast orders. Although Cass couldn't help but notice many of the customers had only come in for coffee. And presumably gossip.

"Enjoy your breakfast." Leighton pointed toward the bag. "Maybe I'll see you later."

"Yeah, sure." Giving up on trying to find a way to approach the subject of the painting in the middle of the crowd, Cass turned away. The mobbed deli was probably not the best time or place to confront the other woman, anyway. She'd have to make sure to catch her alone later.

"Come on, Cass. We have to go." Bee grabbed her arm.

"What's wrong?"

"Nothing. Just walk." He guided her toward the door, weaving through the throng of customers, balancing all three coffees in a cardboard cup holder.

When they reached the sidewalk, Cass tried to stop, but Bee shook his head and kept moving, propelling her toward her car parked a few spots down. He got in the passenger seat without looking back.

She shook her head and followed, then slid into the driver's seat, slammed the door shut, and shoved the bag at Bee. "What is wrong with you?"

"Don't get mad."

"Why would I get—"

"It wasn't my fault."

"What wasn't? What are you talking about?"

Chewing on a thumbnail, he peered over his hand at her. "All right, Bee. Spill it. What happened?"

He cleared his throat, then lowered his hand. "Well . . ." He winced. "I was getting our coffee, and people were gathered around talking about everything, and someone said a ghost told you where the body was, and then someone else said you couldn't have really seen a ghost, because there's no such thing as ghosts, which I actually agree with—mostly—so, of course, I said 'That's true,' just meaning there are no such things as ghosts . . ."

Cass massaged her temples.

"But then this guy I didn't recognize jumped in and said, 'So she's a fake?' And, well, you know how I get when someone says something about one of my girls, so—"

Cass held up a hand. "Stop."

Bee folded his hands in his lap and stared out the windshield.

Great. Now she'd hurt his feelings. She sighed. "Sorry, Bee. I have a pounding headache. Could you just maybe skip the in-between and tell me the part I might be mad at?"

He shrugged. "I kind of told them you weren't a fake, and that you did see a . . . vision . . . and had already discussed it with the police. In my defense, I said 'vision,' not 'ghost.'"

"Ugh . . . Bee, how could you—"

"Hey . . ." Bee pointed toward the sidewalk where a man was walking away from them toward the corner. "That's him. That's the guy who kept provoking me until I blurted out the truth."

"Kept provoking you?"

"Yes." He harrumphed. "Of course, you didn't listen to that part."

Cass sighed again. *This is going to be a long day.*

The stranger stopped at the corner and looked both ways before crossing the street, giving Cass a clear view of his face. The skinny guy with the glasses who'd been grilling her while she was waiting in line for breakfast. What had Rick called him? Brad? No. Wade. That was it. *Hmm . . . why so nosy, Wade?*

She thought briefly about following him, but what purpose would it serve? It wasn't likely he'd lead her to the truth about what had happened to the two skeletons on the beach.

11

Cass unlocked the door to Mystical Musings and pushed it open. "Are you coming?"

"Yeah, yeah." Bee walked past her and dropped the cup holder and bag on the table.

"Hey, wait up." Stephanie ran across the parking lot and up the steps to the boardwalk. "Sorry I'm late."

"That's okay. We just got here. The deli was mobbed."

Stephanie laughed. "What did you expect?"

Stephanie gestured toward Bee, who was still sulking while he unpacked the bag and set their sandwiches out. "What's the matter with him?"

After Stephanie entered, Cass locked the door and left the sign turned to CLOSED. "He opened his mouth when he shouldn't have, and now he's beating himself up over it."

"Ahh . . ."

"I can hear you, you know." Bee shot them a dirty look as they pulled out their chairs and sat down to eat.

Cass sighed. "Are you going to stay in this mood all day?"

He shrugged and flopped onto the chair across from her. "I'm really sorry, Cass."

"I know. You already told me about a hundred times in the car on the way—"

A loud bang from upstairs interrupted her.

Bee drew his eyebrows together and surged to his feet.

Cass shook her head. She had no idea what the noise could have been. As far as she knew, the upstairs was empty.

"Dang." The voice definitely came from upstairs.

Stephanie pulled out her cell phone.

"Hold on a sec. No need to call in the cavalry yet." Moving as stealthily as a better-than-six-foot, two-hundred-pound man could move in platform shoes, Bee crept toward the spiral staircase Emmett had installed in the back corner of the shop. He leaned over the black iron railing and peered up.

"Anything?" Cass whispered.

He shook his head. "Hello?" he yelled up the stairs.

"Hey," a man's voice called back.

Bee jumped back at the unexpected answer and pressed a hand against his heaving chest. "That voice had better be attached to a live person." He pinned Cass with a stare. "Just sayin'."

Cass couldn't help but laugh.

A giggle blurted out of Stephanie, and she offered Bee a sympathetic look.

"I'm glad you both think it's funny."

That only made Cass laugh harder.

Bee rolled his eyes.

"Don't worry about it, Bee." Stephanie stuck her phone back into her pocket and squeezed his arm. "Being afraid of ghosts is perfectly understandable."

He snorted. "First of all, I do not believe in ghosts. Well . . . not really anyway. And, second of all . . ."

Tuning out their bickering, Cass called up the staircase. "Is that you, Emmett?"

"Yup." He emerged from the upstairs landing and started down. "Sorry. Dropped a hammer."

"What are you doing here?"

He reached the bottom and gestured for Cass to go up. "Got a surprise for you."

"A surprise?"

"Sure. Go on up."

She smiled and climbed the stairs. As she rounded the top few steps, a view of the upstairs room Emmett had built came into view. "Oh, my." She looked back down at Emmett coming up behind her with Bee and Stephanie close on his heels. "Is it finished?"

"Yup. It was almost done, and I couldn't sleep, so I came in really early this morning and finished it up. I wanted it to be done in time for the group reading Saturday night. I still have to come back for a few last-minute touches, but you can start setting it up whenever you're ready."

Cass stood in the middle of the huge, open space and turned around. He'd done an amazing job. The walls had been painted a deep maroon with white crown molding. Dark wood floors gleamed in the sunlight coming through the two dormer windows at the back of the shop. Built-in, floor-to-ceiling bookshelves covered the back wall between the windows. "Oh, Emmett. I don't know what to say. It's gorgeous."

Crimson patches blossomed on his cheeks. "I saw stacks of books laying around the back room one day, and I thought these would be helpful." He gestured toward the shelves. "I built them into the wall, so they don't take up any room."

"They're perfect." Tears threatened, but she held them back.

"Oh, and look at the office." He led her across the empty space to a small room in the corner behind the stairs. "It's out of the way, just like you asked, but you won't be able to use it when the shop is open unless you hire help." He opened a set of double, frosted-glass doors.

Cass looked around in the small office. "That's okay. It's just right, exactly what I wanted." A quiet, out of the way space she could go to do her paperwork, which she often did on Wednesdays or early in the morning when the shop was closed. "Thank you so much, Emmett." She threw her arms around him in a big hug. "You're the best."

When she released him, he stepped back and tipped the red baseball cap he always wore. "Glad you like it."

"Like it? I love it." She spun around once more, trying to take in every last detail. "Are you and Sara coming to the reading?"

"Wouldn't miss it." He shoved his wild mane of long, graying hair back and fitted his cap back on.

"This really is amazing." Stephanie poked her head into the small office and looked around.

"You really outdid yourself this time, Emmett." Bee ran a hand over the dark wood shelving. "I'd love something like this in the back room at Dreamweaver."

"Sure thing, Bee. I'd be happy to do it for you."

Bee clapped his hands together. "Perfect."

"I'll stop by one night after you close, and we can work out exactly what you want."

"I can't wait. Thanks."

Emmett nodded and smoothed his goatee. "Anyway, I gotta get going. Gotta get the shop open. I'll see you Saturday."

"Okay. Thank you again, Emmett. And tell Joey I said hi."

Emmett's grin spread from ear to ear at the mention of his son. "Will do."

"It really looks amazing, Cass," Bee said as Emmett headed down the stairs.

"I know. I can't believe how good it looks, and he got it done so fast," Stephanie added.

Cass made one more circuit of the room, then headed for the stairs. "I can't wait to get started setting it up. If I'm not too busy today, I'll start bringing up some of the smaller things."

"Let me know when you want to start moving the tables and stuff up, and I'll come help." Bee sat back down at the table and took the lid off his home fries. At least seeing the new room had helped him get over his earlier funk.

"Thanks." She sat at the table and opened her sandwich.

"We'll have to do it one night this week, if you want to have it ready for the reading Saturday night." Stephanie's cell phone beeped, and she pulled it out of her bag.

"I could do that." Bee opened his sandwich and frowned.

"Something wrong?" Cass asked.

Leaving his sandwich untouched, he cleared his throat and folded his hands on the table. "Nah. Just thinking back to that guy in the deli. He seemed really determined to get me to say you were somehow involved in the investigation."

"Yeah, well, he was hounding me, too, before you came in." She put a hand over his. "If it makes you feel any better, I almost blurted out that I wasn't psychic smack in the middle of gossip central. That would've ruined my business pretty quick."

He smiled. "No kidding."

"Don't worry about it. I'm sure everything will be fine."

He shrugged. "I hope you're right."

"I am."

He laughed. "Is that a premonition of some sort, or are you just being cocky?"

She waggled her eyebrows. "I'll never tell. Now eat your breakfast. It's already late, and I need to get the shop open."

"And I need to run." Stephanie grabbed her coffee and her sandwich and stood. "Sorry, guys. This client is going to drive me crazy."

"Is everything all right?" Cass asked.

"Yeah, yeah." She waved off her concern. "Just the same annoying client who thinks I have nothing else to do but cater to him. I'll catch up with you guys later."

Once Stephanie ran out, the two of them ate in silence for a while, Cass contemplating how to arrange the tables upstairs for the reading, Bee mulling over something— probably still the guy in the deli.

Cass crumpled the wrapper from her breakfast sandwich and tossed it in the garbage. "Are you done?"

A sulking Bee picked at what was left of his sandwich. He shrugged. "I guess."

Apparently she'd been wrong about him feeling better.

"Look, Bee. It's over and done with. You can't change it, so stop worrying about it."

"Easy for you to say, you won't have to deal with Tank."

She grinned, balled up the paper bag their breakfast had come in, and bounced it off his head. "Come on, Bee. It won't be that bad."

He shot her a scowl.

"All right, so it probably will be that bad, but he'll get over it."

The tinkling of the wind chimes Cass kept above the door startled her. Stephanie must have forgotten to lock it behind her.

"Cass?" An elderly woman peered into the shop and spotted Cass. "The sign says CLOSED, but I was hoping to see you before I head home."

A genuine smile tugged at Cass. "Come on in, Grace. How are you?" Cass started toward the woman she'd become quite fond of since the first time she'd come into the shop sheepishly asking for a love potion. The crystals Cass had given her had obviously worked, because Rudy Hastings, the target of her endeavor, followed her into the store.

Grace's gaze landed on Bee. "I hope I'm not interrupting anything."

"Of course not." Cass gave Grace a quick hug, then turned to Rudy and did the same. "How have you been, Rudy?"

He glanced at Grace with such love it melted Cass's heart. "Great, now."

"Oh, go on, now." Grace blushed all the way up to the roots of her blue-gray curls.

Cass laughed. Grace and Rudy could brighten even the worst morning, although last time they'd come in, Grace had been concerned about her granddaughter. She'd been trying so hard to get pregnant and hadn't had any luck. Cass had sent Grace home with a basket for her. "Do you have time to sit and have a cup of tea? I'd love to catch up." Cass led them toward a small, intimate seating arrangement. "How is your granddaughter doing? Sadie, was it?"

"Oh, she's doing wonderfully, thank you. As a matter of fact, she'll be here any minute. She dropped us off by the front door and went to park the car down the road." Grace looked around the empty store and frowned. "Where is everyone?"

"What do you mean?" Cass started toward the counter to make tea, but Bee already had three foam cups lined up and was dropping tea bags into them, so she sank into one of the overstuffed chairs instead.

"The parking lot is packed. I figured the store would be mobbed."

"I meant to flip the sign over after breakfast, but we just finished up." She started to get up.

"No worries, sweetie. I'll get it in a sec." Bee placed a cup of tea on the coffee table in front of each of them and a fourth in front of the empty seat beside Grace on the couch, then he set out a tray of cookies and went to turn the sign around. "Hmm . . . the parking lot is full. It wasn't like that when we got here."

Bee opened the door for a young woman, then walked out onto the porch and let the door fall shut behind him.

"Sadie." Grace stood and held out a hand, which Sadie

took and squeezed with an affectionate smile at her grandmother. It was obvious the two were close. "Come, meet Cass."

Cass stood and held out her hand. "It's a pleasure to meet you, Sadie."

Sadie ignored Cass's proffered hand and wrapped her arms around Cass in a hug, then stepped back, an adorable blush coloring her cheeks. In her face, Cass could see an image of a younger Grace; the features were so similar. Tears shimmered in her eyes. "I'm sorry." She laughed a little. "I'm not usually prone to such random displays of affection, but I am just so thankful to you."

It struck Cass before she had a chance to say anything else. She grinned. "Congratulations. When are you due?"

Sadie's hands fluttered to her flat stomach. "How did you know? I didn't even think I was showing."

"You're not, dear," Grace assured her. "I told you Cass was brilliant."

"Well, I just wanted to come and thank you. I can't say for sure it was the crystals and essential oils you gave Grandma, but my husband and I tried for a long time, and nothing worked. Yet, three months after I started following all of your suggestions, here I am. Pregnant." Happiness radiated from her.

Cass's spirits soared. Nothing compared to playing a part in bringing someone such joy. "Well, for whatever part I might have played, you're very welcome."

"Sit, sit." Grace sat and patted the seat beside her.

Cass returned to her chair, while Sadie sat down beside her grandmother.

"Sadie's not the only one with good news today." She

fluttered her lashes at Rudy. "Rudy and I are getting married."

Cass gasped.

"I know, we haven't been involved romantically for very long, but we were good friends even before . . . well . . . you know, and let's face it, honey, at my age I can't afford to wait."

"I'm so happy for you both." Cass jumped up and kissed Grace's cheek, then Rudy's.

"We really just stopped in to let you know and to make sure you'll come to the wedding."

"Oh, I'd love to. Thank you."

"You can bring your friend, Bee, if you want to. He's such a sweetheart."

"I'll tell him, thank you."

"No, dear, thank you. If not for your crystals, and your support, I'd still be ogling Rudy from afar. I'd never have had the courage to pursue anything more than friendship."

Cass hugged her again, holding back tears.

"Okay, enough of this." Grace sniffed and wiped her eyes, then sat and sipped her tea. "Tell me what you've been up to."

"I had the upstairs of the shop finished off, and I'm going to have a group reading up there on Saturday night. If you'd all like to come, you're welcome."

"Oh, we'd love to."

After a few more minutes of catching up, Grace, Rudy, and Sadie thanked Cass again and said their good-byes with a promise to see Cass on Saturday for the reading.

Cass wished them well, then started cleaning up. It always made her happy when people came back in to share their success stories. The door chimes tinkled, and Cass turned toward them with a smile.

Bee stood in the doorway, his face pale. He shut the door behind him and flipped the sign back to CLOSED. "Uh . . ."

"What's the matter?"

"I think we have a problem."

12

"What do you mean we have a problem?" Cass strode toward him, looking out the front display window past the boardwalk to the parking lot.

Vans, complete with satellite dishes on top and news station logos on their sides, were parked haphazardly throughout the parking lot. "What the heck?"

"Oh, that's nothing. It gets even better." He turned her around and propelled her toward the back window overlooking the beach. "Check out the view out the back."

A small mob of people had gathered on the beach. Some held microphones, others carried cameras, while harried-looking uniformed police officers tried to corral them behind some kind of hastily constructed chicken wire barrier.

"What's going on?" She leaned closer to the window,

trying to get a good view of whatever was going on down the beach. "Don't even tell me they found another body."

"Bite your tongue, honey." Bee leaned over her shoulder, breathing down her neck to see what was going on. "But word of the second body has apparently spread. As has word of your involvement in finding her."

"Her?" Annoyed, she nudged him back and stood. "What are you talking about? As far as I know, they haven't even identified *him or her* yet." She stared at Bee, waiting for him to contradict her, not sure she really wanted to know if they had figured out who was buried out there.

Bee shrugged. "Not that I've heard."

"Mmm . . . hmm . . ." Cass crossed the store and flipped the sign back to OPEN. "And you think you'd have missed that piece of gossip?"

"Probably not," Bee conceded.

She moved behind the polished driftwood counter and opened the register, then started counting out the change.

Bee kept his nose pressed against the glass in the back door. Every once in a while, he huffed out a breath or mumbled something she couldn't quite catch.

After the third time she lost count of the nickels, she dropped them back into the register. "If you're going to hang around, why don't you make yourself useful and start moving the file cabinets to my office upstairs."

He finally turned away from whatever excitement had gripped him out there.

Cass didn't ask. She didn't want to know. She'd had her first dream-free sleep in over a week last night, and she was hoping whatever spirit had been haunting her—or her own overactive imagination—was going to leave her alone now.

"You want the file cabinets up first?"

"And the desk." She closed the register, grabbed her appointment book, and tossed it onto the table. She only had a few appointments scheduled for today, but she couldn't remember the times. "I think it'll be easier to get the office set up first. If we set the tables up first, we'll have to move some of them to get the office stuff up there."

Bee contemplated that for a moment. "Hmm . . . true. I'll tell you what. I'll take the file cabinets up for you now, so you can organize your paperwork in them if you get time today, but then I'm going home to bed. I'll need help moving the desk anyway, so we'll do that later, after you close."

The tinkle of chimes drew her attention. "That would be great. Thanks, Bee."

"No problem." He started off toward the back room.

"Good morning." Cass rounded the counter to greet a customer she didn't recognize.

The young man glanced around. "Um . . . hey."

He seemed nervous, fidgety, but with dark glasses covering his eyes, she couldn't quite tell.

"Can I help you with anything specific?"

"I . . . uh . . . lost something."

A small niggle of fear crept down Cass's back. She couldn't pinpoint the source, but she was sorry Beast wasn't there and very glad Bee still was. "Lost something in here?"

"Oh, no. No. I lost something, and I was hoping you could help me find it. People are saying you can find things."

"Sometimes." Cass shrugged. "Depends on what it is and where you lost it."

The guy nodded. Cass placed him at around twenty-five or twenty-six. It was hard to tell. His too-big shirt hung over loose, baggy jeans, hiding any details of his rail-thin frame. His sunken cheeks gave the impression he was older, but something about his manner seemed young, almost child-like. Acne covered the sides of his face where his shaggy, dark hair hung over it. He glanced over his shoulder. "It's a necklace."

A large crash came from the back room. "Ouch!"

The guy jumped and spun toward the door.

"Excuse me for a minute, please." She stuck her head through the curtain into the back room, which was actually at the side of the store. "Bee? Are you all right?"

He shot her a grin. "Sorry. Dropped something on my foot."

"What did you drop?"

He gestured toward the back corner of the room, where a pile of papers and folders laid scattered across the floor. "I didn't know how to get the drawer out of the file cabinet."

"Well . . . looks like you figured it out."

"Sorry." He bit his lip and looked around at the mess.

It would take hours to reorganize all the paperwork he'd managed to wreck in a matter of seconds. She took a deep breath and bit back a curse. Nothing she could do about it. He was helping her, after all, and accidents happen. "Don't worry about it. I needed to go through it all anyway."

He nodded. "Thanks."

"I have a customer right now, though, so . . ." If the guy hadn't already bolted. She let the curtain fall closed and turned back to the shop.

The guy was leaning over the table, leafing through her appointment book.

Shocked, Cass stopped. "Excuse me!"

He jumped up, stared at her, and gave a nonchalant shrug.

"What are you doing?"

"Um . . . I was just waiting for you to come back. So, what's the deal? Can you help me find the necklace I lost, or what?"

Cass stared at him for another minute. Just nosy, or looking for something specific? What in the world would he be looking for, though? She blew off the paranoia trying to take hold—he was obviously just plain rude—but she did put the book back where it belonged before taking a seat at the table.

"Have a seat, and tell me a little about the necklace, um . . ." She couldn't remember him giving her his name. "I'm sorry, did you say your name?"

"Uh . . . John." His gaze darted to the side.

Yeah right.

He pulled out a velvet-covered chair and sat across the table from her, his gaze roaming over the shop as he spoke. "I have to find this necklace. It's really important."

"When did you last have it?"

He frowned and stared down at his hands fidgeting on the table in front of him. "I last saw it a few months ago."

"What does it look like?"

He shrugged. "It's on a silver chain, and it has, like, a big, whitish stone in the middle of some kind of silver design, and the stone kind of . . . changes color when you move it around."

"An opal?" An opal necklace. Where had she seen one lately? Somewhere, because it sounded familiar; something about it gave her pause.

He shrugged again but didn't offer any more details.

"Where did you last see it?"

"Does that matter?"

She tried to curb her temper, but her patience with this guy was wearing thin. "Of course, it matters. If you want me to help you find it, we have to figure out where you saw it last."

"Okay." He swallowed hard, his Adam's apple bobbing with the effort. "I was working in the art gallery down the boardwalk, and I saw it in there."

An image shimmered behind him, started to form, then dissipated.

She stifled a gasp. Thankfully, the guy was still looking at his hands and didn't notice her surprise. "Did you go in and ask the owner if she's seen it?"

His head shot up. "No . . . uh, you know what . . . this was probably a stupid idea, right? What are the chances you could find something like that, anyway?" He started to stand.

"Wait." Cass reached toward him, but he jerked his hands back.

"D-do you think you could, you know, maybe not say anything to the owner that I was asking?" He stuffed his hands in his pockets, shoulders hunched, and started backing toward the door. "The necklace, it wasn't mine. It belonged to someone else, and I was just wondering if you could find it for me. No big deal. Sorry to waste your time."

"You're not wasting my time—"

He didn't even wait for her to finish her sentence; he just reached the door, ripped it open, and bolted.

The image that had started to form returned. The same woman from her dreams, her bodyless head hovering in front of the door "John" had just fled through. A thought struck. Had he seen her? Is that what had him so spooked?

Surely Cass wasn't the only one who could see the dead. Or something.

The woman winked out of existence an instant later, but just before she did, a glint of something around her neck caught Cass's eye. No way! Could that have been where she'd seen an opal necklace? No. She couldn't remember ever seeing a necklace on the woman in her visions before, and she was certain that wasn't what the glint was, but something tugged at her. Had the woman in the painting in the art gallery window been wearing a necklace like that? Or any necklace? She couldn't remember. Dang. She was going to have to get another look at that painting. But how could she do that? Leighton hadn't exactly welcomed her interest in the painting last time she was there.

"Bee?" Where was he, anyway? She hadn't noticed him taking the file cabinets upstairs, and the back room was surprisingly quiet. She pulled the curtain aside and peeked in.

Bee lay sprawled across the Oriental rug in the middle of the room, snoring softly. At least he'd stacked the papers from the drawer he'd spilled on her desk before conking out in the middle of the room. He must have really been exhausted. Too bad she was going to have to wake him. "Hey, Bee. Wake up."

He jerked awake, shielding his eyes with his hand. "Cass?"

"Yeah, you slacker. What are you doing sleeping on the job?"

He groaned and rolled over.

"Come on, Bee, you have to get up. I need you to do me a favor."

"Honey, the only thing I'm doing when I get up off this floor is going home to bed. It's past my bedtime."

"Well, you'll just have to wait a little while longer. I have to do this while Beast is still at the groomer, and I need you to run interference."

He propped himself up on his elbows and quirked an eyebrow. "Interference?"

Good. She'd piqued his interest. Now to get him to go along with her plan. "Did you see the customer who was just in here?"

"No, sorry. Why?" He rubbed the sleep from his eyes.

"He said he lost a necklace."

Bee shrugged. "So?"

"He said he lost it when he was working in the art gallery."

"He's an artist?"

Hmm . . . She hadn't thought of that. Leighton did say she stocked work by local artists.

"No clue. He was very vague about everything, but he said the necklace wasn't his, then he asked me not to tell Leighton he'd asked about it. Then he got spooked and took off." She frowned. "I don't know if he saw the ghost or—"

"Stop right there, sweetheart. I am so done listening."

"Oh, Bee. Knock it off. You know you want to hear more."

"I definitely want to hear more, but if you want my help, leave out all the heebie-jeebie stuff."

She huffed out a breath. "All right, fine."

He motioned for her to continue.

"Anyway . . ." After giving him an eye roll for good measure, she continued. "When he described the necklace, something seemed familiar about it. For some reason, I think it may have been in the painting I saw in the art gallery window."

"Didn't you say the woman in the painting had on a blouse with a high collar?"

"Yes." She tried to think back. The woman's face popped into her head quickly enough, but everything else was pretty much a blur. Closing her eyes, she tried to bring the image into focus. She could envision the high collar and sort of imagine the blouse's shoulders, but that was it. Try as she might, she couldn't remember if the necklace was there or not. She shook her head. "But something about the necklace seems familiar. I need to get another look at that painting, but the last time I asked Leighton about it, she was . . . snippy, so I don't really want to ask again."

"So what *do* you want to do?"

She offered her best smile.

"Uh-oh."

"Don't *uh-oh* me. You said you wanted to talk to her about a painting for Dreamweaver. All you have to do is go in there and ask about a few paintings. While you get her talking, I'll look around."

Bee drew his bushy eyebrows together. "That's it?"

"That's it."

"What if the painting's not there?"

"We'll worry about that when the time comes. But I can't bring Beast in there, so we have to go now. I'm supposed to pick him up at lunchtime."

Bee shrugged. "Sure. Why not?"

"And whatever you do, don't mention the painting. Or the necklace."

"Are you going to close the shop or see if Stephanie can come back and sit for a few minutes?"

"Nah. Stephanie seems to be a little overwhelmed lately. I'll just close up a little early for lunch, then I'll go get Beast right after the gallery." Cass looked out the back window at the growing crowd. "Seems like everyone's more interested in whatever's going on at the beach than coming in here, anyway."

Bee squeezed in beside her by the window. "Hmm . . . looks like that little nap on your back room floor is going to have to last me awhile."

"Don't get any ideas about stopping out there, mister." She grinned at him. "At least, not until we get back."

{ 13 }

Cass hurried down the boardwalk with Bee at her side. Considering the mob scene on the beach, the boardwalk was fairly deserted. A woman on a bike sped past them. An older man walking a golden retriever stopped to look in the window of the ice cream shop, then looked down at his dog and resumed his walk. Seagulls screamed, and she could picture them diving into the choppy waves of the bay, or more likely, scavenging bits of bread and french fries people in the crowd would inevitably drop.

She slowed as she passed Dreamweaver. "The window looks stunning, Bee." She gestured toward a black slip dress she couldn't remember seeing before. "Is that a new piece? I didn't notice it last time."

"I just finished it. You like?"

"Are you kidding? I love it." Thin double straps separated as they dipped over the mannequin's shoulders. Bee's dresses were known for their bare backs with elaborate strap designs. "What do those straps do in the back?"

"Uh-uh. You'll have to come in and see them."

"Seriously?"

"Seriously, sweetie. Trust me, words don't do them justice." He started to turn away from the window.

"Mr. Maxwell?"

Cass turned toward the voice that had called from across the street.

Tim Daughtry crossed the street and jogged up the few steps to the boardwalk. He extended a hand. "Hi, Cass."

She took his hand and shook. "Hi, Tim. How are you doing? Done with school already?"

"Just finished for the summer." He turned to Bee and held out his hand, twin spots of crimson flaming on his pale cheeks. "That's actually what I was coming down here for, Mr. Maxwell. I was hoping to talk to you. Do you have a minute?"

Bee took his hand and glanced at Cass, and she nodded. "Sure. What did you want to talk about?"

"I was hoping to talk you into allowing me to do an internship with you this summer." Tim had just finished his first year at a college in Philadelphia where he was studying fashion design, a program Bee had helped him get into. "I'm taking a few summer courses in the mornings, and I know you don't usually open the shop before noon, so I thought maybe you'd let me work a few hours in the afternoon with you."

Bee studied him. Although Bee always opened in the summer months, when the beach and boardwalk were most crowded, he sometimes didn't bother opening when there weren't likely to be many shoppers stopping in. A good portion of his inventory went to buyers, and a large part of his business was done by appointment only.

"I'll do anything you need me to. I don't even mind cleaning up and running errands."

Bee smiled. "Sure, Tim. I'd love to have you for the summer."

A huge smile spread across Tim's face. "Thank you so much, Mr. Maxwell."

Sometimes Bee was such a sweetheart. While Bee and Tim started to work out a few of the details, Cass returned her attention to the black dress in the window. She wondered if it was a special order, or if it was available. Luke would be coming this weekend. Of course, she had to do the reading Saturday night, which would probably run late, but maybe they could still go somewhere nice for dinner on Sunday. She had a pair of killer red heels that would look amazing with that dress, and she was dying to see the back. She'd bet anything it dipped low, and she'd already been working on her tan.

A flicker of movement reflected in the window pulled her focus from drooling over the dress. Goose bumps prickled the back of her neck. She turned slowly, keeping her gaze from landing directly on the figure standing against the alley side of the ice-cream shop.

She watched from her peripheral vision as a beefy guy in a loose black T-shirt peered around the side of the newspaper he was holding discreetly—or so he probably thought, but did anyone even read papers anymore?—to block his face.

It didn't matter, anyway; she'd have recognized Artie Becker's build from a block away, even if she couldn't see his face. But what was he doing there? Obviously trying to keep an eye on something, but what? From where he stood, he'd have a clear view of the art gallery, but he'd also have Mystical Musings under surveillance.

"Bye, Cass."

"Huh?" She turned and waved to Tim. "Oh. See ya, Tim."

"Thanks, Mr. Maxwell. I'll stop in tomorrow afternoon."

Bee waved, but his attention had already turned to Cass. "Are you okay?"

"Uh . . ." She tried to shake off her apprehension. "Yeah, why?"

"'Cause you're pale. You look like you just saw a gho— Oh . . ." Bee looked over his shoulder and whispered, "You didn't, did you?"

Cass laughed. She couldn't help it. The fearful expression on his face was priceless. "Nope. No ghosts, but I did see something."

She angled herself to see Artie without letting him know she'd recognized him and was looking at him. She needn't have bothered. He was gone.

"Well, are you going to tell me what it was you saw or leave me standing here in suspense all day?"

"Oh, sorry." She hooked her arm through his and started toward the art gallery. "Artie Becker was just standing across the street with a newspaper covering his face."

Bee looked at her and lifted a brow.

"I know it sounds crazy, but I'm sure it was him."

He looked across the street to the spot Cass had indicated and shrugged. "I didn't see anyone."

Doubt started to creep in. Could she really be sure it was him? She'd been so sure when she'd first spotted him, but now . . . she couldn't say a hundred percent it was him. The feeling someone was watching her followed her down to the art gallery, and she was glad to finally walk inside and close the door behind her.

The sweet, piney scent of turpentine enveloped her. Paintings lined the walls and sat on easels and stands spread sporadically throughout the shop. She leaned close to Bee and whispered, "You know what to do, right?"

"I got this."

Cass certainly hoped so. Discretion wasn't one of Bee's strong suits.

Leighton rounded the counter and strode toward them. "Hi, Cass."

"Hi there." She gestured toward Bee. "This is Bee Maxwell. He owns Dreamweaver Designs."

"Oh, hi. It's nice to meet you, Bee. I was just admiring that black dress you have in the window on my way in this morning."

"Thank you." He smiled, always thrilled when anyone complimented his designs.

Uh-oh. No way was she getting that dress. "Don't you love it? I'm picking it up tomorrow to wear out this weekend."

If Bee was surprised, he hid it well. Maybe he was getting better at being discreet. "I designed it specifically with Cass's gorgeous red shoes in mind."

Or maybe he was telling the truth. It was hard to tell with Bee.

"Oh, that's too bad. I definitely had my eye on it." She waved it off. As if a dress that stunning could be dismissed so easily. "Oh, well, maybe next time."

Together, they browsed through the shop. The paintings inside leaned more toward landscapes, especially beaches, lighthouses, and forests, mostly done in dark tones. Angry seas, run-down, abandoned-looking lighthouses and keeper's cottages, gnarled, twisted tree trunks with leafless branches, skies filled with black and gray storm clouds casting a somber pall over everything they touched. The woman was obviously extremely talented, though her tastes ran a little too dark and brooding for Cass. You couldn't help but feel the forlorn nature of her work, along with something else, as well. A sense of fear, foreboding. She lost herself in all the dark beauty.

"I love it." Bee's voice pulled her back to reality.

She shook off the weird melancholy that had gripped her and looked around. A quick scan of the gallery told Cass all she needed to know. The painting she was looking for wasn't there.

Bee honed in on a sunset painting, done in beautiful shades of blue, pink, and lavender, a bit brighter than most of the others. "Oh, that's beautiful." He studied the painting displayed on an easel beside the counter. "Do you take custom orders?"

"Yes, actually, but I do charge more."

"That's fine." Bee waved it off. "Do you think you could do something similar to this, but with a little less lavender, a little deeper blue, and maybe brighten up the pink a little, so it really pops? Actually, you know what? Maybe it would be better if you walked down to the shop with me. Then I could show you the wall I want the painting for, and maybe you could give me a better idea for the colors."

Leighton hesitated, though whether it was from fear of going somewhere with an unknown man or reluctance to leave the shop, Cass couldn't tell.

"It'll be fine. Cass can keep an eye on the shop in case anyone comes in." Bee shot Cass a pointed warning glare. "It'll just take a couple of minutes."

"Oh, sure. I don't mind. I wanted to browse a little more, anyway, while I don't have Beast with me. That doesn't happen often." She tried for a grin but figured it probably came off more like a grimace. She just wasn't good at lying. Sweat trickled down her back. It didn't seem right, snooping through Leighton's things, but what else could she do? She'd already asked about the painting, and Leighton wouldn't give her any information. And she had to get one more look at that painting, had to know for sure if it was the same woman who'd been appearing in her visions. She wasn't sure exactly what she expected to gain from the knowledge, when she could very well have conjured the woman after seeing the painting in the window, but the need to know hammered her relentlessly.

"I don't know . . ." Leighton looked around the empty shop.

"I'll tell you what . . ." Bee started guiding her toward the counter. "Dreamweaver is only a few doors down. You could give Cass your cell phone number. If any customers come in, she can tell them you just stepped out for a moment, then call you." He lifted a pad and pen from the counter beside the register and held them out to her. "Besides . . ." He looked around and lowered his voice. "I doubt anyone will be coming in right now anyway. They're all gathered on the beach down by Mystical Musings. Cops, reporters, citizens, maybe even a killer."

Leighton glanced at Cass once more before writing her number on the top page and setting it on the counter.

Bee led her toward the door, the promise of good dirt apparently all the bait she needed. "What do you mean, a killer?"

He nodded knowingly. "Well, I've heard killers often return to the scene of the crime, sometimes even try to insert themselves into the investigation, so who's to say whoever buried those skeletons out on the beach didn't come back to witness his handiwork?"

Leighton gasped. "You don't really think—"

The door fell shut behind them, and Cass forced herself to stay put and count to twenty before bolting for the back room and shoving open the door. When the door closed behind her, she propped it open with a chair. She *had* promised to keep an eye on the shop, and she didn't want anyone coming in and making off with anything when Leighton had trusted her. A pang of guilt tried to surface, but she tamped it down. She didn't have time for her conscience right now.

She scanned the small back room, hoping to come across the painting quickly. No such luck. An assortment of canvases, some empty, others partially painted, were spread across the room. The smell of turpentine and paint were much thicker in the back room, almost gagging her. Spools of thick twine in every color imaginable hung on pegs suspended from one sidewall above an unfinished wood countertop, its surface stained with a variety of paint splotches and spills. Paintbrushes stood in mismatched containers on a shelf that ran along the back of the countertop, just beneath the twine. Cass cracked open a door at the side of the stockroom. Just a bathroom. Then she opened the cabinet doors beneath the center island. Blank canvases were lined neatly across the space. She returned to her search of the small stockroom, almost ready to accept defeat.

Along the back wall stood a row of easels holding what looked like six or seven completed paintings. Maybe Leighton had left them there to dry? The last easel in line had been turned to face the wall. She glanced over her shoulder out into the shop. They'd already been gone at least five minutes. With Bee's warning that they'd be back in a few minutes etched in her mind, she ran across the room and peeked over the top of the canvas. Disappointment surged. The entire top half of the canvas was white. Blank?

She gripped the side of the canvas and turned it a little to get a better look, and gasped. The bottom half of the painting, depicting a woman's shoulders, was the same as the one she'd seen in the display window. She was positive. Almost. But the woman's face had been painted over with white. As had the top of the high collar she'd been wearing. But a bit of the dress between the woman's shoulders was still visible, and there, dead center, hung a large opal surrounded by an intricate pattern of silver.

Her cell phone beeped, and she nearly jumped out of her skin, quickly shoving the painting back into place. She pulled the phone from her pocket and went to swipe for her new message, then spotted the white mark on her thumb. *Uh-oh*. She checked the text from Bee.

Coming.

Ah jeez. She shoved the phone back into her pocket and stared at her thumb again as if the spot would have disappeared. She glanced frantically around the studio for something to wipe the paint off. Her gaze landed on the back of the painting. *Oh. Oh no.*

She leaned around the side, careful not to touch the surface again. A perfect thumbprint, smack in the corner of the canvas. Sweat sprang out on her forehead and dripped into her eyes. She wiped it away and searched the room again, desperate for some way to clean up the mess she'd made. Dreamweaver was only a few doors down.

She whipped out her cell phone and typed Stall, then hit send and prayed Bee would get it in time and be able to do something. Discreetly. *Ugh* . . .

She yanked the bathroom door open, unrolled some toilet paper, and used it to wipe her thumb. It succeeded in smearing the paint. She ran toward the painting with the wad of toilet paper in hand. She had to do something. She might not be able to fix it so Leighton wouldn't notice anything, but she definitely did not need to leave her thumbprint, for crying out loud. Her conscience chose that moment to start battering her. She didn't need the reminder that her fingerprints were already on file thanks to the last crime she was accused of committing.

There had to be some way to get out of this mess. On the verge of tears, Cass tried to focus. The paintbrushes grabbed her attention. "Okay, maybe I can fix this."

She yanked a brush from a holder and ran to the painting. Careful to only touch the bottom that hadn't been painted over, she turned it enough to face the light. Using gentle strokes, her hand shaking wildly, she used the paintbrush to try to spread the surrounding paint over the incriminating print.

Bee's overly loud laugh outside the front door interrupted her efforts.

Dang! Resigned to the fact she was out of time, she

quickly spun the painting back around, shoved the paint-brush in her jeans pocket, and arranged her oversize tunic top so it covered the evidence of her guilt, then ran for the front room, huffing and puffing as if she'd just run a marathon.

She made it before them, but a quick glance over her shoulder told her she wasn't out of the woods yet.

Bee's bulky silhouette barred the shop entrance, and Cass ran back to the stockroom door, kicked the chair she'd used to prop the door open out of the way, ran back, and skidded to a stop by the register even as the door burst open and Bee poked his head in.

Ugh . . . way to be discreet, Bee. Of course, he hadn't left his thumbprint on anything. So there was that. She quickly hooked her incriminating thumb in her jeans pocket, holding the paintbrush in place to keep it from falling out.

Bee took one look at her, and his eyes widened. Thankfully, he kept talking with only a small hitch in his voice. "That would be perfect if you could have it done by the end of the summer, just in time for the buyers to be in town for my annual fashion show."

He held the door open and Leighton strolled through, quickly surveying the shop as she entered. Her gaze landed on Cass, and she frowned.

Cass tried for a smile, still breathing a little hard through her teeth. "So, how'd it go?"

"Fantastic," Bee gushed. "Leighton is going to do a sunset for the wall where my beach wedding line is displayed."

"Oh, that's great." She hooked Bee's arm with her free hand. "Come on, though, I've got to run. Everything was quiet while you were gone, Leighton." She started to pull her cell phone out of her pocket to check the time, but then thought better of it. No way could she explain the paint smudge on her thumb. "Uh . . . I have to go get Beast. I was supposed to pick him up a little while ago."

Bee's eyebrows pulled into a bushy *V*, but he turned to Leighton without questioning Cass. "Could you write up the order, and I'll stop in tomorrow and leave a deposit?"

"Sure."

"Thanks."

When they got outside, he lit into her the instant the door closed. "What on earth happened to you?"

She scoffed and started speed walking toward Mystical Musings, which was no easy task with one hand hooked through Bee's arm and the other stuffed in her pocket. "I don't know what you're talking about."

"Oh, please. You have got to be kidding me. Your hair is soaked with sweat and you look like you just—" He paled and waved a hand dismissively. "Never mind. If you were breathing any harder when I walked in there, you'd have probably passed out. So, something obviously happened. Now, are you going to tell me what it was or not?"

She twisted her face up in an expression that hopefully told him he couldn't be more wrong, but probably screamed *I'm guilty as hell*.

14

Bee maintained a moody silence all the way back to Mystical Musings. When Cass unlocked the door and held it open for him, he simply crossed his arms, leaned back against the railing, and pinned her with *the look*. He obviously wasn't going anywhere without answers. And he *had* run interference for her. As much as she hated admitting how badly she'd screwed up, he deserved the truth. "Fine."

Bee smirked, and she had half a mind to walk away without saying anything. But she really wanted another opinion as to why Leighton would have painted over the portrait Cass had asked her about, especially just after she'd seen Artie Becker leaving the gallery.

Still holding the door open, she gestured toward the shop. "Come in, though. I want to see if the reporters are still out back."

He pushed away from the railing and pointed toward the side of the shop where the boardwalk ended and the edge of the parking lot met hard-packed sand. "If that's any indication, it's worse than before."

"But we weren't even gone long." She let the door fall closed and peered around the corner of the shop. More news vans were packed into the cramped space, along with a few police cruisers, their lights flashing. "Do you think something else happened?"

Bee shrugged and started toward the door. "No idea, but I'll make the rounds if we can't figure anything out."

An idea struck. "Any chance you'd pick up Beast for me while you're out, and I'll try to figure out what's going on?"

"Not a chance, honey." He winked.

Cass couldn't help but laugh. As long as there was drama in her backyard, Bee wouldn't be going anywhere. Not even for gossip. Beast would be okay for a couple more minutes. She'd run and get him as soon as she checked out the beach. And she'd make sure to give the groomer a generous tip.

On the way in the door, she flipped the sign to OPEN, then crossed the shop and started to turn the sign on the back door over. One look at the beach out the back window stopped her short. They'd removed the chicken wire, and the reporters were crammed together yelling questions over one another. The new police chief stood with Tank and Harry on either side of her. Doctor Jones, a local doctor who doubled as the medical examiner, stood beside Tank, his usually friendly expression grim.

Apparently they'd missed whatever announcement he'd made, but maybe they could figure something out from the questions being asked. Unable to hear more than a chaotic rumble through the closed door, Cass opened the door and strolled onto the porch with Bee right on her heels.

". . . serial killer . . . bodies . . . safe?"

She struggled to sort through the barrage of questions.

When the police chief pointed to a petite woman with dark hair toward the middle of the pack, the other questions died down.

"What precautions are you taking to keep the community safe?" she yelled, in a much more forceful voice than Cass would have expected from the delicate woman.

"We have no reason to believe any of our citizens are in danger . . ." the chief started.

The murmur that rushed through the crowd told Cass they didn't agree with her assessment.

"Please . . ." She held her hands up. "Please. We have very little information right now, and it's way too early in the investigation to jump to any conclusions. As soon as we know more, we'll let you know. For now, though, there's no reason to panic."

After a second or two of silence, when it became obvious she wasn't going to elaborate, the volley of questions started again.

Cass rested her elbows on the railing and scanned the group of what she'd originally thought were mostly reporters. It seemed a number of Bay Island's citizens were among the crowd. Tony and his wife, Gina, who co-owned the bakery; a few employees from the diner; Rick, who owned the deli; and several business owners from along the boardwalk. Apparently, the situation was more concerning than Cass had realized.

She spotted another vaguely familiar face among the

throng of people. The skinny guy from the deli leaned against a lamppost toward the back of the crowd, hands stuffed into the pockets of his baggy khakis. Wade something.

His gaze shot to hers as if he'd sensed the weight of her stare, and a slow grin spread across his face. Without breaking eye contact, he leaned toward a heavyset man standing next to him and spoke briefly.

The other man turned toward Cass, staring openly, and nodded, then moved through the crowd until he reached the petite woman with the big voice. He gripped her shoulder and leaned close to her ear. If the rapid movement of his lips was any indication, he was excited about something.

Uh-oh. Cass stood and backed toward the door.

"Miss Donovan!" The woman honed in on her before Cass even finished crossing the porch and started shoving her way through the crowd toward Mystical Musings. "Aren't you Cass Donovan?"

Cass froze. "Uh . . ."

Bee grabbed her shoulders from behind and whispered in her ear, "On second thought, someone really should go get Beast," then fled. His heavy footsteps retreated across the porch, and the wind chimes tinkled as he opened the door.

"Aren't you the woman who found the first body?"

The police chief rolled her eyes, smiled, and took the opportunity to quickly thank everyone for coming, then she shot Cass a warning stare and took off.

Tank's jaw clenched, the only indication he wasn't happy with the situation . . . or her . . . or something.

Harry simply tilted his head and looked amused.

With no idea what she was supposed to say, she resorted to the standard line they always used on TV. "No comment?"

"Did a spirit actually lead you to the body?"

Cass shook her head but refrained from repeating herself.

"Can you really talk to ghosts?" another reporter yelled.

The barrage of questions overwhelmed her.

"There are reports you've worked with the police before. Are you working with them on this case?"

"What?" Caught off guard, Cass forgot her no comment mantra.

Tank shook his head and moved toward her.

If she didn't put a stop to the all the rumors and speculation flying around, she'd never be left alone. She'd have to worry constantly that the killer—or Tank—would come after her. She couldn't live looking over her shoulder every two seconds. "Look. I don't know where you're getting your information from . . ."

She scanned the crowd for the troublemaker who'd set the reporters on her, but he seemed to have disappeared. "But I'm not consulting with the police in any professional capacity. I was walking my dog on the beach, and he picked up a bone. When I realized what it was, I called nine-one-one. That's it."

Voices raised in competition for her attention. Did these people just not get it?

She backed up until she hit the door Bee had closed behind him. *Thanks a lot, Bee.* She felt behind her for the handle.

"Do you have reason to believe the woman who contacted you was Kelly Becker?"

Ah jeez . . . Who were these people talking to, and why did they seem to have so much information?

"You had an appointment with Artie Becker on Friday evening . . ."

Shock slammed through her. An image of "John" hunched over her appointment book flashed before her.

"Did Mr. Becker give you a clue that led you to his daughter's whereabouts?"

Anger started to simmer. How dare that guy come into her shop, go through her things, and then pass on information to reporters?

The rapid-fire questions continued to pummel her, coming so quickly she had no hope of sorting through them, or even making sense of them.

She opened her mouth, intent on giving these people a piece of her mind, then snapped it shut just as quickly. If she blurted out that she wasn't psychic, she may as well lock her doors and move back to the city right now. If she admitted to any sort of psychic ability, they'd be all over her. Besides, a spirit—or something—had actually led her to the body. Maybe. Okay, she definitely couldn't say that. Of course, business *would* probably pick up if she did.

She was saved from having to say anything else by a firm grip around her arm. She spun toward the hold, tried to jerk away, and came face-to-face with a stone-faced Tank. *Oh, boy. This isn't going to be pretty.* She offered a winning— she hoped—smile.

Tank just rolled his eyes and tightened his grip while he announced the end of her impromptu press conference. Then he turned and ushered her through the store. "Lock up."

"Lock up? I can't close the store in the middle of the afternoon."

Tank turned the sign on the back door to CLOSED. "As long as you're open, we'll never be able to get rid of the reporters. Besides, we need to talk."

"Why can't we talk here?"

He stared at her with his brow lifted, then pulled out his cell phone and started texting.

Cass reluctantly locked the back door, then strode toward the front. A few of the reporters had already made their way around to the front and were lingering on the porch. One guy cupped his hands and pressed his face against the display window, trying to see in. Though she hated to admit it, and she wouldn't tell him, Tank was right. She'd never be able to work this way.

"Come on." Tank placed a gentle hand on her back and guided her toward the door. "Once we get you out of here, maybe we can get control of this mess."

The frustration in his voice made her glance over and take a good look at him for the first time. He looked more tired than she'd ever seen him. Dark circles ringed his eyes, deep lines bracketed his mouth, and his posture was just a little slouched, not enough that you'd notice without studying him, but Cass made a career of noticing things like that.

"Tank?"

He watched out the front door, obviously distracted. "Yeah?"

"Are you okay?"

He looked at her for a moment, surprise apparent in his expression, then nodded. "Yeah, I'm okay, just tired." He rubbed a circle on her back. "Thanks for caring, though. Even though you frustrate the crap out of me, you're a good friend."

"Thanks." Cass laughed. "I think."

He grinned. "Come on, let's get out of here. Do you have the key?"

She handed it to him as she watched the crowd out front grow.

"Where's your car?"

"Bee drove with me from the deli. He must have taken it to go get Beast."

Harry pulled up out front and hurried—as fast as Harry hurried anywhere—up the boardwalk to the front porch. Two uniformed officers flanked him, keeping the reporters back.

Tank leaned close. "Keep your focus straight ahead and, whatever you do, don't say a word."

He opened the front door, and she walked onto the porch. Harry took her arm and guided her toward the car.

A moment later, after locking the door, Tank caught up and picked up the pace.

A man standing beside a black car in the parking lot caught her attention. *John.* Or whatever his real name was. She hesitated, but Tank propelled her forward. "Wait. That's him."

Tank tried to follow her gaze with his own. "Who?"

"The guy who came into the shop and was looking through my appointment book." She tried to head toward him, but Tank's iron grip kept her on track.

Harry opened the car door.

"But wait, you have to . . ." Before she could finish the

statement, the guy spotted her looking at him and melted into the crowd toward the beach. "He's getting—"

"Not here, Cass. I'll meet you at the station." Tank helped her into the car, then slammed the door.

"Station? Wait, what station? Tank?"

But he was already walking away. Harry slid in next to her and took off.

Great. She pulled her phone out of her pocket and texted Bee. He'd just have to take care of Beast until she could straighten all of this out, whatever all of this was.

When the phone beeped with his answer, she didn't even bother reading it. She already knew he wouldn't be happy, between having to keep Beast and not knowing what was happening, but what else could she do?

Resigned to her fate for the next little while, Cass sighed. "So, how are things going, Harry?"

He smiled and shook his head. "I'll tell ya, this is the last thing I needed two weeks before retirement." He glanced at her from the corner of his eye. "You couldn't have waited two lousy weeks before calling this in, Cass? Really?"

She shrugged. "Sorry, Harry. I'll do better next time."

"Bite your tongue, girl. There'd better not be a next time." His good humor fled.

"What exactly is going on? I heard another body was found."

He studied her for a moment. "You can't say anything to anyone about any of this."

"I won't." She slid her crossed fingers beneath her leg. Of course, she'd tell Bee and Stephanie, but she figured he probably expected that.

He heaved his bulk up a little, probably getting more

comfortable, then hit the turn signal as they pulled onto the main road, which only allowed for one lane of traffic in each direction, and headed through the town. "The first body, the one you found, seems to be old. And we're fairly certain it's a man. We can't tell for sure, but it seems that way. But the second body . . ." He shook his head and stared out the windshield.

Cass watched the scenery go by as she waited to see if he'd continue. After a long cold winter, everything was just starting to bloom. Daffodils surrounded the trees that lined the side streets. The trees that had stood bare all winter now held buds that would soon form canopies over the roads. Sunlight flickered as the branches swayed in the gentle bay breeze.

"It wasn't found far from the first, just a little farther into the dunes, and we're certain it's a woman, though we haven't verified her identity yet." He stared at Cass, his scrutiny long and hard enough to make her squirm in her seat. "If you'd have followed her a little farther, you'd have stumbled right over her."

Cass gasped.

"The rumors are true, aren't they? You followed a woman into the dunes and found the first body?"

She didn't know what to say. Harry's paunchy appearance and laid-back—lazy, if she were to be perfectly honest—attitude made it easy to forget how smart he was. And how observant.

"My cousin and her husband were guests at the old Madison Estate when the spirit you conjured appeared over the fireplace."

Cass racked her brain to think of who his cousin could

be, but she hadn't yet been back on Bay Island long enough to have learned all of the family connections.

"My cousin and I are very close, more like brother and sister, so aside from Tank's high praise and glowing recommendation, I also researched you after the trouble up there. I didn't find anything to make me think you are a fraud, nor did I find anything to indicate you were crazy. Millie is a smart woman, not given to theatrics, and she told me in no uncertain terms, if rumor has it a spirit guided you to the body, then it probably did." He shrugged. "So, I'm asking. Did you have help finding the body?"

15

Uncomfortable under his stare, Cass turned and looked out the side window.

Harry pulled into the parking lot and parked in a reserved spot in front of the police station. He cracked the windows open, turned off the car, and sat, waiting.

Memories of the last time she'd been there swamped her, and she made no move to get out of the car. If she never set foot in that station again, it would be too soon. "Yes."

"I'm sorry?" he asked, though she was pretty sure he knew exactly what she meant.

She heaved in a breath and slouched back against the seat. "Yes, I followed a . . . I don't know exactly, but something, into the dunes. The vision hit me after I took the bone from Beast. I followed her, but the woman disappeared behind the dune. Then I found the pile of bones Beast had dug up."

"So you didn't actually see the exact spot where the image vanished?"

She shook her head.

"So it could have been a few dozen feet farther into the dunes?"

Cass thought about it. She'd been hesitant, afraid of what she'd find, and she'd paused before the woman disappeared. "Yes. It could have been."

He seemed to turn the information over in his mind. He reached for the door handle.

"Wait."

With his hand perched on the handle, he stopped.

"That's it?"

He shrugged. "For now."

"And you believe me?"

"No reason not to." He reached across the seat and patted her arm, then hauled his bulk out of the car.

Before she could say anything else, Tank pulled in beside them. He got out and opened Cass's door.

She climbed from the car, feeling like she was caught up in a bad episode of *The Ghost Whisperer,* and followed Harry and Tank up the front steps and into the building.

"You okay?" Tank whispered just after they crossed the threshold.

She nodded and kept walking, her gaze focused firmly in front of her.

Tank ushered her into a corner office—thankfully, one she'd never been in before—and gestured to a chair at a small round table. "Have a seat, and I'll be right back."

Harry seemed to have disappeared somewhere.

She pulled out a chair and sat. Resting her elbows on the

table, she cradled her head in her hands and searched for focus. Things had spiraled so far out of control, she had no clue what to do to straighten them out. She didn't know what Tank wanted to talk to her about. A small niggle of fear tried to creep in, but she brushed it aside. Even if Leighton had already noticed the damage she'd done to the painting, there hadn't been time for her to call the police or for them to investigate and match the smudge to her thumbprint, if they even could still match it after she'd smeared it the best she could with the paintbrush. Okay. She took a deep breath and blew it out slowly. Obviously, focusing internally was an epic failure.

She looked around the room. Lush green ferns adorned a multisurface planter beneath the window. A small, scratched desk sat in one corner, papers strewn haphazardly across its surface. Not once did it cross her mind to shuffle through them to see what they were. Of course, she had no interest in their contents. If she did, she'd probably have used the moment alone to take a peek. Was that all "John" had done, taken a peek into something that had been left lying around that he thought might be interesting? Or had his interest been more calculated than that? It didn't seem likely that he'd come in intent on finding her appointment book. That had to have just been a bonus, yet her gut told her he'd been there for something. But what?

The door squeaked as it opened and Tank walked in with the chief of police, a tall, handsome woman who appeared to be in her late forties or so. Her meticulously pressed suit hung from slim shoulders and hips. Her salt-and-pepper hair had been pulled back into a tight bun, sharpening her already angular features. She reminded Cass of her grade-school principal, back when she'd been afraid of authority figures.

Cass stood.

"Cass, this is Chief Rawlins."

Cass stepped forward and offered her hand. "It's nice to meet you."

The chief nodded. "Nice to meet you. Sit, please. Would you like a cup of coffee?"

Cass's stomach turned over at the thought. "No, thank you."

Chief Rawlins pulled out a seat across from Cass and sat, maintaining eye contact the whole time. "I've been hearing rumors about you."

Cass struggled not to squirm beneath the weight of her stare. She remained silent. No way she'd offer any information at all unless she was asked a direct question. She clasped her hands on the table in front of her and waited, the picture of calm, or so she hoped.

"I can't even stop for a decent cup of coffee without your name coming up, so I figured it was time we met." She smiled and folded her hands on the table in front of her.

Heat crept into Cass's cheeks. She hated being the focus of the rumor mill.

"Since I don't believe in gossip and prefer to get my information directly from the source, would you please walk me through the events that led to you finding the skeleton on the beach?"

"Um . . ." Her gaze flickered to Tank, who stood stone-faced beside the door, hands clasped in front of him. Apparently he hadn't been invited to join their chat.

"Would you please give us a moment alone, Detective?"

He studied Cass, and she nodded. "Of course, Chief. Let

me know when you're done, Cass, and I'll call Stephanie to pick you up."

"Sure. Thanks."

"Cass?" The chief's voice softened just a little.

"Yes?"

She stared hard at Cass. "I understand your reluctance to talk to me, but there's no need to feel hesitant . . . or threatened. Sometimes, especially in small towns, where there's not a lot of crime and things have been done the same way for generations, it can be hard for people to, shall we say, think outside the box? But I'm not from a small town. My last position was in a big city, where we often consulted with . . . well, anyone who might have information, no matter how they might have obtained it." Her warm smile lessened the harshness of her personality. "Now, talk to me."

Her southern accent reminded her a little of Luke's, and sincerity radiated from her. Although Cass had always been good at judging people's character, she still found it hard to trust them, even when she thought the person she was speaking to was being completely honest and genuine. But she did trust Tank, and she didn't think he'd have brought her into the station or left her alone with Chief Rawlins if he didn't trust her.

Heck, half the town already thought she was crazy, what difference did it really make what this woman thought of her? "I was walking on the beach with Beast, my dog, and he dug the bones up and brought me one. When I touched it . . ." She shivered at the memory. "I've been having dreams lately, about a woman who seems to be trying to tell me something. When I grabbed the bone, I got a vision of the woman."

The chief uncrossed her legs and perched on the edge of her chair, leaning forward against the table. "And?"

Cass shrugged. "I followed her into the dunes and found the bones."

Chief Rawlins pursed her lips and slid back in the chair. "You had a visit from a man named Artie Becker."

She nodded, unsure of what to make of the abrupt change of subject.

"Did he show you a photograph of his daughter?"

"Yes."

"Was it the same woman?"

The thought had tormented Cass since she'd stumbled across the body. "I just don't know. The picture was old, from when she was a young teenager. She had a long bob, hanging around her face. The image of the woman I saw was older and had her hair pulled back. Plus, it was shadowy." Cass shook her head. She just couldn't say for sure. "It was hard to even tell what color it was, though if I had to guess, I'd say dirty blond or light brown."

The chief studied her a moment longer, then stood and extended her hand. "Thank you for coming in. If you think of anything else that could be helpful to us, I'd appreciate you contacting me." She released Cass's hand and pulled a leather business card holder from her jacket pocket. She removed a card and handed it to Cass. "It would be best if you contact me directly. Others in the department might not be quite so open-minded."

Cass had a strong suspicion this woman knew exactly what each and every member of her department thought.

"Thank you."

She smiled and left. A moment later, Tank walked in. "Stephanie is on her way."

"Thank you."

"You okay?" he asked.

"Yeah, just tired."

He squeezed her arm and walked with her to the front door. She couldn't help but notice the sideways glances and even a few not-so-discreet stares from the other officers in the station, some of whom even stopped what they were doing to ogle her. Beginning to feel like some kind of freak, Cass hurried toward the door.

Somehow, it seemed odd to have people think she actually communicated with the dead. Of course, that's what they were all supposed to think. She'd worked hard to build a reputation as a medium and a psychic. But up until recently, she'd thought her instincts were just that, instincts. Now, however, she might have to face the fact that she was receiving some sort of otherworldly intervention. Her head started to pound.

She had to admit to a certain amount of relief when they exited the building and the door fell shut behind them, blocking the stares.

A flash of light blinded her for an instant and left spots in front of her eyes.

"Hey," Tank yelled, but remained at her side.

Someone jumped into the passenger side of a white van and took off.

Tank mumbled something that sounded suspiciously like "idiot," and Cass hoped he was referring to the guy with the camera. "Stephanie should be here any minute. Will you be all right until then?"

She inhaled deeply, the humid, salty air failing to relieve

any tension. "I'm fine. But don't you want to wait and see Stephanie?"

"I'd love to. Unfortunately, I can't right now. I have to go." He kissed her cheek and walked away. Weird. Tank never missed a chance to say hello to his wife. Either there was definitely trouble brewing, or this case was taking its toll.

Cass stood on the sidewalk and pulled out her cell phone to text Bee, but there was already a message waiting for her. It simply said, Call me.

She pressed Bee's name and put the phone to her ear.

"It's about time. Where are you?"

"I'm still at the police station. Stephanie's on her way to pick me up. Did you pick Beast up?"

"Well, I got there, but there was a slight issue."

"What do you mean? What happened?"

"He's okay, but he chewed up a bottle of shampoo. Unfortunately, it was full."

"Is he all right?"

"I took him over to the vet when you didn't call back." His voice held a slight reprimand, but Cass ignored it. "Doc said he'd be fine, but he's keeping him overnight for observation."

"All right. Thank you for taking him, Bee."

"You're welcome. There's one little problem, though."

"Just one?"

"Ha-ha, smarty-pants. I was just going to warn you, he threw up all over the car before we made it to the vet. I left the windows open, but, well, yeah . . ."

"Okay." She sighed. This day just got better and better. "I'll clean it up when I get there. Where are you?"

"I'm at the shop. I came back here to move the file cabinets and your paperwork upstairs."

In other words, he went back to the shop to see what was going on. "Are the reporters still there?"

"A few are still hanging around, but most of them already took off. Probably wanted to get on the ferry and head back to the mainland before dark."

Stephanie's car rounded the corner, so Cass cut her conversation with Bee short and shoved the phone into her pocket. Stephanie pulled up to the curb, and Cass slid into the passenger seat. "Thanks for coming to get me."

"No problem." Stephanie checked her side-view mirror and pulled out.

"Tank said he had to run." She studied Stephanie's profile, but didn't see any change in her expression at the mention of Tank.

"I know, thanks. When he called he said he wouldn't be able to wait."

"He usually does. Wait, I mean."

Stephanie glanced at her. "He usually doesn't have two bodies on the beach."

She couldn't argue that.

"How are you doing?" Stephanie asked.

Cass shrugged but accepted the change of subject. "It's been a rough day. I'll feel better after dinner and a hot bath." Though she was beyond exhausted, the thought of sleep brought only anxiety.

"Do you want to go out?"

She thought about it for a few minutes, but the thought of going out didn't really appeal. Between her lack of sleep, Beast stuck at the vet overnight—again—the episode at the art gallery, and her apparent involvement in a case she'd tried to stay out of, she didn't feel like doing anything. It was too late to stop at the vet and see Beast, so she'd have to settle for calling the doctor and asking about him. She could stop by and see him on the way to the shop in the morning. "Would you mind dropping me off at home?"

Stephanie glanced at her but, thankfully, refrained from asking questions Cass didn't feel like answering. "Sure. Where's your car?"

"Bee has it. He went back to the shop to start moving stuff upstairs. If I ask him to meet us at the house, would you drop him off at the deli to pick up his car?" Hopefully he wouldn't balk at driving it again before she could clean it up. Not an appealing thought.

"Are you going to have the group reading upstairs Saturday?"

A bit of excitement fluttered in her stomach. "I'm hoping to, if we can get it set up in time."

"All you really need up there are the tables and chairs, right?"

"Pretty much. Eventually, I'd like to have a counter for coffee and dessert, but we can do that downstairs this time."

"Or you could set up a table along one wall."

"True." She perked up at the thought of Saturday's reading. She loved the group readings, which had evolved into social events. She'd go home, get a good night's sleep, then pick up Beast in the morning and head into the shop. Tomorrow would be a better day.

16

The woman came closer, fear etched in her taut features. Cass reached out and tried to touch her, but her image dissipated into a cloudy haze beneath her fingers, only to reappear a moment later.

Cass's gaze shot to the woman's mouth. Not the pouty, full lips from the portrait in the gallery window, but a thin, tight line, her lips pressed firmly together. Did that mean Cass was dreaming? She didn't feel like she was asleep. And yet . . .

"Help me." The woman's voice sounded in Cass's head, even though her mouth never moved.

"I don't know how." Had she said that out loud? It felt like it, but she couldn't be sure.

"Help me!" The voice took on an angry edge, more insistent this time. The woman's eyes darkened.

Fear gripped Cass, but she wrestled it down. This needed to end, and the only way she could think to end it was to find out what the woman wanted and try to help. And if it was only a dream, well, it still couldn't hurt to ask. "What can I do?"

The woman held out a hand, and Cass reached for it. Their fingers met. An ice-cold chill penetrated Cass's hand and ran up her arm, the pain excruciating. She yanked her hand back.

The woman let out a silent scream, her features contorting into a grotesque mask of pain and anger, then she vanished.

Cass jerked upright and launched herself from the bed. Sweat soaked her shirt. Strands of damp hair stuck to her neck and wrapped around her throat. She pulled at it, desperately trying to untangle herself, needing air. Holding her hair up behind her, she sucked in a deep breath.

She looked for Beast in his usual spot at the foot of the bed, then remembered he was at the vet and wished he was there to comfort her. And to confirm he sensed a presence.

She shook off the last remnants of sleep and rubbed her arm where the phantom pain still lingered. No way was she getting back in that bed. She stumbled to the kitchen, turning on all the lights as she went, grabbed a bottle of water from the fridge, and sucked down half of it. Then she perched on the edge of a chair and put the bottle down in front of her. Propping her elbows on the table, she dropped her head into her hands and tried to bring the vision of the woman back into focus.

She was fairly certain it was the same woman from the painting in the gallery. The mouth had thrown her.

Cass had purposely looked for the necklace this time. Since she saw it in the painting in Leighton's back room, she knew exactly what she was looking for and where to look. But the woman in her visions was definitely not wearing the necklace "John" had been searching for. She had no doubt that was an important clue, but with no idea what it meant, all she could do was file it away for now.

A sound like a motor kicked on and Cass jerked out of the chair. The refrigerator. Okay, more like a soft hum than a motor, but in the silence and her current state of mind, it had sounded way louder than normal. She pressed a shaky hand to her chest to still her hammering heart. She couldn't take much more of this. Her nerves were shot. The clock on the stove read 3:00 A.M. The house was too lonely without Beast, too quiet. She wasn't hanging around alone for another minute.

Luke was currently working days, and though she had no doubt he'd wake up to talk to her, she didn't really want to worry him with a middle-of-the-night phone call. Who knew what hours Tank was working lately? And if he'd managed to get home and get a few hours of sleep or spend some time with Stephanie, she didn't want to interrupt. With the need to do something normal weighing on her, Cass picked up the phone and dialed Bee's number. Her need to hear another voice—another *live, human* voice—was worth the risk of earning Bee's wrath.

He answered on the first ring. "How dare you interrupt my genius?"

Cass forced a laugh. "Come on, Bee. We both know if

you were lost in the zone, you'd never have answered the phone."

"Ahh . . . Touché. Now what can I do for you, beautiful?"

Even over the phone, the strong tenor of Bee's voice brought comfort. "What are you doing right now?"

"Actually, nothing. I've been working on some new designs, but nothing seems to be coming to me. Maybe I'm just not feeling creative. Why? What's up?"

"Maybe some physical labor will stir the creative juices."

Bee's warm laughter embraced her. "Okay, sweetie, just spit it out. What sort of physical labor do you have in mind that can't wait until morning?"

"The kind I need your help for, and you won't be up in the morning."

"Oh, fine. I'm not getting anything done here anyway." An unusual note of frustration tinged Bee's tone.

"Everything okay?"

"Yeah, yeah. I think I'm just exhausted. I'll be fine after I get some sleep."

"If you'd rather go home and go to bed, I can—"

"Nah. I'm fine. If I go to bed too early, it screws up my schedule. So let me guess, you want the tables moved upstairs for Saturday's reading."

She grinned. No one knew her like Bee did. "I want to make sure I can have the reading upstairs, and if I'm busy all week, we won't get to it."

"Fine. Let me clean up here, and I'll stop at 7-Eleven for coffee and meet you at the shop in about half an hour, but afterward, you're buying me breakfast at the diner."

"You got it. I'll see you there." She disconnected the call, already feeling better. It hadn't escaped her notice that Bee didn't ask what she was doing up. He'd have known what was on her mind, of course, but he'd let her talk about it in her own time—if she wanted to. Which, right now, she didn't.

In no hurry to return to the bedroom, she ran into the laundry room off the kitchen, stripped off her sweat-soaked tank top, replaced it with a sports bra, then grabbed an oversize T-shirt from the drying rack and pulled it over the yoga pants she'd worn to bed. She could always stop back with Bee when they were done and change before heading out to breakfast. She hefted her large leather bag over her shoulder, grabbed the keys from the hook beside the door, then remembered her cell phone was charging on the nightstand. She thought briefly about going without it, but with Beast at the vet, she had to be reachable. Ugh . . . she was going to have to go back in there for it.

Keeping her focus firmly in front of her, she ran into the bedroom, grabbed the phone, and yanked it from the charger. Relief coursed through her as she spun back toward the door . . . and froze in her tracks.

The woman hovered a couple of feet in front of her, smack in the middle of the doorway. There was not a chance in the world she was walking through the specter, which she'd have to do if she wanted to get out of the room. Instead, she opted for the window.

Cass opened the door to Mystical Musings and turned on the light. A prickle at the back of her neck held her frozen for an instant, then she shook off her fear. This wasn't the first time she'd worked into the wee hours of the morning, and it certainly wouldn't be the last. If whatever was haunting her showed up this time, it'd just have to wait until Cass was finished.

She locked the door behind her, crossed the room, and dropped her bag on the table. She kept several round tables, as well as a bunch of folding tables and chairs, in the storeroom on the side of the shop. She'd have to pick up more tablecloths, though. Oh, and more foam coffee cups.

As tired as she was, she'd never remember everything if she didn't write it down. She grabbed a sheet of paper and a colored pencil from a basket on the shelf behind the table. She leaned over the counter to start a list, but the red pencil in her hand gave her pause. A random choice of color? Or a warning of danger?

Cass had made a living—first at her psychiatric practice, and then again at Mystical Musings—by following her instincts. Of course, in the end, her instincts had failed her, and one of her patients had committed suicide soon after leaving her office. And they'd failed her again when she hadn't realized her husband and her best friend had more than just friendship between them.

An image of the brick that had been thrown through her window brought beads of sweat to her forehead. Ghosts were one thing; she was getting used to those. Sort of. But an apparition couldn't throw a brick. Though the ghost did manage to leave a mark on her hand at the beach. And then there'd been the incident with the Ouija board. She still couldn't explain the welt that had appeared on her arm after she'd used one.

Okay, now I'm just spooking myself.

If she was going to accomplish anything at all, she'd have to stop standing there. Bee would arrive any moment with coffee. Surely company and caffeine would dampen the lingering effects of her recent . . . visits.

Ignoring her exhaustion and the increasing sense of foreboding, she grabbed the edge of the curtain that separated the main area from the storeroom, then hesitated.

The feeling that she wasn't alone nagged at her, and she glanced over her shoulder. The empty shop did nothing to alleviate the portent of impending danger. A premonition, or just middle-of-the-night jitters?

Something clattered against the floor upstairs, followed by a hushed curse.

Her gaze shot to the spiral staircase a few feet away. She crept toward it. Maybe Emmett had returned to finish off the room for Saturday. He'd said he'd do it one night that week. Or Bee could have arrived early and started moving more stuff upstairs. She refrained from calling out. Just in case.

She leaned over the railing and peered up into pitch darkness. Deafening silence surrounded her. If it were Emmett or Bee, there's no way they'd be working in the dark.

Okay, that's enough. I'm outta here.

She took a step back and turned to run, her breathing so loud she was sure whoever was up there had to know she'd realized something was wrong.

Footsteps pounded against the iron stairs at her back.

She spun toward the sound, scanning the shop for anything she could use as a weapon.

A black figure catapulted itself from the second step and barreled into her, knocking her down. The back of her head smacked the hardwood floor. The weight of the figure on top of her threatened to crush her, but then it scrambled up and off her and headed toward the back of the shop.

She tried to sit up, to follow it, but whomever—or whatever—it was bolted out the back door before she could even roll over.

Nausea threatened, and bile crept up the back of her throat. A dark eddy intruded on her peripheral vision. She laid her cheek against the cool floor as blackness overwhelmed her.

{17}

She floated in darkness. An overpowering sense of peace embraced her. Her limbs felt so light, as if she were drifting on a cloud.

"Cass?"

Pain tore through her head, ripping her forcefully from the sense of bliss enveloping her.

"Cass!" Bee's voice was more insistent this time.

Ugh . . . she was going to have to answer, but the pounding in her head wouldn't even allow her to form words.

Bee's shaky voice moved away. "No. I mean, yes. She's breathing, but she's not answering. You have to hurry."

Was he crying?

She rolled onto her side and tamped down the roiling in her stomach. Hadn't she been on her side? The last thing she remembered was the cool feel of the wood pressed against the side of her face.

"Cass?" Bee grabbed her arms. "Are you okay? What happened? Did you fall?"

If he didn't stop battering her with questions, she was going to vomit. She reached up and touched the back of her head. Her hand came away wet. Tentatively slitting open one eye, she brought her fingers in front of her face. Blood.

How hard had she fallen?

"Oh, dear. Wait here."

Where would I go?

The sound of Bee's platform shoes running on the wood floor beat a steady rhythm through her entire body, culminating in a crescendo in her head.

She closed her eyes again and tried to lift her head. She had to get it off the floor before he returned from wherever he'd gone. She put her hand down in a wet, sticky puddle.

Ah jeez. How badly was she bleeding?

Bee returned with all the grace of a stampeding elephant. "Here, honey. Put this on your head." He pressed something cold and hard against the back of her head. "Are you all right? What happened?"

"Stop." She held up a hand. "Please." She felt bad. He was so concerned and trying so hard to help her, and she appreciated him so much, but she had to get her bearings. She couldn't even think straight. The overwhelming scent of coffee almost made her hurl.

A low moan echoed through the shop.

Oh, wait. That was me.

Bee crouched down in front of her and stared into her eyes. "Cass?"

His stare gave her something to focus on, and she held his gaze.

He blinked, and tears dripped from his puffy, bloodshot eyes and rolled down his cheeks.

Ah, Bee. She lifted a hand to wipe his tears. Pain radiated from the back of her head, straight through to her eye sockets. She winced, but quickly gained control. "I'm okay, Bee."

"Are you sure?"

She started to nod, but thought better of moving her head. "Yeah. Just a bit of a headache."

"What happened? Did you fall?"

"How bad am I bleeding?"

Bee moved the compress aside, gently parted some of her hair, and studied her head wound. "Not that bad. Head wounds bleed a lot."

What was he talking about? There was blood all over the floor. Careful not to jolt her head, she scanned the floor around her. "What on earth?"

"I'm sorry. I'll get it cleaned up as soon as you're okay." His cheeks flushed a deep red. "When I came in and saw you on the floor, I dropped the coffees."

Coffee? She'd had visions of a river of blood covering the wood floors. Cass stared into his somber expression, and a laugh bubbled up.

He frowned.

"I'm sorry, Bee, I thought—" She hiccupped and almost choked as she started to laugh harder. Sucking in a deep, steadying breath, she struggled for some semblance of control.

Bee huffed, looking insulted.

"I'm sorry. I-I thought it was blood." She gestured toward the puddle.

Bee's mouth fell open.

She laughed harder, pressing a hand to the stitch in her side.

Bee simply stared at her as if she were some kind of lunatic and pressed the compress back against her head.

Ouch!

"Calm down, honey. The ambulance is almost here."

"What!"

The volume of sirens she hadn't noticed in the background increased as they came closer.

"You called an ambulance?" Panic gripped her throat, threatening to cut off her airway. "Cancel it."

"What?"

"I said cancel it. I'm not going to the hospital, and I certainly am not going by ambulance." She tried to stand, but a wave of dizziness sent her right back to the floor.

"Mmm . . . hmm."

"Oh, shut up."

"Just sit still. Let them check you out, and then you can decide what to do."

"Fine." She shrugged, more annoyed with the situation than with Bee. If he would just give her a minute, she'd be able to get up. Probably. "Whatever."

"Here. Hold this." Bee guided her hand to the cloth on the back of her head, then sat on the floor in front of her and crossed his legs, his expression serious. "Now, what happened?"

Thinking hurt her brain. Still, she tried to recall what she'd been doing before she ended up sprawled on the floor. After a moment, the memory of what had happened rushed back full force. "Oh. Oh no."

"What?"

"There was someone upstairs when I got here. Whoever it was barreled down the stairs and plowed me over, then I smacked my head on the floor."

Bee's eyes widened, and he fished his cell phone from his pocket.

Cass narrowed her eyes—carefully. "Who do you think you're calling?"

Ignoring her, he dialed, pressed the phone to his ear, and held his finger up in a *one minute* gesture. "Tank?"

"Ah jeez." She started to roll her eyes, caught herself mid-roll, and halted the gesture, but not before another bout of dizziness hit, bringing with it a wave of nausea. She settled, instead, for sticking her tongue out at him.

The rat turned his back on her.

Commotion at the doorway pulled her attention from the tattletale on the phone.

"Are you okay, Cass?" Rick's knees cracked as he squatted down in front of her and looked into her eyes. Not only did Rick own the deli, he was also a volunteer EMT. Many of the business owners on Bay Island offered their services to the all-volunteer Bay Island Fire Department and Ambulance Company.

"I'm fine. I just needed a minute to sit."

Rick stood and leaned over her, then lifted the cloth from her head and set it aside. "That's quite a knock on the head. You're going to need a few stitches."

Great. "Can you just do them here?"

He laughed, so she figured that meant *no*.

"Well, do I have to go in the ambulance? Can't I just drive myself?"

"Sure, honey. Right after you stand up and walk in a straight line. Come on." He held out a hand.

She accepted his hand and stood, then swayed and grabbed the stair railing.

"Uh-huh." Rick shook his head and smiled. "Still want to drive?"

"Maybe Bee could drive me," she said softly, though she already knew she'd lost the argument. No way was he letting her go.

Tank strode through the emergency room doors and straight to Cass's cubicle. He pulled the curtain closed behind him, tossed a newspaper onto the counter, and focused his full attention on her. "You okay?"

"Yes." She nodded, then hesitated. Nope, no dizziness. The nausea had passed, too. Since they'd numbed her head to stitch it up, even that injury didn't hurt. But she had a whopping headache. She turned and let her legs dangle over the stretcher. She'd try to get up in a minute.

Tank pulled her into a tight embrace and dropped a kiss on the top of her head. Then he stepped back and studied her. "Tell me what happened."

She shrugged. "There's not much to tell. I'm sure it's too late to catch anyone now."

"I've already spoken to Bee, and he told me what happened. We already have people searching the beach, but so far we haven't found anything. There was no sign of a break-in, and Bee swears he locked up before he left earlier. But I'd like to hear from you about what happened."

She ran through the events of the night, leaving out the early morning visit from her phantom. "How could there be no sign of a break-in? How did he get in?"

"We don't know. Is Bee usually good about locking up? Maybe he forgot to lock the back?"

Cass was already shaking her head. "Bee is completely OCD about locking up his own shop and mine, or I never would have given him a key. There's no way he forgot."

"Which door did you enter through tonight?"

"The front."

"Did you unlock the back at any point?"

"No."

"Are you sure?"

Was she? "Yes. Positive. I had no reason to open it."

"But the attacker fled out the back door?"

"Yes." She frowned. "At least, I think so." She tried to remember which direction he was headed. "He plowed me over, and it seemed like he was headed toward the back of the shop, but I can't be sure."

"All right. The doctor said you can go home. Do you feel up to going back to the shop and checking to see if anything is missing?"

The pounding at her temples begged her to go home. "Will it matter if I do it tomorrow?"

"No. Bee's going to drive you home and stay with you for the rest of the night . . . well, morning, I guess. When you're ready to go into the shop, give me a call, and I'll pick you up and go in with you. Bee looked around, but he didn't notice anything missing. You would know better if anything was taken." Tank helped her to her feet and stood with her for a moment to make sure she was steady.

"Do you think this has anything to do with the bones I found on the beach?"

He ran a hand over his crew cut. "I honestly don't know. I don't think that press conference fiasco you pulled yesterday afternoon helped matters, but I can't say it had anything to do with the break-in."

"Did you figure out if the second set of bones belongs to Artie Becker's daughter?"

He shook his head.

"That skeleton wasn't old, was it?"

He blew out a breath, glanced over his shoulder, and lowered his voice. "It wasn't a skeleton. It was a woman's body."

Cass gasped. Harry had referred to it as a body as well, but he'd also referred to the first skeleton as a body, so she'd just assumed—

"You have to stay out of this, Cass." Tank grabbed the paper he'd tossed on the counter and handed it to her.

She opened it and stared at the picture of her coming out of the police station on the front page and the headline above it: "Local Psychic Aids Police in Murder Investigation." "Ah jeez."

"Maybe you could close the shop up for a few days and go away with Luke or something."

"You didn't involve Luke in this, did you?" That was the last thing she needed. She was having enough trouble building any sort of relationship with him without him thinking he had to play babysitter. She folded the paper and tossed it in the trash can.

"No. At least not yet."

"What do you mean, 'not yet'? How can you even be sure

the woman was murdered?" All right, so that was probably a stupid question, considering she'd been found buried on the beach, but still . . .

He sighed. "This is between us, and *nobody* else. I mean it, Cass. Nobody."

She nodded.

"The first skeleton was tangled in a large net. There are several ways, both sinister and not, that could have happened. But the woman was found with a plastic bag covering her head and red string tied around her neck to hold it in place. That couldn't have happened accidentally."

Cass struggled to swallow the lump blocking her throat, but she still only managed a hoarse croak. "Artie Becker's daughter?"

"We haven't identified her yet." He studied her for a moment, seeming to weigh how much he wanted to say. "She does fit the description, though, so it's a possibility. Now, will you please make yourself scarce and stay out of this?"

"I'll do my best, but I can't close the shop, Tank."

He smoothed the goatee he'd been wearing for the past couple of weeks and nodded. "I understand, but I don't want you there alone at night anymore. Fair enough?"

That was an easy enough concession to make, since she was in no hurry to confront another intruder. "Sure. Thanks, Tank."

He pulled the curtain aside and walked with her toward the waiting room.

The instant they pushed through the double doors, Bee hovered over her. "Oh, dear. Are you all right, sweetie? Here, let me help you." He put his arm around her and guided her toward the doors.

Tank winked at her. "Well, I can see you're in good hands, so I'll see you in a few hours." He nodded to Bee, then headed back into the emergency room.

"Where's he going?"

Bee looked after him for a moment. "I don't know. Maybe he wanted to talk to the doctor. Anyway . . ." Bee waved a hand dismissively. "Let's get you home. Do you want to stop for coffee?"

Her stomach flip-flopped, and sour bile burned the back of her throat. "Definitely not. I just want to get home and lie down. Hopefully, I can sleep now."

"I'll be on the couch if you need me."

She stopped and turned to him, being sure to hold his gaze. "Thank you, Bee. You really are a great friend."

He pulled her into his arms. "You're my best friend, Cass. I'd do anything for you."

She rested her cheek against his broad chest, taking comfort from his strength.

18

Cass checked the rearview mirror, hit the turn signal, and pulled into the parking lot at Mystical Musings. Tank was supposed to pick her up, but he'd gotten sidetracked with something, and she'd gotten tired of waiting. He could just meet her there later. Besides, she couldn't wait any longer to stop and see Beast. She'd been worried sick about him. She ruffled his mane, thrilled the vet had released him this morning with a firm admonishment about getting him trained. She'd assured him that she'd scheduled an appointment with Herb Cox.

She was already over an hour late to open the shop. Although she'd only slept a few hours, it had been dream free, and she felt more rested than she had in a while. Except for the pain in her head, but at least that was manageable.

Leaving the car windows open to air out the stench of Beast's vomit, which still lingered despite last night's and this morning's scrubbings, she slammed the door and strode toward the shop with Beast trotting excitedly beside her. "Behave yourself."

He tilted his head in an expression she might have taken for innocence if she didn't know him better.

Several people were already milling around on the front porch. Hopefully they were customers and not reporters.

"Hi. Sorry I'm late." She unlocked the door and held it open for the small group to precede her. "Feel free to have a look around while I open up."

She left them to browse and crossed the shop to open the back door. Thankfully, the beach seemed fairly empty other than a few kids playing and a couple of women chatting. None of the reporters from yesterday were hanging around. Maybe the thick black clouds hanging overhead were driving people off.

After settling Beast with a bone, she turned over the OPEN sign, started a pot of coffee and water for tea, and set out a couple of trays of cookies. She found people didn't mind waiting if she made them comfortable, and that was a big part of the atmosphere she'd worked so hard to create.

She then opened the register, carefully counting out the change to be sure none had been stolen. It hadn't.

With that done, she turned her attention to her customers, walking through the shop, greeting everyone, and offering refreshments. A few of the faces were familiar, but many were not. One woman in particular stood out. She was middle-aged. She seemed nervous, out of place. She was alone, and instead of browsing as most of the others were, she stood to the side, making herself as inconspicuous as possible, arms wrapped tightly across her stomach.

Cass approached her first. "Good morning. I'm Cass. Can I help you with anything special today?"

A tremor shook her hand as she patted her perfectly coifed hair. "I hope so." She offered a tentative smile. "I'm Trish."

"Do you know what you're looking for? Or what you hope to accomplish?"

"Actually, I have no idea what I'm looking for. As for what I'm hoping to accomplish . . ." She cast a quick look around the shop and lowered her voice. "I'm very much hoping to find out if my husband is being unfaithful."

"Do you have reason to believe he is?"

She nodded but didn't expand. This woman didn't need to discover anything; she already knew.

"Come with me. I may have something that will help." Cass led her toward a small seating arrangement. "Would you like a cup of tea?"

She shook her head.

Cass left her sitting on the love seat long enough to pull out a few trays of stones, a suede pouch, and a leather cord, then she returned and sat next to her. Though she was confident her customers would wait, and she didn't want to rush the woman, she didn't like to keep anyone waiting too long. "I'm a little busy right now, but I'd love to do a reading for you if you have time to come back later."

Trish clasped and unclasped her hands. "Would it help?"

"It might help us get to the bottom of what's going on, but for now, I have some stones you can carry that might help you feel better."

"Okay." She nodded. "I'll come back."

"Good." Cass patted her entwined hands and watched

her carefully. "Now, what do you hope to accomplish? Let's just say, for argument's sake, he is cheating on you. How do you want to handle it?"

She needn't have bothered looking for subtle tells; Trish's pain was written all over her face. "I love my husband," she whispered.

"Okay, then. Let's do this . . ." She sorted through the stones, lifting some, turning them over in her hand. Some she returned to the bins. Others, the ones that felt just right to bring this woman comfort, she set atop the suede pouch she'd laid on the table.

When she was satisfied she had the correct combination to help attract love, but also give her the strength to accept the truth and the confidence to move on if need be, she set the rest aside. She held a greenish-blue stone up between her thumb and forefinger. "This is Lapis Lazuli. It does many things, but one of the things it's known for is enhancing love and fidelity within a marriage."

Trish's eyes widened. "Really? Stones can help with that?"

"Sure. There are crystals that aid with all sorts of things: love, healing, strength . . . confidence." Cass had hoped for a reaction to the last one, but she was disappointed. That was the one thing she felt Trish needed more than anything else. Well, she'd do what she could, but faith in herself was something Trish would have to discover on her own.

She held up an amber crystal. "Amber is considered a good luck charm for love and marriage." It also helped bring clarity of thought and wisdom.

Next came a rose quartz, one of Cass's favorite stones. Its beautiful pink color always brought her a sense of peace and calm. "Rose quartz is known as the love stone. It brings all kinds of love, as well as soothing energy. It also lowers stress."

For the first time, Trish offered a tentative smile. "I could definitely use that one."

Cass smiled back, glad to see she might finally be reacting a little. "Okay, this one is a little different." She held up an abalone with gorgeous iridescent whirls of silver, pink, and blue. "It's a seashell, and it's not only known for its soothing and healing qualities, but also for offering guidance in relationships."

Cass slid the handful of stones into the pouch and told Trish to turn around. She tied the top with the leather cord, then handed it to Trish. "Hold this over your heart." When she did as instructed, Cass tied the leather cord around her neck. "There. Hopefully, that will help some, but I'd still love for you to come back in for the reading."

"You bet I will." She threw her arms around Cass's neck in a quick hug. "Thank you so much."

"You're very welcome. I hope everything works out."

She smiled, her fingers wrapped tightly around the bag against her chest. "It will."

Cass's heart soared. Maybe Trish hadn't lacked confidence as much as she'd lacked hope. Good. Maybe now she'd take charge and work things out.

Cass scheduled an appointment for Trish's reading, rang up her purchase, and bid her good-bye. Then she turned to the other customers milling about the shop.

When there was finally a lull, she ran upstairs. A cursory walk of the perimeter didn't show anything out of place. Bee had moved the file cabinets into her office and put her papers in the drawers. She'd have to go through and reorganize it when she had time, but for now at least it was upstairs and they could concentrate on getting the room ready for Saturday. Unfortunately, there was no way to tell if anything was missing.

The tinkle of wind chimes as someone entered the shop cut her search short. She headed down the stairs. Maybe Tank had finally arrived. If not, she'd give him a call and tell him not to bother. Nothing seemed out of place. She had no clue what the intruder had been looking for.

Leighton crouched next to Beast, petting his head. When she spotted Cass, she stood and brushed off her hands. "Oh, hi."

Cass's heart skipped a beat. Had she noticed the smudge Cass had left on the painting? Her tone was too neutral to tell. "Hi."

"I heard about what happened last night, and I wanted to stop in and see how you were feeling."

Relief rushed through her. "Oh, thanks. I feel all right. A couple of stitches and a little sore, but that's about it." Cass grinned. "Where'd you hear about it?"

"The deli, not long after they opened." Leighton's soft chuckle echoed in the shop. "I have no clue how news spreads so fast on this island."

Cass joined her laughter. "Me neither, but it certainly does. Can I get you something? Coffee? Tea?"

"A cup of tea sounds great."

"Sit, I'll get it." Cass gestured toward the back table she used for readings. *Hmm* . . . An idea started to form. If she could talk Leighton into a reading, maybe she could get a better feeling for the woman. Or even better, maybe she could lead the conversation to the painting and get her to open up a little.

"I love your shop. It's so cozy."

"Thank you." A surge of pride shot through her. She dropped tea bags into two foam cups, poured water over them, then set them on the table. "Milk or sugar?"

"No, nothing, thanks."

Cass took her usual seat directly across from Leighton. "So, how's business?"

Leighton's stormy gray eyes showed no emotion, making it difficult for Cass to get a read on her. She shrugged. "It's not bad. I'm hoping it'll pick up over the summer."

"It will. The boardwalk and beach are crowded with tourists all summer long. The rush starts in the spring and lingers into the fall, but summer is when most of us make the bulk of our sales."

"Winters must be tough."

Cass blew on her tea and nodded. "They are."

"This will be my first winter on Bay Island, so I'm hoping to establish myself and maybe sell to some of the galleries on Long Island before it starts getting cold."

Cass searched for an opening to bring up the painting. "Do you often sell to galleries?"

"Occasionally."

Her interest piqued. "Bee designs most of his lines and then sells them to buyers, but sometimes he'll design something specifically for someone. Is that how it works with paintings?"

Leighton squeezed her tea bag out against her spoon, then set it aside and sipped her tea. "My business is about half and half. I paint what I like, and often people buy the paintings. I've gotten to know what will sell, so that helps. But some paintings, like the one I'm doing for Bee, and often portraits, are special order."

It was now or never. Trying to appear casual, Cass asked, "So, the portrait I saw in your window, did someone commission that one?" She lifted her cup to take a sip while she waited for an answer, but her shaking hand probably gave away her nerves.

Leighton picked at the top of the foam cup, breaking off little pieces and coaxing them into a small pile, wiping off those that stuck to her fingers with static. Keeping her gaze averted, she turned the cup to the other side and sipped her tea.

Cass waited. There was obviously some problem she was hesitant to talk about, but years of practice had taught Cass silence was sometimes the best way to get someone to talk. She steadied her hand and took another sip of tea, the heat almost scorching her throat. It took all of her willpower to give Leighton the time she needed and to keep her gaze from shooting to the doors, hoping desperately no one would come in and interrupt.

"That painting was commissioned by the woman's boyfriend."

Yes! Now to figure out if it was Artie Becker's daughter. "Did the woman pose for you, or was it done from a picture?"

"No, she came in and posed for the portrait."

"Do you know her name?"

She ignored the question.

Dang.

"Let *me* ask *you* a question now."

Uh-oh. Cass shrugged. "Sure." How in the world could she explain the smudge? Maybe she could just play dumb.

"Why are you so interested in that painting?" She tilted her head, her expression hard.

Cass took a deep breath and let it out slowly. "All right. I am going to be completely honest with you." *Since I just cannot come up with a good enough lie to explain my interest.* "I don't know if you believe in anything . . . otherworldly, as Bee would call it . . ."

She watched for a reaction, but Leighton gave nothing away.

"But I've been dreaming of a woman lately, a woman who asks me for help, and when I saw the portrait in your window, I was almost certain it was the same woman."

Leighton frowned. "How long have you been having the dreams?"

"A little over a week now."

"So you think the woman I painted really needs help?"

"I don't know what to think." She wasn't quite ready to share her suspicions that the woman from the portrait was the same woman who was found on the beach. "But I'd like to try to find the woman and at least make sure she's okay."

Leighton smiled. "Sure."

"Sure?"

"Yes. I'll help you—if I can. I don't have much information. The woman and her boyfriend came in and asked me to do the painting. I agreed. She posed for a while, then they left. That was it. They were supposed to return the following week to pick it up, but they never showed up."

"How long ago was that?"

"About a month ago."

"Do you remember the woman's name?"

"I don't remember. I think it was Kathy or Kerry or something like that."

She was lying. The certainty plowed through Cass with a vengeance. "Do you remember the boyfriend's name? Or could you look it up?"

"When they didn't show up for the portrait, after I tried to reach them several times, I just tossed the paperwork and painted over the portrait. No sense wasting a perfectly good canvas. I do remember the man's name, though. Vincent DiSilva. He's from Long Island. East Hampton, if I'm not mistaken."

If the calculated look in her eye was any indication, she was not mistaken. Cass chose to ignore the lies. No sense calling her on them when she couldn't prove anything.

Besides, if Cass went about it the right way, she could probably get the information on her own anyway. "Have you ever had a reading before?"

Leighton frowned. "What do you mean?"

"A psychic reading." She offered a smile as she stood and took the crystal ball from the counter behind her. "I'd be happy to do one for you. It'll be fun."

"I don't know."

Cass sat and placed the ball in front of her. She didn't waste time trying to get comfortable; she was anxious to get started before Leighton could say no.

She stared into the depths of the ball. She'd used the same one since she was a teenager working the beach and the boardwalk to save money for college. What could she see about Leighton? What was she hiding? Something about her manner struck Cass as devious, or at least deceptive. She couldn't very well say that.

Leighton fidgeted in her seat. She slid forward and uncrossed her legs. She'd been nervous about something since she'd walked in, but now she seemed even worse.

"You enjoy your work."

A tentative smile formed. "Yes."

Reading someone as closed up as Leighton was difficult under the best of circumstances, but with Leighton purposely keeping her expression and her body language neutral, it was close to impossible. She had to find a way to connect with her. She'd noticed most of Leighton's work consisted of dark, stormy landscapes and beach scenes, which she now knew were not commissioned. They evoked a sense of turmoil.

"You display your emotions in your paintings."

"Mostly."

The stormy painting she'd noticed in Leighton's window came to mind: the violent sea, waves crashing against the stones, sending their spray against the lighthouse, the dark color choices. "When did you paint the lighthouse in the window?"

She stiffened.

Something was there, if Cass could just grab hold of it.

Leighton shifted her gaze away from Cass's. "Last month."

"It's beautiful. And . . . angry." Cass frowned. Something about the darkness made the painting seem almost alive. She could envision the waves breaking one after another, hear the ebb and flow of the sea's roar. Powerful. The deep rumble of thunder rattled the windows.

"I . . . was going through a tough time."

Cass waited, but it seemed Leighton had nothing more to say. What would evoke such strong feelings of anger? Something personal. Something she was determined to keep hidden. Had she been angry enough to kill? It was a long shot, but . . . "You were angry with someone."

Leighton turned her cup around and around on the table. "Yes," she said softly.

Male or female? Cass couldn't tell. If she guessed and got it wrong, she might lose Leighton's trust. Trust. "Someone you trusted."

A tear leaked out and slid down Leighton's cheek. She swiped it away a bit harder than necessary. She nodded, keeping her gaze riveted on the foam cup. "Why is it always the ones we trust who hurt us most?"

"Because we don't expect it from them." A vision of her ex and his mistress tried to surface, but she tamped it down. She didn't have time for that. She had to get more from Leighton. There would be time to wallow in self-pity later. "Because then it's a double whammy. Whatever they did to lose your trust, plus the pain of betrayal."

Leighton's gaze shot to Cass. "Yes. Exactly."

Cass bit back the urge to offer comfort or ask questions. She simply waited, giving Leighton the space to figure out how to share her feelings. An old trick, but quite effective.

"I never expected it from him," she whispered softly, almost to herself.

"Expected what?"

"I never expected him to cheat on—"

The chimes over the door interrupted, cutting the connection and announcing Bee and Stephanie's arrival.

Leighton jumped up. "You know what? I have to run,

anyway. It was good to see you, Cass. This does seem fun; we'll have to try it again sometime."

"Wait." Dang. She'd been onto something. She was sure of it. She grabbed a business card and handed it to Leighton. "I have a group reading on Saturday night. It's the first one I'm doing in the upstairs room. I'd love to have you if you'd like to attend."

Leighton glanced at the card and shoved it into her skirt pocket. "Sure. I'll see if I can make it."

In other words, *no*.

"You'll enjoy it, and you'll get to meet a lot of people. Many of the business owners come."

"I'll be there," Bee interjected, smiling warmly. "We have a good time."

Cass shot him a *thank-you* look. He must have realized Cass wanted Leighton there for some reason, because Bee hated the group readings.

While Bee introduced Leighton to Stephanie and the three talked for a moment, Cass studied Leighton, trying her hardest to figure out what she could be hiding. A transparent woman's image shimmered into view directly in front of Leighton, allowing Cass a hazy, distorted vision of the other woman. It grew brighter and brighter. Cass shielded her eyes, still trying to understand what she was seeing. Then the vision vanished, leaving a dark shadow in its place. A premonition of death? Or simply the darkness that's often left after a bright flash of light?

Bee saw Leighton out, shut the door behind her, and turned on Cass. "Okay, what gives? You're pale as a ghost. Are you feeling all right?"

"I feel fine; thanks, Bee. But I need help." She caught her

bottom lip between her teeth and looked hopefully back and forth between her two best friends. Her gaze ultimately landed on Bee, since he would need convincing. She knew without asking that Stephanie would be all over the idea that had begun to take shape.

"No." Bee held up a hand. "Whatever it is, I want no part of it."

"Oh, come on, Bee. You can't let me do this alone. It might be dangerous, and I need a big, strong man to help me."

Bee tossed his silk scarf over his shoulder and fluttered his lashes. "Then call Tank."

Stephanie laughed. "Nice try, Bee. But you know as well as I do you're going to give in. May as well do it without the theatrics this time. Cass looks tired."

He studied her for a moment, then threw his hands in the air and stalked toward the table. "Fine. I'll help with whatever it is, but I'm not doing anything without coffee." He flopped into one of the large, velvet-covered chairs, crossed his arms over his chest, and sulked. "Tony's coffee. And whichever one of you is going out"—he waved a finger back and forth between the two of them—"you'd better get donuts."

19

Cass hefted the large canvas bag higher onto her shoulder as she trudged down the beach toward Mystical Musings. Very little moonlight spilled through the storm clouds still threatening to unleash their fury. Thunder rumbled softly in the distance, lightning rippled among the clouds, and the pungent scent of ozone warned her she'd better hurry.

"I still don't understand why we have to do this at all, never mind at Leighton's shop in the middle of the night," Bee grumbled, plodding along next to her, head down, feet dragging.

"She already explained it, Bee." Stephanie patted his arm sympathetically. "Don't worry. Everything will be fine."

"I have to get as close to the spot where the woman died as I can. Souls are most receptive to contact at the point of departure." That might be true, but even if it wasn't, she still had to get into that shop.

"Then why not do it on the beach where her body was found?"

Cass thought it through again. The somber feeling she'd had in Leighton's shop and when she'd tried to do Leighton's reading bothered her. Even in the dunes where the bodies were discovered, she hadn't experienced the same sense of dread and fear she had around Leighton. "I have the definite impression Leighton is keeping secrets."

Bee glared at her. "People have secrets, Cass. Not all of them are sinister."

The reprimand stung, but she shook it off. "Look . . ." She stopped and faced them. "Tank told me something I wasn't supposed to tell anyone, but it's bothering me."

Bee perked up considerably at the prospect of good dirt

She looked directly into Bee's eyes. "You cannot repeat this."

"Of course, I won't repeat it."

"Promise?"

He held up a hand. "Promise."

Since they were standing on a wet, chilly beach with her at close to three o'clock in the morning, she at least owed them an explanation for why they were there. Stephanie probably wouldn't say anything, though there was always a chance she'd slip and mention it to Tank. And she was reasonably sure Bee wouldn't say anything, as long as he wasn't forced to defend her.

Thunder boomed, and she glanced up at the gathering clouds.

She didn't have much time. "The second woman was found with a bag over her head. It was tied down around her neck with a red string. If she died on the beach, it had to have been premeditated, and the killer had to have brought those things with him. Unless, of course, he'd been lucky enough to happen across them on the beach. So it seems more likely that she was killed somewhere else and buried on the beach after the fact."

The fine mist leftover from the afternoon storms dampened her skin. At least that's what she told herself. It could also have something to do with the cold sweat that had sprung out at the thought of breaking into Leighton's shop. "There is a rack in the back of the art gallery with all different colors of thick twine. I don't recall seeing red, but I wasn't really paying that much attention either."

Stephanie chewed on her thumbnail, not seeming quite as comfortable as she had before Cass mentioned Tank.

"Is that why you need to get into the shop?" Bee asked. "To see if there's red twine? Heck, I'll stop by and visit her tomorrow and ask to use the restroom." He turned and started back toward Cass's house.

"Not so fast, buddy. I still have to do the séance, remember? I don't know any other way to try and contact the woman. She appears whenever she feels like it, but I don't know how to summon her."

"Well, here's a novel idea at three in the morning: why don't you go home and go to sleep and see if she shows up? That's when she usually makes contact."

Cass was already shaking her head. "I need to be in control of the interaction for once. I have to see if I can get her to answer my questions."

Stephanie looked around the deserted beach. "You could always try the Ouija board."

"No," Cass and Bee cried together.

"Oh, fine. It was just a suggestion."

Bee raked his hands through his hair, pushing the damp, bleached blond strands off his face.

Thunder rolled down the beach, closer than it had been before.

"Just out of curiosity . . ." Stephanie started. "Why not call the police and let them investigate?"

Cass searched for patience. Stephanie meant well, but she always wanted to call the police. "And tell them what? That Leighton has string in the art gallery? Or that a shadow fell on her when she was leaving the shop?"

Although Chief Rawlins might be receptive if Cass reached out, she was still hesitant. She'd prefer to have something a little more concrete to approach her with.

"You didn't mention the shadow before." Bee sulked.

"No. That changes things." Stephanie moved closer to Cass.

"Yeah, well . . . Come on. We have to get going." Cass started to cut across the dunes, angling toward the art gallery with Stephanie at her side.

"Oh, fine. Let's just get this over with. And someone's buying me breakfast when we're done. At the diner." Bee stayed glued to her other side.

Stephanie grabbed her arm. "You know, if Bee can get into the shop tomorrow to check for the twine, maybe we don't need to break in after all."

Cass frowned. She was already having enough trouble with Bee; the last thing she needed was Stephanie balking, too. "What do you mean? I just explained—"

"Hang on. If anyone was killed in the gallery and dragged out onto the beach, maybe staying just outside the shop will be close enough."

Bee bit his lip but remained silent, though hope filled his eyes.

Cass looked up at the back of the gallery. They were only a few feet from the wooden walkway that would lead them through the remainder of the dunes and onto the gallery's back deck. Would it be close enough? "All right. I'll try it from the outside."

Bee's breath whooshed out.

She shot him a dirty look, but she couldn't deny the bit of relief she felt. Breaking in had never sat well with her, but she couldn't let another woman die if she could avoid it. "We'll have to get as close to the shop as we can, though. I know you guys don't really understand why I have to do this, but the shadow I saw over Leighton scared me. What if she's the next victim of a serial killer and she dies because I didn't try to figure out what his last victim was trying to tell me?"

She shook her head and looked down at the wet sand, then wiped the tears tracking down her face. "I can't live with that guilt again." The guilt of losing her patient after seeing a shadow pass over him, after ignoring her gut instincts to check on him, after missing the desperation that must have been in his voice when she'd last spoken to him, still weighed heavier than she could bear. "If you guys don't want to come, I'll understand, but I have to do this. Maybe you could just keep watch for me."

Bee took the bag from her shoulder. "Come on. We'll try it up there and if it doesn't work we'll get you into the shop."

He gestured toward a few dunes that butted up against the gallery and the boardwalk, creating a quiet little corner that should be completely private even if someone did happen to be walking along the beach that early.

She smiled through the tears. "Thanks, Bee. You're the best."

"Yeah, well don't forget it, because when we go to Southampton on Monday, I want to go to the beach."

Cass grinned. That would be an easy enough request to grant, since she'd already planned on going anyway. "Sure thing."

"Hey, what about me?" Stephanie pouted.

"You're the best, too." She squeezed Stephanie's hand and they started toward the gallery.

Bee skirted one of the small dunes and headed into the corner.

Cass looked around for a flat spot to set up. She hadn't planned on doing the séance outside, and the wind from the approaching storm was already starting to kick up. "I don't know if the candles will stay lit out here."

"Would this work?" Bee stood around the side of the building in a small dip created by the runoff from Leighton's gutters. "The wind is mostly blocked on this side."

Cass moved into the sort-of-protected space between the side of the building and the boardwalk. The wind tearing off the bay was somewhat diminished in the little corner. "We'll give it a try."

"Yeah, just do me a favor, and don't burn the building down, because I am not hanging around to explain that one to Tank." Bee lifted a brow and stared at her.

Cass laughed softly. "I'll do my best, Bee."

She'd brought towels to clean up any mess they made on Leighton's floor, and she pulled them out of her bag and handed one to Bee and one to Stephanie. "Sit on those, so you don't get soaked."

Cass drew a circle in the wet sand and pointed out a spot for each of them to sit. She pulled out several candles from her bag, dug them into the sand and, with Bee and Stephanie shielding them from the bit of wind funneling around the corner, managed to get them lit. She preferred to sit directly on the ground, so she slid off her shoes, sat, and dug her toes into the sand.

Since she'd never actually tried to contact a spirit before, she just sat there and tried to focus on the woman. A few minutes passed, and nothing happened.

Bee readjusted his position, grunting with the effort, then whispered, "I don't think you're doing it right."

"Shh." Stephanie slapped his arm. "Let her concentrate so we can get out of here."

While she appreciated Stephanie's help, Bee was obviously right, but Cass wasn't about to admit that, so she ignored him. She took her crystal ball out of the bag and set it in the center of the circle in front of her. The flames from the candles flickered and danced within the ball. A flash of lightning reflected off its surface.

She had managed to conjure a spirit once before—maybe—but she hadn't been trying. It had just sort of happened on its own, so she had no clue how she'd done it—if she even had.

The flames seemed to recede deeper into the ball. Even though she'd never actually seen a vision in the crystal ball, the distorted reflections off its surface helped her to focus.

The temperature plummeted suddenly, raising goose bumps and making her shiver. "Do you guys feel that?"

"Feel what?" Stephanie looked around.

"The chill?"

Stephanie and Bee both shook their heads, and Bee shifted onto his knees on the towel. Probably preparing to make a quick getaway.

"Okay." She glanced toward the gallery. Maybe she'd made a mistake trying to contact the woman from outside. She could always send Bee and Stephanie home and break in herself. She tried to shake off her uncertainty. No use second-guessing herself. She returned her attention to the depths of the crystal.

Fear touched her, but it was probably her own. Or maybe Bee's.

A shadow appeared in her peripheral vision, but she resisted the urge to turn her head and look at it. Instead, she kept her head perfectly still and tracked the shadow from the corner of her eye.

The figure crept stealthily through the dunes, keeping as low as possible in the dips between them. Odd; the woman in her visions had never made any attempt to sneak up on her before. When the figure rounded the walkway, Cass stared at Bee and Stephanie, put her finger to her lips, then gestured toward the figure. She moved quickly and snuffed out the candles before it emerged again.

Bee and Stephanie both nodded their understanding and remained silently rooted in place—except for Bee's hyperventilating, but nothing could be done about that.

The shadow leaped over the railing, caught its foot, faceplanted onto the walkway, and cursed.

Bee's breathing slowed. Even in his near-hysterical state, he could probably tell this was no ghost, nor anything else supernatural.

The figure mumbled as it scuttled up the walkway toward the back of the shop. Then he detoured, heading across the back deck.

Cass stayed perfectly still and willed herself invisible as he snuck straight toward them. She took shallow breaths through her mouth. When he reached the back corner of the deck, where the three of them would be perfectly visible even in the dark if not for the heavy cloud cover, he stopped and bent over. He came up with a small flowerpot and hefted the weight in his hand. Giving up any pretense of stealth, he took three long strides toward the back of the shop and threw the flowerpot. It shattered the window in the back door.

Cass covered her mouth and stifled a gasp.

After picking out some of the larger glass remnants, the figure reached through and unlocked the door, then disappeared into the dark interior of the art gallery.

"Can you believe he just broke in?" Bee whispered against her ear. His indignation was laughable considering they had come to the beach with the same intention.

Stephanie pulled out her cell phone, its lighted screen blaring like a beacon in the dark night.

"Cover that thing up. What are you doing?" Cass hissed.

She pressed the screen against her leg. "The guy just broke in. I'm calling the police."

"Are you crazy? What are you going to tell them we're doing here? Just hanging out on the beach in the dark?"

"In the rain," Bee added in a hushed whisper. "Let's just get out of here."

"Is that what you'd want someone to do if they witnessed a break-in at Dreamweaver?"

Bee stayed quiet a moment, then sighed.

Stephanie took it as a sign of agreement and dialed what Cass assumed was Tank's number. She moved toward the front of the gallery, ducking beneath the boardwalk as best she could to stay out of view.

Cass turned and stared at the shop.

Bee stuffed everything back into Cass's bag and handed it to her. "Do you think it's the same guy who broke into your shop?"

She'd thought of that. "Maybe he's targeting shops along the boardwalk, and I just happened to walk in at the wrong time."

"I guess." Bee shrugged.

The back door creaked as it opened.

"Get down." Bee grabbed her shoulder and pulled her down with him.

The figure poked his head out the door, looked around, then closed the door behind him and sauntered down the walkway.

They couldn't let him leave. The police hadn't arrived yet. She couldn't decide what to do. If she confronted him, they might be able to find out what was going on. If they let him get away, they'd never know.

Bee took the decision out of her hands when he sprang up and took off—faster than Cass would have thought possible—and jumped onto the walkway, his platform shoes slamming against the wood decking with the volume of small explosions in the silence.

The figure spun around and Bee plowed his shoulder into the guy's gut. The two of them tumbled over the railing and landed in the sand with a grunt.

$\left\{ 20 \right\}$

Cass ran around the end of the walkway and found Bee and the intruder tangled together, rolling around the sand.

The guy swung his elbow back and clipped Bee's jaw.

Bee jerked back but didn't loosen his hold.

Stephanie stopped beside Cass, huffing and puffing. "What is going on?"

"The burglar tried to leave, so Bee stopped him."

Bee threaded his arm beneath the guy's neck and held him in a choke hold, forcing his head into the sand, finally gaining the upper hand.

"Get off me, you big oaf." A black ski mask muffled the words, but they were clear enough to understand.

Bee snorted and tightened his hold.

Sirens blared in the distance. *Finally.*

Of course, that meant she'd only have a couple of minutes to talk to him before the police arrived. She ran over, ripped the mask off his head, and wasn't the least bit surprised to find herself face-to-face with "John."

He stared at her for a moment, mouth agape.

Cass recovered her senses first. "What were you doing in the art gallery?"

"Looking for something."

"The necklace?"

The guy shrugged as best he could with more than two hundred pounds of Bee wrapped around his neck.

"What's so important about the necklace?"

He stared at her, his expression a hard mask of defiance, his lips pressed together in a tight line.

The sirens screamed louder.

All right. Think. Think. Think.

"The woman who disappeared was wearing that necklace."

His eyes widened, but he still didn't answer.

"Did you know her?"

Nothing.

"Did you have anything to do with her disappearance?"

He scoffed but still didn't answer.

"Look, if you tell me what's going on, I might be able to help you." Okay, that might be a total lie, but it could also be true, depending on what he told her. The guy was pretty young, probably not more than his midtwenties, but he had a hard edge about him. But still, a killer? She couldn't be sure.

A car door slammed.

Urgency beat at her. "This is your last chance."

"Fine." His voice was no more than a hoarse whisper, probably something to do with Bee's hold on his neck. "You want to help? Find out why Artie Becker was in the gallery having a heated exchange with Leighton Mills."

"What? When?"

He finally stopped resisting Bee's grip and laid his cheek against the wet sand, obviously accepting his fate.

"What's going on here?" The officer's voice startled Cass, not because she hadn't expected it, but because it wasn't Tank.

"Uh . . ." She stared at him for a moment then glanced at Stephanie.

The young cop laughed. "Oh, don't worry. He's on his way."

Cass cringed.

"Are you two going to stand there chatting all night, or is someone gonna get this old goof off me?" The guy tried to squirm out from beneath Bee.

The officer's partner was already trying to untangle them, but he wasn't having much luck hauling Bee off him.

Bee only tightened his hold. "Old? Who are you calling old?"

The young cop ran to help.

Bee finally released the kid's neck. "Ha. Old. I took you down, didn't I?"

The kid snorted and tried to brush himself off as the officers helped him to his feet.

Bee propped a hand on his cocked hip and fanned himself with the end of his scarf.

One of the officers led the kid a short distance away, and the other moved away with Stephanie. Presumably, she'd tell him what happened.

Cass put a hand on Bee's shoulder. "You did great, Bee. Thank you."

He smiled. "Anytime." His expression sobered. "What do you think he meant about Artie Becker?"

She frowned. "I don't know. He was coming out of the gallery one day and standing across the street from it another day, so something's up there."

Bee pursed his lips. "Remember I said there was a skinny guy asking around about Kelly Becker?"

"Yeah."

Tank's arrival distracted her. He pulled Stephanie into his arms and glared over her head at Cass. *Oh, boy.*

"Do you think he's the guy that was asking the questions? I assumed it was the guy I spoke to in the deli."

"Uh, what?" She returned her focus to Bee.

He huffed out an impatient breath, or maybe he was just still winded from his tussle. Either way, he seemed annoyed she wasn't paying attention, so she tried harder.

"A skinny guy with glasses and shaggy hair was asking around about Kelly Becker. Remember I told you that was the rumor going around?"

"Oh, yeah. I assumed it was the guy who confronted me in the deli. I figured he was a reporter or something when I saw him at the press conference." Could be he was just posing as a reporter.

"So did I, but maybe he wasn't." He looked after "John" as the young officer put his hands on top of his head and guided him into the back seat of the cruiser.

Although he didn't look like the guy from the deli, the skinny, shaggy hair, and glasses description did match.

Tank honed in on her and started down the beach.

She sighed, resigned to the coming confrontation.

"What part of 'stay out of this' did you not understand?"

So much for the niceties. "I wasn't trying to be involved. It just sort of . . . happened."

"And what were you doing on the beach in the middle of the night? Taking a stroll with Curly and Moe?" He gestured at Bee and Stephanie, crowded together far enough away to avoid any spillover of Tank's temper tantrum.

Cowards.

He rubbed a hand over his head, a sure sign he was agitated. "Look, Cass. A woman was murdered. You've already been targeted. Twice. If I can't trust you to stay out of this, I'm going to have to resort to extreme measures."

She narrowed her eyes at him. "You wouldn't dare."

He held her stare. "Try me."

Dang. He had her. No way would she let him call Luke and ask him to babysit her, and he knew it. "Fine. I'll try to stay out of it."

"You'd better do more than try." He turned and walked away, but she didn't miss the twinkle in his eyes. He had her, and he knew it. *Smart aleck.*

Stephanie and Bee waited for him to cross the beach before approaching her.

She pinned them with her hardest stare. "Chickens."

"Yup," Bee agreed with a grin.

Stephanie held up her hands. "Don't look at me. I have to live with him."

"So, what do you want to do? Go to the diner?" Bee asked.

Gray light was already seeping onto the horizon. Another

cloudy day. And a wasted night, since she didn't get to accomplish what she'd set out to do, thanks to "John's" midnight break-in. "I have to take Beast to the trainer this morning. Either of you want to come?"

"No thanks." Stephanie smiled and fluttered her lashes.

"I'd rather stay here and contact ghosts." Bee smirked.

"Maybe I'll just reschedule it."

"No!" Stephanie and Bee yelled in unison.

Cass pouted all the way back to the house. She thought about canceling the training class and climbing into bed and pulling the covers over her head, but they were right. Beast really needed to get trained before he got hurt.

At least she didn't have to open the shop after. Since weekends were her busiest times, she always took Wednesdays off. She could go home and relax after the class.

Or she could try to figure out what Artie Becker had been arguing with Leighton about.

"You have to be good here, Beast." Cass clipped Beast's leash to his collar and looked him straight in the eye. "Please."

She watched the other dog owners climbing out of their cars, their dogs, mostly puppies, trotting eagerly beside them. She recognized a golden retriever puppy, its paws too big for its furry, golden body, and what she thought was a German shepherd.

The German shepherd barked at a little gray ball of fluff, who in turn ran beneath his owner's legs. The young woman tripped over him, then scooped him up in her arms and shot the German shepherd's owner a dirty look.

How in the world did I let myself get talked into this?

Cass cracked open the car door, just enough to get out without letting Beast escape, and slid tentatively from the driver's seat. She wound Beast's leash around her hand a couple of times, so she wouldn't lose him if he took off, and looked around for Herb Cox, hesitant to leave the relative safety of her position. Wedged between the door and the seat as she was, Beast wasn't going anywhere unless he knocked her over. "Don't even think about it."

He wiggled frantically in the driver's seat, tongue hanging out, eager to be somewhere new. He practically vibrated with energy as he bounced back and forth from one side to the other in the cramped space.

She must be crazy.

The others crunched along the gravel driveway, passed Herb's small ranch, climbed two small steps to a lawn that had seen better days, and continued to trudge toward a small corral surrounded by a weathered, split-rail fence at the back of the property. It seemed about ten dogs were enrolled in the class. Eleven, if her guess was correct, and the woman with the big straw hat had a tiny dog in her shoulder bag.

She'd wanted a private session, just her and Beast, but Doc had assured her it was better for Beast to be enrolled in a class so he could be properly socialized with other dogs.

Herb appeared from behind the house and strode toward the corral with two more dogs on his heels.

Cass inched the car door open.

Beast's whole back end wagged. He crouched.

"Stay," Cass commanded, her voice stern.

He crouched lower, ready to spring.

"I'm going to open the door now, Beast. You stay calm. Understand?"

He glanced back and forth between her and the excitement out back.

She opened the door all the way.

Excitement won out. Beast tore from the car like a maniac, running full tilt for the enclosure, tightening the leash around Cass's hand.

She tried to dig her feet in and hold him back, but the gravel only slid out from under her feet, leaving her no choice but to try to keep up while trying to loosen the leash enough to free her hand. It was no use. She settled for holding on with both hands and running after him while Beast bounded toward the corral.

All of the others were now staring at her, some shaking their heads, others laughing, and a few kind souls offering sympathetic looks.

When she hit the steps, her feet couldn't move fast enough to keep up, and she tripped, belly flopping onto the scratchy, brown grass.

Beast finally stopped and looked behind him.

She took advantage of the moment's respite and unwound the leash, then rubbed the deep red indentations it had left in her hand and wrist.

Herb emerged from the enclosure, closed the gate behind him, and approached Cass. "You okay?" Humor tinged his voice, but to his credit, he didn't laugh.

"Yeah." She sat up, more than ready to accept Beast's first training class was a complete and total failure and go home to a nice hot bath. "Sorry."

"Don't worry about it. That's what you're here for." He

helped her to her feet, then grabbed Beast's leash and petted his head before finally giving in to the chuckle. "Believe me, you're not the first person to face-plant coming up those steps behind an overeager dog. I keep telling myself I need to make a ramp or something, but I never remember."

She gave him a sheepish smile. "Thanks."

He handed her Beast's leash. "Come on. Let's get started."

She took the leash and patted Beast's head. It wasn't his fault; he just got excited.

"Ms. Donovan?"

She glanced over her shoulder.

The petite reporter from the beach stood staring at her.

A man stood behind her aiming a small video camera and a huge grin right at Cass.

"I tried to catch you at home, but I arrived just as you were leaving." She offered her hand. "I'm Stevie Rhymes."

Cass eyed the cameraman while she switched Beast's leash to her left hand—with half a mind to drop the leash and let Beast knock him over so she could grab the camera and run. Instead, she shook the woman's hand.

"Would you answer a few questions?"

"Um . . . I'm kind of busy."

"It'll only take a few minutes."

Herb had already returned to the corral and was trying to gain some semblance of control. Some of the dogs had jumped up and rested their front paws on the fence, peeking between the slats to watch the chaos; others chased one another in circles; and one rolled over and over in the dirt, all while their owners tried to rein them in.

"I'm sorry. This isn't a good time." *Not to mention Tank would have my head.*

"Cass," Herb yelled over the howling and barking. "I have to start."

"Coming, sorry."

Even some of the people who had originally seemed sympathetic were shifting back and forth with growing impatience.

"I have to go. You shouldn't have followed me here."

"Can I come into the shop tomorrow?"

"Um . . . sure, whatever." She waved them off and jogged toward the corral with Beast. If the woman showed up, she'd find a way to blow her off. Right now she had more pressing things to worry about. She had to get Beast trained, she had to get Mystical Musings ready for Saturday night's reading, and she still had to go back to the beach and collect stones, glass, sand, and sticks for her centerpieces. Plus, she had to pick up her new dress from Bee for her date with Luke on Sunday. She smiled at the reminder as she lifted her arm to open the gate. A twinge in her lower back stopped her. *Ouch.*

The top priority was to finish Beast's training class, then pop a couple of ibuprofen, and take a long, hot bath. She'd do what Tank had asked and leave the investigating to the police. At least for now.

21

Cass spread a deep blue tablecloth over a round table in the far corner of her new upstairs room in Mystical Musings, then smoothed the wrinkles and placed one of her homemade mason jar centerpieces on top. She'd made extras with things she'd collected from the beach and displayed them on a table along the sidewall. Hopefully some would sell after the reading.

"What do you think, Beast?" She surveyed the end results. Tables were scattered sporadically throughout the room, with plenty of space for her to walk between them and interact with the crowd. The beach-themed centerpieces atop the deep blue tablecloths added warmth to the large, open, otherwise-empty area. The lights she'd strung above would allow her to turn off the overheads and set the mood.

A couple of paintings would help make the room feel cozier.

Maybe she'd look for an artist to talk to about commissioning a beach and a lighthouse scene, not one of the dark, foreboding ones Leighton displayed in her window, but something light and breezy, something that brought the viewer a sense of peace, something that would complement Cass's new stress-free attitude.

Since she'd decided to leave the investigating to the police and denied Stevie Rhymes's repeated requests for interviews, the rest of her week had been pleasantly uneventful, and she had every intention of keeping it that way. The phone rang, and she lifted it from one of the tables, still distracted by her to-do list. She was pretty sure she had everything ready, and it was time to open the shop for the day. "Mystical Musings, how may I help you?"

"Hey there, beautiful."

Warmth flooded her at Luke's slow, easy drawl. "Hey yourself."

She glanced at the rustic clock made from weathered boards that hung over the door. "Are you here already? The first ferry didn't even come in yet."

"Uh, not exactly. About that . . ."

Disappointment surged.

"Something came up this morning . . ."

It seemed something always came up lately.

"I'm going to try to get there later, but I can't promise. I'm really sorry, Cass."

His words dampened the sense of peace she'd worked so hard for. "Don't worry about it. I'm sure you couldn't help it."

"Actually, a great opportunity presented itself, and I can't pass it up, so I need to be here today to go over the details with my boss. If I can get out later, I will. Promise."

"Sure, I understand." And she did, but that didn't mean she had to like it. "I'm going to be crazy busy today setting up for tonight's reading, anyway. Speaking of which, I'd better get going. I spent all morning setting up the room for the reading, and I have to get the shop open."

"Hopefully I'll see you tonight. I want to be there for your first reading in the new room."

"That would be nice." They said their good-byes, and Cass placed the phone in the charger.

She knew he really did want to be there, and it wasn't always his fault they couldn't get together. During the winter, it was easier to close the shop, since she wasn't that busy, but during the spring and fall months, she could only afford to take Wednesdays off. Sometimes during the summer, she didn't even take that. And then there was Beast. She couldn't leave him alone all day to go to the mainland. But Luke's job as a detective was also important, and she couldn't always expect him to drop everything and run to Bay Island.

She sighed. As much as she liked Luke and wanted a chance to see where their relationship was going, it might be time to cut her losses and move on. She hadn't really been ready for a relationship anyway. She still had trust issues to work out. Maybe it was time to take a break. She'd see how the weekend played out, then talk to him about it.

"Looks like it might be just you and me for a while longer, Beast." The sadness that thought brought came as a bit of a surprise. Maybe she was finally moving past the betrayal her ex-husband's affair with her ex–best friend had brought.

She unlocked the doors, turned the signs over, and counted out the register, then pulled out her to-do list. She checked off *make centerpieces* and *set up tables*.

She still had to bring up the coffeemakers, but she couldn't do that until she closed the shop. The long table was already set up for the caterer, so there was nothing more she could do there until Isabella Trapani showed up with the trays of food.

Bee was supposed to come by and set up the sound system when he got up, so they'd have soft background music after the actual reading.

The wind chimes tinkled, and she looked up from her list. Her smile died when her gaze fell on Artie Becker strolling into the shop. He stopped and turned the sign to CLOSED before he strode toward her, his face red, one thick vein throbbing at the side of his temple.

Good thing I decided on a more stress-free lifestyle.

Beast growled.

"Shut that thing up. I'm in no mood for it."

Cass bristled. Who did he think he was? She had half a mind to let Beast bite his nasty . . . She reined in her temper. "It's okay, Beast."

She tried for a smile, but she couldn't manage to conjure one, so she just settled for not going off on him. "What can I do for you, Mr. Becker?"

Beast moved beside her and sat, but thankfully refrained from growling again and escalating the situation.

She put a hand on his head, her need to comfort him as strong as the need for her own comfort.

"I need answers."

"About?"

"Is that Kelly they found on the beach?"

"You'd need to ask the police that, Mr. Becker."

"I did ask. They won't give me any answers. Now I'm

asking you." He splayed his hands on the driftwood countertop and leaned forward. "And I want answers."

Cass took a step back.

Beast issued another low warning growl.

It did nothing to faze Artie. He leaned farther over the counter. "Now."

"Look, Mr. Becker, I'm not sure what I can tell you. The police haven't told me who the bod—uh, woman—they found on the beach is . . ."

"So, it was a woman? That's what I've heard, but the police wouldn't confirm it."

Oh, dang. "I meant person. I . . . um . . . I just didn't want to say body, you know . . . just in case." All right, kind of lame but the best she could do under current circumstances.

His eyebrows drew together, but he didn't comment further on her slipup.

"So, I'm afraid there's not much I can do for you." She inched her way toward the side of the counter, intent on seeing him out.

"I want you to contact her . . . the woman on the beach. Everyone is saying she led you to her body. Even the news reporters. That means you can find out if it's Kelly."

Hmm . . . Actually, the idea kind of piqued her interest again. But as hard as she'd tried to contact the woman on the beach with Bee and Stephanie, she'd failed. Besides, what if Artie Becker was the killer? Of course, if Artie had killed his daughter, he'd already know it was her buried on the beach.

"It doesn't really work that way—"

"Does that mean you won't help me?"

For the first time Cass looked past the anger that emanated

from him in waves and saw something else in the depths of his eyes. Sadness.

She was going to relent. She could feel it coming, despite her own admonishments and Tank's irate voice screaming in her head. Had Artie just continued his temper tantrum, she'd have been able to say no and either escort him out or call the police. As it was . . . It was the sheer agony in his eyes that did her in. She just didn't have it in her to turn away someone in pain.

She sighed. "I'll see what I can do."

He nodded once, then shoved away from the counter and paced.

She thought of sending him away, but she'd tried to contact the woman with the séance on the beach and hadn't been able to. Of course, that had turned into a fiasco, but still . . . Maybe with her father in the shop, if it was Kelly, Cass could convince her to show up. "Have a seat at the table, but I need you to do something for me."

"What?"

"You have to try to be calm. It's hard for me to concentrate when you're . . . agitated, and it might scare Kelly away." She had no idea if the second part was true, but she didn't need him pitching a fit in her shop either. "Would you like something to drink?"

"I'm fine." He pulled out a chair and sat.

Beast tilted his head at her and whined.

She ruffled his fur and reassured him it was okay, then lit a thick, white pillar candle and placed it on the side of the table. She'd already done a color reading with Artie, without much luck, so she took the crystal ball from the shelf, even though that hadn't helped much either lately. She placed it on the table and took a seat across from him.

She inhaled deeply and blocked all of the negative energy Artie had brought in with him. She concentrated on the woman's image as she remembered it.

The air shimmered, and a vague distortion of color appeared. Intense fear invaded Cass. She gasped.

"Is she here?"

She struggled to maintain whatever shallow connection she'd achieved and nodded.

"Can I talk to her? Will she hear me?"

Cass nodded again, trying to pinpoint the source of the all-encompassing fear surrounding her.

"I just want to say I'm sorry, Kelly. I should have done better by you. I knew what your mother was, knew she was hurting you, but I loved her so much." He looked down at his hands clasped together in a white-knuckled grip on the table. "The drugs did things to her, and I should have protected you."

He sniffed. "I should have come looking for you sooner, but I figured maybe you were better off. Then your mother up and disappeared, and the police thought I had something to do with it, and I just couldn't deal with it all."

His shoulders slumped beneath the weight of burdens he'd carried far too long. "Then, when I found you here with that . . . loser . . ." He shook his head. "I should have handled it better, shouldn't have threatened him . . . or you . . ."

Blood roared in Cass's ears. Her hands shook violently, and she stuffed them under the table so Artie wouldn't notice. Artie had told Cass he hadn't seen his daughter in years.

He'd lied. Fear evolved into stark terror. Her own? She didn't think so, and yet . . . was that a premonition?

"Anyway. I just wanted the chance to tell you, I'm sorry. For everything." He shoved his chair back, stood, and walked out of the shop without another word.

Cass sat perfectly still, fear holding her hostage in a way she didn't understand.

She had no idea how much time had passed when the chimes tinkled, ripping her from her trance.

"Hey, Cass." Emmett turned the sign to OPEN. "I just have a few last-minute things to do upstairs, then I'll be outta your hair." He started toward the stairs, then grunted and detoured to the counter, pulled her shop key from his pocket, and held it up before placing it beside the register. "I almost forgot. I'll leave the key on the counter, since I won't be needing it anymore."

She nodded, then forced out a thank-you as he jogged up the stairs.

How long had she been sitting there? She glanced at the clock, shocked to see a little more than an hour had passed since she'd sat down with Artie Becker. Even given the time she'd spent with him, and possibly Kelly, she'd still been sitting unaware of anything for more than forty-five minutes. The fear she'd experienced before blacking out was gone, as was the shimmer of color she'd attributed to Kelly, but a new dread had begun to creep in. Was she going crazy?

Cass stood, the stiffness in her joints confirming what the clock had already told her. She grabbed the key Emmett had left on the register, flipped her appointment book open to the folder in the back where she always kept a couple of spare keys, and went to drop it in. It was empty. The second spare key she kept was gone. And she only knew of one person who'd touched her appointment book. She had two choices. She could contact Tank and let the police handle it. Or she could find the little rat and see what he wanted from her shop. So much for letting the police handle the investigation.

22

The shop had maintained a steady flow of customers throughout the day, but Cass finally managed a minute to call Tank and tell him about the missing key. "The guy who broke into Leighton's gallery was in here looking through my appointment book. He's the only one who could have taken the key, so he must have been the one to break in."

Tank's frustrated breath echoed through the phone. "I understand that, Cass, and I'm not saying he didn't take it. Or that he wasn't the intruder. I'm just saying I can't arrest him for breaking into your shop without any kind of evidence."

"He wasn't wearing gloves when he came in for the reading and he was looking through my book."

"We've been over this already, Cass. He was there as a customer. The book was sitting on the table. Touching it isn't a crime. If we caught him with the key, we'd be able to do something, but as it is . . ."

Knowing he was right didn't dampen her anger. "Did you find out who he is, at least?"

"His name's Vincent DiSilva."

His name hit her like a punch in the gut. Cass sucked in a breath.

"You know him?"

"Uh . . ." She rushed to connect the dots.

"Cass." His tone held a note of warning.

"No. I don't know him, but I have heard the name. Did you ask Leighton about him?"

"Yes. She said she didn't know him."

What! Her mind raced. Leighton had told her he was the woman from the portrait's boyfriend. When he'd been in Mystical Musings asking her to help him find the necklace, he'd said he'd been working in the art gallery.

"When he was in the shop that day, he said he worked at the gallery."

"Hmm . . . I'll look into that. You said you've heard his name before?"

"Oh, yeah." Dang. She was hoping he'd forget she'd blurted that out. If he went to the gallery and searched for the painting, they might still be able to retrieve her thumbprint. But what had Tank said? He couldn't arrest Vincent for breaking into Cass's shop, even though his prints were on her appointment book, because he'd been there for a legitimate reason? Hopefully, the same went for her. "I was asking Leighton about a portrait she painted. It was displayed in the art gallery window, and it bore a striking resemblance to the woman . . ." She swallowed hard, still

253 254 254 254 254 254 254 254 254 254 254 254 254 254 254 254 254 254 254 254 254 254 254 254 254 254 254 254 254 254 254 254 254 254 254 254 254 254 254 254 254 254 254 254 254 254 254 254 254 254 254 254 254 254 254 254 254 254 254 254 254 254 254 254 254 254 254 254 254 254 254 254 254 254 254 254 254 254 254

uncomfortable discussing anything relating to spirits with Tank.

He saved her the trouble. "The woman you've been seeing in your . . . uh . . ."

"Yeah, her. Leighton said she came in with her boyfriend, Vincent DiSilva, to commission the painting, but neither of them ever returned to pick it up, and she wasn't able to contact either of them."

Tank didn't say anything at first.

Cass just waited.

"All right. Let me talk to Chief Rawlins about it. Maybe we can bring him back in and ask a few more questions. Oh, and by the way, Emmett's coming over later to change your locks."

"Sure. Thanks, Tank."

"No problem. I'll see you tonight."

Warmth surged through her. Of course, he'd be there for her tonight. "Great, thanks. See ya then."

The chimes sounded, and Cass jumped, still a little unnerved by the episode with Artie Becker. For a few moments early on, she'd been sure he wasn't the killer. By the time he left, well . . . she had no clue what to think, but she was terrified of having another blackout. She should have told Tank about their conversation, but she hadn't thought of it. Dang. She'd have to call him back.

"Hey, there." Bee hugged her.

"Hi."

Stephanie hugged her next. "So, are you ready for tonight?" As she stepped back, she glanced at Bee over Cass's shoulder.

When Cass turned to Bee, he jerked his gaze away from Stephanie and smiled at her.

Cass nailed them with a glare. "Okay, spill it."

Bee's eyes widened innocently. A little too innocently. "What are you talking about?"

"It's obvious there's something going on between you two. What is it?"

Bee huffed. "You tell her, Stephanie."

"Uh-uh. Not me. You're the gossipmonger," Stephanie countered.

He grinned. "Well, that is true, but since this isn't exactly gossip, I'll let you do the honors."

"What do you mean it isn't gossip? Everyone is talking about it."

Cass massaged her temples. "I don't care which one of you tells me, but I don't have time to listen to you two bicker. One of you, tell me."

"Oh, all right." Bee offered a sympathetic look and rubbed her arm.

Uh-oh. This could not be good.

"You know that reporter, Stevie Rhymes?"

"Yeah. I've been dodging her for days. She wanted to do an interview with me, but I refused."

Bee winced. "Maybe you should have just agreed to the interview."

"Are you kidding? Tank would have killed me."

"That's true."

She shot Stephanie a look.

Stephanie only shrugged.

Cass waved it off. "Anyway, what did she do?"

"She does a series on the local news about local events, businesses, people, stuff like that, you know?"

"Uh-oh."

"Uh-oh is right. Last night's piece was on Herb Cox's dog training program and how people are falling over themselves to get in."

A vision of the man hovering behind Stevie, his camera ready, flashed before her. "Please don't tell me the camera was running when Beast pulled me down."

He pressed his lips into a thin line and laughter danced in his eyes.

"Don't you dare laugh."

"Oh, honey. Would I laugh at you?"

She stared at him.

He lowered his gaze. His shoulders shook. "*With* you, honey. I would never laugh at you, only with you." He finally recovered himself enough to look up. "Surely you can see the humor here?"

"Not really."

"Besides, you know what they say . . ."

"Enlighten me, Bee. What do they say?"

"There's no such thing as bad publicity." He waggled his eyebrows.

"He might be right, Cass. Everyone I've talked to today is planning to attend the group reading tonight. Even with the new room upstairs, you might still have to turn people away," Stephanie said.

Bee huffed. "Yeah, well, some of that interest might have more to do with a ghost leading Cass to her body than any video Stevie Rhymes put out."

The wind chimes interrupted any further discussion of her TV debut.

"Hey, Cass." Emmett held up his toolbox. "I'm just going to take care of these locks now. Don't want to miss any of the reading."

"Is Sara coming?"

"Yup. Said she'd meet me here."

Cass shrugged off her humiliation. "All right. Let's get started. There's too much to do for me to worry about this right now."

"That's a good attitude," Bee said.

Cass glared at him.

He just grinned.

At that moment Isabella stuck her head in the door. "Anyone have a free hand?"

"I do." Together, Bee and Stephanie made a beeline for the front door.

Now she was going to have to stand up in front of all these people knowing most, if not all of them, had witnessed her fall. Cass needed a moment to compose herself. She opened the small refrigerator beneath the counter at the back of the shop and took out a bottle of water, then shook two ibuprofen into her hand and swallowed them. If she didn't get rid of her headache, she'd never get through the night.

Isabella preceded Bee into the shop and held the door open while he carried in a five-foot hero wrapped in cellophane. Stephanie followed behind with a box of salads.

Cass's mouth started to water. With the shop being so busy, she hadn't eaten all day.

"There's still another hero in the car, Cass. I decided to

do two when I heard how many people were coming." Isabella caught her bottom lip between her teeth while she watched Bee maneuver the hero up the spiral staircase. "Hope that's okay."

"Great, thanks. Both Italian?"

"Yup, that's what always goes. But I do have the smaller American one we talked about."

"Perfect." Cass preferred Italian herself. Pepperoni, salami, capicola, bologna, provolone, lettuce, tomato, onions, and Italian dressing on a five-foot-long, soft Italian hero roll. Her stomach growled, and she pressed her hand against it. Maybe they should eat before the reading.

"Where do you want this, Cass?" Bee had returned and he stood by the stairway with the coffeemaker in hand.

"I set up a table in the far corner for the coffee."

"You got it."

Isabella and Stephanie followed him up, their hands full of paper plates, paper cups, utensils, and napkins.

Cass shook off her mood. She'd been looking forward to this all week. No way she'd let anything as foolish as her pride interfere.

Stephanie stopped at the bottom of the stairs and stared at her. "Hey, you okay?"

Cass sighed. "Yeah. I just have a pounding headache."

"Did you take something for it?"

"I just took ibuprofen."

"Have you had your caffeine fix yet today? I could put on a pot of coffee."

Cass's stomach roiled. "That's okay. Thanks, though."

Stephanie frowned as she moved closer. "Have you eaten anything?"

"Actually, no. I was swamped all day and didn't get a chance."

"That's probably what's wrong." Stephanie dug through her bag and pulled out a protein bar, then grinned. "It tastes awful, but I keep them for times when I just can't get a chance to eat anything. They help."

"Thanks. I don't care what it tastes like if it helps get rid of this headache." Cass took the protein bar and unwrapped it. Maybe hunger had had something to do with the time she'd lost this afternoon after Artie's visit. She hoped so. The other option was too scary to contemplate at the moment. She ate the protein bar, then pulled out her to-do list and started checking things off and seeing to the last-minute arrangements.

Guests started arriving, some familiar, others not, and she moved forward to greet them. Thankfully, her headache had finally started to recede. Now maybe she could at least enjoy the evening.

Grace and Rudy walked in with Sadie and a man Cass didn't recognize. Sadie introduced him as her husband, and Cass bid them a warm welcome and moved on. Sara stood holding hands with Emmett. Cass hadn't seen her come in, but she smiled and waved. They made the cutest couple.

As Bee and Stephanie ushered people to their seats, Cass moved through the room smiling and saying hello, but mostly trying to get a feel for people. Excitement sizzled in the air. She caught snippets of conversations and tried to hone in on the people she'd try to *read* tonight.

A woman stood in the corner with her hand against her flat stomach, giggling softly with a group of friends. Her complexion glowed, radiating warmth and happiness. Cass approached her. "Congratulations."

The woman's mouth fell open. "Am I showing already?"

"Nope, you look fantastic."

"Go ahead." One of her friends nudged her and laughed. "Ask."

The woman's cheeks reddened. "Can you tell what it is?"

Cass studied the woman. The certainty she was having a girl had already come to Cass, but she could never be sure. Though even she had to admit, her guesses were surprisingly accurate. "If I had to guess, I'd say a girl."

The woman's friend squealed. "I knew it."

Cass kept small baskets of lotions and crystals made up for expectant mothers. She'd have to remember to give the woman one on her way out.

Stephanie motioned for her.

Cass bid the woman good luck and moved on. "Everything ready?"

"Pretty much." Stephanie glanced at her cell phone screen. "You have about ten minutes before you have to start, but we're trying to get everyone seated. The rest of the people will sit once we dim the lights and turn off the music."

Cass swallowed hard. The room was completely full. Chairs from Dreamweaver had even been added to some of the tables and along one wall to accommodate unexpected guests.

Tank walked in and put an arm around Stephanie. "How's everything?"

She smiled at him. "Great. We're almost ready to start. But I do have a few last-minute things to do, so I'll catch up with you in a little bit."

He kissed her, and she strode across the room, her smile still lingering.

Good. Cass hated seeing the two of them having problems.

Tank kissed Cass's cheek. He'd never said he believed in any of what Cass did, but he was always supportive and always showed up when something special was going on. "The room looks great."

"Thanks."

"I hope it's okay I brought a few friends." He gestured toward a table in the farthest corner where Chief Rawlins sat talking with another woman Cass didn't recognize.

"Wow. That's weird." She didn't know what to think.

Tank shrugged. "She said she wanted to see what you could do. She seemed sincere, so I figured it'd be okay."

"Of course, it is. Thanks, Tank."

"Anytime. Do you have a minute?"

Bee and Stephanie seemed to have everything under control, and Cass had a few questions for Tank, anyway, so she nodded and followed him down the stairs.

When he reached the bottom, he stepped aside and gestured ahead of him. "I brought you a surprise."

"Wha—"

Luke Morgan leaned against the counter, his arms folded across his chest. His shaggy, dark hair, which had grown even longer since she'd seen him last, was now hanging just past his collar, and she longed to rake her fingers through it.

She smiled at the thought. "Luke. You made it."

He strolled toward her and opened his arms. "Did you think I'd miss your big moment?"

Cass slid into his arms and smiled. Maybe she wasn't quite ready to break things off with him after all. "Thank you."

He hugged her close and dropped a kiss on her head. "I'm sorry I couldn't get here this morning."

"It's all right, I understand."

"I know you do, and that makes me feel worse." He set her back and caught her gaze. "Getting to know each other long-distance is harder than I expected."

Cass just shrugged. What could she say?

"But I do want to get to know you, Cass." Heat sizzled in the depths of his dark blue eyes.

A shiver tore through her.

He tucked her hair behind her ear in a gesture that had become familiar and let his fingers linger along the side of her neck. "I want to make this work between us."

She nodded, unable to speak past the lump in her throat, terrified he was going to break up with her, even though she'd been thinking the same thing. Now she found she wasn't quite ready to let Luke go.

"If you tell me it's what you want, I'll try to find a way for us to spend more time together. But you have to be sure, Cass."

"I'm sure." Her voice came out a raspy whisper.

He brushed his lips against hers, then stepped back and grinned. "Good."

She struggled to regain her composure. How did he always manage to do that to her? He left her with her limbs weak and her heart racing. If they were going to make this work, she'd have to develop some kind of resistance to his good-ole-boy charm.

He looked around and frowned. Apparently their intimate moment was over. For now, anyway. "Where's Beast?"

"I can't trust him not to eat the food, so he's gated in the back room." Herb had suggested crating him, but putting him in a cage still didn't sit right with Cass. So she'd stacked two baby gates, one on top of the other, in the doorway. "Hopefully he's not chewing the gates apart."

$$23$$

At the last minute, Stevie Rhymes walked in with Wade and her photographer in tow and slid into a seat at the back of the room.

Bee gestured toward them and raised a brow.

Cass shook her head. Why have Bee throw them out, when she could do it perfectly well herself?

Stevie smirked as Cass approached. "Well, hello, Ms. Donovan."

"Ms. Rhymes." Cass offered a professional smile. "Can I help you with something?"

"I came to see what all the fuss was about." She tilted her head. "Is that a problem?"

Cass bit back the urge to toss them all on their cans. Stevie Rhymes didn't matter to her one way or the other, but she did want to know what her friend Wade's deal was. "No problem, but you'll have to give your camera to my friend. I'm sorry, but I don't allow videotape of my group readings."

"Oh, why's that? Afraid your tricks won't appear so spectacular on camera?"

"No. I just don't believe in invading other people's privacy. My customers deserve respect, and I ensure they receive it."

Bee had come up behind them and held out a hand. "You can have it back afterward."

The cameraman looked back and forth between Stevie and her companion.

Stevie shrugged, and the cameraman handed it to Bee.

"Thank you." Cass turned her back and walked away. She already knew Bee would keep an eye on them throughout the reading, and since Stephanie was leaning over Tank's table speaking to him, Luke, and the chief, she assumed they'd be watching as well.

Bee dimmed the lights, and Stephanie straightened, moved to the center of the room, and called for everyone's attention.

Excited whispers buzzed through the room as everyone settled in.

Cass smoothed her long skirt and took a deep breath, reminding herself this was no different from the readings she hosted every month.

Stephanie looked over to be sure she was ready. When Cass nodded her assent, Stephanie introduced her.

Cass entered to an enthusiastic round of applause. Bee let out a shrill whistle, and Cass couldn't help but laugh. Some of her tension seeped away. A good portion of these people were not only her customers, they were also her friends. Hopefully, by the end of the night, the rest would be as well.

She looked over the room while she opened with her traditional remarks, trying to make everyone feel welcome and letting them know how the group readings worked. "As I move through the room, I get impressions, which I will share with you. I can't answer any specific questions during a group reading, but if you'd like to discuss an individual reading, you can see me afterward."

A man, his face lined with grief, stood out to her. She passed him over. Just for now. She'd have to come back to him later; she couldn't bear the thought of leaving him suffering, but she needed something a little lighter to start.

A guy seated toward the front caught her attention. He sat with an older woman, his posture stiff, her hand lying atop his. A gesture of support? There seemed to be something between them. They weren't a couple, but maybe mother and son. The woman looked at him and patted his hand.

Cass approached. "Hi. I'm Cass."

The woman patted the guy's hand again and released it, then sat back. "Hello. I'm Mary, and this is my son, Trevor."

Trevor nodded. He couldn't be more than eighteen or nineteen. He slid back in his seat and looked away from his mother. Was he hiding something? Ashamed to face his mother? There was definitely tension between them.

"I sense there's something the two of you need to talk about."

Mary nodded.

Trevor's cheeks reddened. This wasn't the time or place

for their discussion, but Cass could at least open the door for them to step through later when they were alone.

Since there wasn't an empty seat available, Cass leaned against the table, focusing her full attention on the young man. "You're afraid your mother won't approve of something."

He gasped and glanced at his mother.

"And her approval is important to you."

He nodded.

A tear rolled down the woman's cheek and she twisted what looked like a wedding band around her finger, a nervous habit Cass had seen often enough.

The kid seemed genuinely concerned about his mother's feelings, and she looked at him with the most loving expression. The way he held himself, the way he'd positioned himself to face the doorway, the way he studied the room, all reminded her of a cop or a soldier. If she kept her observations vague enough, she might be able to hit on the problem. "I see something to do with law enforcement or the military."

The guy's guilt-riddled gaze shot to his mother. "Mom . . ."

"It's okay, honey. I already know."

"You do? How? No one else knows I enlisted."

She waved it off. "It doesn't matter. All that matters is that I'm so proud of you, and Dad would be, too."

"Why didn't you say anything?" he asked.

She shrugged. "I figured you'd tell me in your own way, in your own time." She grinned at Cass. "But I got tired of waiting, so I figured I'd bring you here and try to give you a little nudge, figured maybe your dad would help out."

Trevor stood and took his mother's hand, then pulled her into his arms. Tears tracked down her cheeks, but she didn't wipe them, just clung tightly to her son. When he stepped back, she reached up and cupped his cheek. "I love you, Trevor."

"I love you, too, Mom."

She nodded. "I know, son. You're a good boy. And you'll make a great soldier, just like your dad did."

Satisfied they would find their way to a happy ending, Cass moved away to a smattering of applause. So much for starting with something light.

She couldn't help discreetly glancing at Stevie and Wade. Wade appeared curious, but Stevie had her gaze riveted on him. Hmm . . . should she call her out on her feelings for him in front of everyone? Embarrass her as she'd embarrassed Cass by running that video?

Cass sighed and moved on. It would just be petty, and her paying customers deserved better than that.

She passed the grieving man again and didn't have the heart to keep going if she could offer him comfort. He seemed to be alone, and there was an empty seat beside him, so Cass turned the chair to face him and sat. "What's your name?"

He cleared his throat. "Alfred."

"I feel like there's someone here for you." His grief was easy to read, but she wasn't getting much else.

"Is it my Marilyn?"

"Is there something you need to talk to Marilyn about?"

He shook his head. "I'd just like to tell her I miss her."

Cass took both of his hands in hers and searched for the right words to comfort him. "How long has she been gone?"

"Two long years." He sighed.

"She'll always be with you."

A small smile played at the corner of his mouth. "She used to tell me that when she was sick. She'd say 'I'll be with you always.'" He squeezed Cass's hands. "Thank you for giving me the chance to say hello."

She smiled. "You're welcome. If you'd like to come in for an individual reading, I'll see what I can do."

He nodded. "I'd like that."

She'd done the best she could for him. Sometimes there just wasn't anything to be done. She'd make sure to talk to him afterward and tell him she'd do the individual reading at no cost. Whenever she suggested a private reading to someone who seemed especially vulnerable at one of her group readings, she didn't charge. It just didn't feel right. Too much like taking advantage of people.

A young woman bounced up and down in her chair, all but waving her hand in the air. Cass studied her. She vibrated with energy. Excitement danced in her eyes. Cass approached.

"What's your name?"

"Reece."

"It's nice to meet you, Reece."

"It's nice to meet you, too. I'm so excited to be here."

"I can see that."

Soft laughter rippled through the room.

Reece grinned. "I actually came to you once before. When my sister was getting married, she brought her bridal party for a reading."

"Oh, yes. I remember you. Your sister originally came in with her fiancé. They were going to get married by the lighthouse."

"Yes."

"How are they doing?"

"Awesome, they just got back from their honeymoon."

"That's great. They made a beautiful couple." It always brought her a rush of joy to hear her customers were doing well. "Is there something specific you wanted to ask about today?"

"Actually, yes."

She didn't usually answer specific questions for people at a group reading, but this girl was so excited, and Cass needed to lighten the atmosphere a little.

"I just got accepted at two colleges, and I can't decide which one to go to. Can you see which would be the best choice for me?"

Movement by the stairway caught her attention, and she squinted to bring the figure into focus in the dim light. Leighton weaved between a couple of tables and took an empty seat.

"Uh . . ." She dragged her focus back to Reece.

Hope filled the girl's eyes.

Cass smiled. This girl knew exactly which school she wanted to go to. She was just looking for confirmation that she'd made the right choice. "You've made the right decision."

Reece squealed and bounced up and down, obviously pleased with Cass's agreement. "I knew it. My mom keeps telling me to go away to school, to experience the world, but the local school I've chosen is less expensive and closer to home."

Oops. "You've got a good head on your shoulders. I'm sure you'll do well no matter where you go."

"Thank you."

Cass moved on, searching out people she could read, those whose emotions were clearly expressed in their expressions and body language.

Leighton slouched low in her chair, arms folded across her chest. Hmm . . . interesting. The desire to delve into her mind prodded Cass, but she ignored it and moved on.

Two older women sat together at Leighton's table. One of them held her lower lip caught between her teeth, her focus internal.

"Hi. What's your name?"

The woman jerked her head up as if startled. "Oh, uh . . . Sue."

Cass offered a warm smile.

A gentleman at the table next to them stood and offered Cass his seat.

She thanked him and positioned the chair where she could keep Leighton in her peripheral vision and still sit face-to-face with the woman. "You're worried about something."

The woman nodded, her cheeks flushed.

"Would you like me to try to help?" Some people didn't want attention drawn to them, and Cass was always careful to respect that.

She glanced around the room, then nodded. "Yes, please."

"Okay, let's see what we can do for you."

Before Cass had approached, Sue had been very focused on something. The way she'd been startled when Cass had spoken told her she was right in her original assessment, that focus had been internal. "You are trying to remember something."

Leighton stiffened.

Sue's gaze darted to the friend sitting next to her, only for an instant, but enough to tell Cass she was right.

Cass always watched carefully for a reaction so she'd know if she was on the right track. If it seemed she veered off, she'd backtrack a little and try a different direction. Thankfully, this woman was very easy to read, because Cass's attention was too split for her to focus properly.

"Something you can't find."

Sue's eyes widened.

Bingo.

Leighton leaned forward, resting her elbows on the table. Was her interest piqued?

"When was the last time you saw it?"

"My son left it with me last month. He wanted me to put it in a safe place." She looked down and shook her head. A tremor shook her.

The woman beside her reached over and squeezed her hand.

Cass frowned. What could her son have left with her? "Something very important."

"Yes," she whispered.

She needed more information, but how to get it. She changed tracks. "He trusted you."

She nodded.

"You're afraid of betraying his trust, afraid he won't trust you again."

"Yes."

"He doesn't know you lost it yet."

She jerked her head back up. "No."

"Well, let's find it before you have to tell him, then."

Her posture relaxed, and she nodded and offered a semismile.

"Where did he give it to you?"

"In my kitchen." She frowned, narrowing her eyes, and Cass waited to see if she'd elaborate. "His girlfriend is coming home from college on Friday." She grabbed Cass's hand. "Please. I have to find it before then."

What could be *that* important? Something that the woman couldn't just replace. Inspiration struck. "Is he asking her on Friday?"

Sue gasped. "Yes. How did you know?"

Cass ignored the question.

"Close your eyes and try to relax."

She did as instructed.

"Now, envision him handing you the ring box." Cass held her breath. She'd figured out it was an engagement ring, but she had no clue if he'd given it to his mother in the box. It seemed he would.

Sue held out her hand as if accepting the ring box. "He handed it to me and asked me to keep it safe. I was so excited for him; his girlfriend is such a sweetheart, very good for him—"

"Bring your focus back to the box in your hand." Cass coaxed her gently to keep her on track. If her mind wandered off in every direction whenever she tried to find the ring, it was no wonder she couldn't find it.

"Oh, right. I got up and hugged him."

"Were you still holding the box?"

"Yes."

"Then what?"

"He left, and I got up to go put the ring in my jewelry box, but it's not there. I've looked a hundred . . ." Her eyes shot open. "Oh, my . . ."

Cass smiled and relaxed back in her seat. "You remember."

"Yes, yes. I was thinking about celebrating their engagement, and wondering if I still had champagne in the cabinet. I keep it in the cabinet above the refrigerator because we never really use it . . ."

This time, Cass allowed her the moment to ramble. It wouldn't matter at this point, since she'd already remembered where the ring was, and it gave Cass a moment to take a peek at Leighton. As soon as she shifted her attention, Leighton's gaze crashed into hers.

Leighton studied her a moment, then looked away.

Cass thought again about reading her but remembered how she'd balked at the individual reading. No way she'd be comfortable with a reading in front of a roomful of people.

". . . and put the box down to get to the bottles in the back, and it's still there. Right there in the cabinet." She jumped up and ran around the table.

Cass stood to accept the hug.

"I can't ever thank you enough."

"I'm glad I could help."

She continued to wander through the room, seeking out the people who seemed to need her help. After nearly two hours of helping people find things they'd misplaced, talk to dearly departed loved ones, make decisions they'd already made on their own, and find love, she wrapped up the reading and thanked everyone for coming.

"Please feel free to hang around and have something to eat." Hopefully, they'd make purchases and set up individual readings as well.

As soon as she was done, Leighton sought her out. "That was . . . impressive."

"Thank you."

"I'll have to come again."

"I'd love to have you. You're welcome to bring your fiancé next time if you'd like."

"My . . ." She frowned.

Cass gestured to the diamond on her left hand.

"Oh, right." She gave a tight smile, thanked Cass again, and left.

Bee squeezed her shoulder. "That went really well."

"Thanks, Bee." She patted his hand. "Do you know where Stevie Rhymes and her crew disappeared to?"

"Nah. They left right after you finished, but she seemed totally engrossed in everything you were saying."

"Really?" She lifted a brow. "The only thing she seemed engrossed in to me was that guy she brought with her."

"I know, right? She couldn't take her eyes off him, and she was practically drooling."

"Did you give the guy's camera back?"

"Yeah, though I had half a mind to lose it." He winked.

She laughed. Bee's loyalty always touched her. "Want to walk downstairs with me for a minute? I have to check on Beast."

"Sure, dear." He started down the stairs with Cass right behind him.

Stephanie had already gone down and was ringing up a customer.

Cass stopped to offer her business card, thank the couple for coming, and say good-bye.

"Everything went great." Stephanie started toward the back room with her and Bee.

"Do you think so?"

"Oh, yeah. People were really happy. I came down to

help any customers, but most of them are still upstairs having something to eat."

"That's great. The longer—"

Several loud pops sounded. Holes appeared in the back window, surrounded by weblike cracks in the glass.

Beast went ballistic, barking and howling in the closed-off room. She had to get to him.

She started to spin around.

Another pop, and the shelves behind them shattered, then crashed down in an explosion of glass and stones.

She froze.

"I'm hit!" Bee screamed, his hand pressed to the side of his head. "Oh, my . . . I've been shot."

He swayed on his feet and Cass and Stephanie ran to him. Blood gushed down his cheek and neck.

Footsteps pounded down the iron stairway.

Beast's barks turned hoarse with the strain.

"Bee, are you all right?"

He pulled his blood-covered hand away from his head and stared at it a moment, then his eyes rolled back into his head, his knees buckled, and he dropped straight down.

24

Cass and Stephanie tried to catch Bee as he fell. They managed to break his fall a little, but not enough to keep his head from smacking the floor a bit too hard, then laid him flat on his back.

Cass knelt next to him. "Bee! Bee! Wake up!"

Chief Rawlins leaned over her shoulder, gun in hand. "Is anyone else hurt?"

The woman who'd been sitting with the chief already had her phone pressed against her ear, relaying rapid-fire details.

Luke and Tank bolted out the back door, guns drawn.

"I'll get a cloth." Stephanie started to get up.

Chief Rawlins stepped over Bee, gripped her shoulder and shoved her back down to the floor, then crouched beside her opposite Cass. "Stay down! Nobody move. Let me see him."

Stephanie scooted to the side, allowing the chief to get closer to Bee.

"It's okay, Bee." Cass gripped his hand and held it against her chest. Sobs shook her. "You're going to be all right."

"Everyone calm down." Chief Rawlins studied his head. "What happened to him?"

The other woman handed her a dish towel. "The ambulance is on its way."

"Thanks, Jen."

"He w-w-was shot." Stephanie's voice shook with the effort to speak through her tears.

Cass hugged his hand tighter. This was all her fault. She should have stayed out of anything to do with the bodies on the beach, should have listened to Tank about it being dangerous. She'd never forgive herself for Bee getting hurt. She rocked back and forth, pain squeezing her chest while she held Bee's hand.

Voices mumbled in the background, but Cass ignored them. An EMT leaned over her, then knelt beside her.

She ignored the newcomer, her mind lost in memories of Bee being . . . well, Bee. Her best friend. She cried harder.

"Cass." Stephanie leaned across Bee and shook Cass's shoulders. "Cass. Listen to me."

Cass looked up into Stephanie's eyes.

Tears tracked down her cheeks, but she smiled through them. "Did you hear Chief Rawlins?"

Cass shook her head.

"He's going to be okay, Cass." She finally released Cass's shoulders and sat back on her heels, laughing and crying at the same time. "He wasn't shot."

"He wasn't?"

Stephanie shook her head and wiped her cheeks. "Something hit him in the head when the shelves crashed down."

A wave of relief surged through her as she looked down at Bee's serene features. He lay with his eyes closed. Bloody streaks had dried on his cheek and matted his hair. "It knocked him out?"

"Nah . . ." Rick, the EMT who'd knelt beside her, now held a blood-soaked cloth pressed against Bee's head as another EMT opened a box and started pulling out gauze and bandages. "Head wounds bleed a lot. He probably took one look at all the blood and passed out."

"So, he's going to be okay?"

"A few stitches, and he should be good. They may keep him overnight in case he has a concussion. Did he hit his head when he fell?"

"Uh . . ." Cass tried to think back. Her brain was pretty much fried. Now that she knew Bee would be all right, Beast's whimpering intruded on her thoughts.

Stephanie answered for her. "We caught him, but he still hit his head."

"Okay." He returned to working on Bee.

"Stephanie, could you check on Beast?"

"I already did. He's fine. Not happy, but fine. I pushed a few chairs in front of the gates so he can't get out. There's too much glass everywhere."

"Oh. Right." She hadn't thought of that, hadn't thought of anything but Bee.

"Come on now, Cass. Let's give them room to work." Chief Rawlins helped her to her feet and put an arm around her shoulder. "I need to ask you some questions."

Glass crunched beneath their feet as the chief led her to

the table in the back corner. The glass shelves had come down like dominoes, shattering as they fell. Stones lay scattered amid the debris, as did remnants of glass knickknacks and broken bottles, their contents spilled out over the mess.

Chief Rawlins pulled out a chair. "Sit."

Cass eyed the back window, a reflection of the chaos staring back at her.

"Don't worry. It's safe. The beach is already secure."

Ignoring the offer of a chair, Cass continued to stare at the window, trying to see out through the destruction. Blackness stared back at her. "Did they catch whoever it was?"

The chief's reflection firmed its mouth into a tight line as she shook her head. "Did you see anyone?"

"No. I didn't even know what was happening."

Rick and his partner loaded Bee onto a stretcher.

His eyes fluttered open, and he moaned.

Stephanie leaned close to him and said something as they rolled him out the door.

"I'll take you to the hospital as soon as I can leave here," Chief Rawlins assured her. "Do you know of anyone who would want to hurt you?"

"I have no idea." She shook her head, then remembered Artie's visit. She'd never gotten the chance to discuss it with Tank earlier. "Artie Becker was in today."

"What did he want?"

"He wanted me to try to contact Kelly."

Chief Rawlins tilted her head and cocked a brow. "And did you?"

"Did I try?" Cass held the other woman's gaze, trying to determine how much information she wanted . . . and how much she'd believe. Then she decided it didn't matter what the other woman believed and went with complete honesty. Who knows? If she'd been honest about everything in the first place, maybe this wouldn't have happened. "Yes."

"And?"

Cass took a deep breath and dove in. "I believe I was successful."

The chief looked around for a minute, then grabbed a sheet of paper and a colored pencil from the basket beneath the counter, shook some glass shards off the paper, and sat at the table. Poised to write, she looked up. "Tell me."

Cass sighed and sat across from her. "It was weird. I had this overwhelming sense of fear, and yet I didn't feel afraid. I can't really explain it."

The chief only nodded.

"He wanted to talk to Kelly, to apologize for not taking better care of her. He mentioned his wife's disappearance, said the police thought he had something to do with it." She frowned, trying to remember everything, but she couldn't. At least, not right now. She'd have to settle for the highlights. "The biggest thing that struck me was when he told her he shouldn't have threatened her or the loser he found her with. I don't know what he meant by that, or who he was referring to, but when he first came in last Friday, he told me he hadn't seen Kelly in years."

"Did you tell Tank about this?"

"No. I meant to, but then I forgot, and I was going to call him back, but things were crazy today and I never thought of it."

The chief patted her hand. "It's all right. Is that all you remember?"

"Yes." Cass stood. "Right now, anyway. If I remember

anything else, I'll call you, but I can't answer any more questions right now. I have to tend to my dog, and I have to get to the hospital to see Bee."

She started to walk away, then turned back, ashamed she hadn't given any thought to her other guests before that moment. "Is everyone else all right?"

Chief Rawlins stood, folded the paper, and tucked it into her skirt pocket. "Yes. No one else was down here at the time, and the upstairs wasn't hit."

Cass nodded. "Thank you." She picked her way across the mess to the back room. Beast's whimpers had finally died off, but she had to see him, had to reassure herself he was all right. She pulled the curtain aside.

Beast scrambled to his feet the instant he spotted her.

"Hey, boy. You okay?" She moved the chairs, took one of the gates down, and stepped over the other. She still needed to keep him confined so he wouldn't hurt himself.

He jumped up on her and whined.

This time, she didn't reprimand him. Instead, she wrapped her arms around him and hugged him close, then sank down on the floor next to him.

He plopped down with her and lowered his head into her lap.

Thankfully, the windows in the back room actually faced the side of the building, not the beach where the suspect had fired from. "I'm sorry, boy. I know you were probably scared, but Bee got hurt, and he needed me."

Beast rolled over for a belly rub. Apparently she was forgiven. Not that she deserved it.

"I don't deserve you, or Bee for that matter. I put everyone I love in danger." Her tears dripped onto his thick fur.

"Is this a private pity party, or is anyone welcome?" Luke stepped over the gate and sat down next to her. He petted Beast's head, then picked up the front of Cass's shirt between his thumb and forefinger. "Please tell me this isn't yours."

She looked down at the blood she hadn't even noticed on the front of her shirt. "It's Bee's."

Luke nodded and settled beside her, leaning against the wall and wrapping his arms around her. "I told Chief Rawlins I'd take you to the hospital."

She laid her cheek against his chest, letting the strong beat of his heart steady her. "Thank you. I just have to drop Beast off at home first."

"No problem."

"You're sure you don't mind? This isn't exactly how I'd envisioned this weekend."

"No, me neither." His soft laughter caught her off guard. "But I will say this, things are never dull with you around."

Cass huffed out a breath.

He gripped her chin and tilted her head up until he stared into her eyes, his expression unguarded in a way it rarely was. "I know life has interfered with us getting to know each other better, but I have deep feelings for you, Cass. When I heard those shots fired . . ." He shook his head, released her chin, and pulled her back into his embrace, resting his chin on her head. "My heart just about stopped."

She snuggled closer to him, inhaling the woodsy scent that would always remind her of Luke, enjoying one moment of losing herself in him.

"But we have plenty of time to figure that out." He stood and held his hand out to her. "Right now, let's get to the hospital."

Tank poked his head around the corner.

She stiffened, expecting him to be furious with her for putting everyone, especially Stephanie, in danger.

"You okay?" He hugged her and dropped a kiss on the top of her head.

She nodded against him.

He set her back and studied her. "Chief Rawlins told me about Artie Becker—"

"I'm sorry, Tank, I meant to tell you—"

He held up a hand to stop her. "I know, Cass. The chief already told me. It's okay. It's partly my fault you didn't feel comfortable talking to me about this stuff, as the chief reminded me . . . not so gently." He glanced at Luke, humor lighting his eyes. "And I'm sorry. I should have taken you more seriously."

She threw her arms around his neck and hugged him.

"Now come on." He started toward the door. "Stephanie went to the hospital with Bee, so I haven't seen her since all of this started, and I really need to."

(25)

Cass stood on the front porch of Cayden and Sophie's weekend rental home and rang the bell. She glanced over her shoulder at her car parked in the driveway.

Bee waved to her from the passenger seat. After spending the remainder of Saturday night in the hospital, he'd been released Sunday morning and had spent the day at Cass's with her and Luke. She'd meant to go to Southampton alone, since it turned out Luke had to go to work once they got off the ferry, but Bee had balked, saying he was looking forward to getting away and spending some time on the beach. While that could possibly be true, she'd also overheard him telling Luke he didn't want her to be alone.

Tears threatened, and she thought about skipping Sophie's mother's reading and heading straight for the beach.

The front door squeaked open.

"Hi, Cass." Sophie greeted her with a hug. "Thank you

so much for coming. Mom's out back in the garden." She led Cass through the breezeway toward the back of the house. Though the house was beautiful, it lacked the cozy feeling of home. Generic paintings on the walls, sparse furnishings, and the lack of personal belongings left her feeling cold. Or maybe that was just her own mood.

The garden was a different story, though. A gorgeous array of colors surrounded a kidney-shaped, in-ground pool. A small waterfall poured over stacked rocks in the far corner; the soft sound of rushing water was soothing.

Sophie approached her mother, who was sitting on a wrought iron bench at the far end of the pool, leaned over, and kissed her cheek. "Mom, this is Cass. Remember I told you about her?"

She smiled, her eyes filled with sadness. "It's nice to meet you, Cass. I'm Estelle."

"Hi, Estelle." Cass sat in a chair facing her. "How are you?"

"I'll leave you two alone."

Estelle watched Sophie close the door gently behind her before speaking. "I'm okay. Sophie said you can talk to ghosts. Is that true?"

That wasn't exactly how Cass would describe it, but if that's what would allow Estelle to accept her help, then so be it. "Sort of."

She frowned. "What do you mean, 'sort of'?"

"Well, it's not like having a conversation . . ." She gestured back and forth between them. "I can't just sit and talk with them like this. It's more like, I get . . . impressions . . . of what spirits want me to know. Then it's up to you to help me interpret them. Would you like to try?"

"It's been ten years since the last time I talked to my Tom." Tears welled in her eyes.

Cass's heart ached for her. "Just because someone is gone doesn't mean we can't still talk to them, can't still feel their presence."

Estelle lowered her gaze to her clasped hands, and the tears spilled over.

Cass slid her chair closer and gripped Estelle's ice-cold hands. "What would you like to say to Tom?"

She jerked back. "Is he here?"

Cass nodded. She figured in some way he probably was.

"Oh, Tom, I'm so sorry. I love you so much, and I am so, so sorry." Violent sobs tore through her. "It was all my fault, and now you're gone, and I can't fix it."

Cass continued to hold her hands, rubbing warmth into them. "What's your fault, Estelle?"

Her sobs died off into soft cries, and Cass wasn't sure she would answer. She waited, studying the deep lines years of pain had etched into her face.

"We were married for sixty years, through lots of good and lots of bad. But through it all, we loved each other deeply." She sucked in a deep, steadying breath. "That day . . ."

Cass didn't say a word; she barely even breathed.

"We had a terrible fight. I was so angry I blurted out . . ." Anguish twisted her features. "I blurted out that I couldn't stand him anymore. It wasn't true. I loved that man with every ounce of my being for more than sixty years. I would have done anything for him. I would have died in his place if I could have." She broke down, sobbing uncontrollably.

Sophie and Cayden peeked out the back door.

Cass shook her head and waved them off. Being interrupted was the last thing Estelle needed just then, especially by the people she loved most, the people she'd feel guilty for still being with while her husband was gone.

Once she regained her composure, she spoke softly, as if drained. "He stormed off in a huff, as he was prone to do when we argued." She stared into Cass's eyes. "And I let him."

Cass remained silent but squeezed her hands.

"There was an accident . . ."

Cass got up, moved to the bench, and wrapped an arm around her.

"He never came home. I never got to tell him I loved him."

"He knows."

She glanced at Cass, her red-rimmed eyes swollen almost shut.

"He knows you love him. And he knows you didn't mean what you said. He forgives you for it, Estelle."

"How can you be sure?"

Cass smiled. "It's what I do, remember?"

"Is he really here with us?"

How could she answer that without lying? She couldn't. Not really. Because she had no idea if Tom was there or not, but she did know he'd forgive her. She couldn't explain how, but she was very sure. If he loved his wife even half as much as she loved him, how could he not? "His spirit is here, his essence, however you look at it. But it's more a feeling I have in my gut, a feeling of . . . acceptance, of love and forgiveness, and . . ." She frowned. There was something else, something odd. "Concern. Is something wrong, Estelle?"

She ignored Cass's question. "Are you absolutely positive he forgives me?"

"I am."

She leaned into Cass's arms and cried softly.

"Now you have to forgive yourself, Estelle." Guilt gripped Cass. Would she have forgiven herself if Bee had really been shot? What if he'd died because of her? Would she have been able to forgive herself then?

This time when Sophie looked in, Cass waved her over.

Cass got up and let Sophie take her place, then left them talking quietly as she strode through the house in search of Cayden. She found him in the living room feeding the baby.

He set the bottle aside and stood. "How did it go?"

Cass shrugged. "I think it went well. It's a start anyway, but she's going to need more help. I'll call you later with the number of a good counselor for her."

Cayden swallowed hard and nodded. "Thank you."

"Call me if you need me. Anytime."

He nodded and started toward the front door.

She put a hand on his arm to stop him. "Go to them. I can see myself out."

The sudden need to get to Bee battered her. She had no doubt Bee knew how she felt about him, but what if she'd lost him? She'd have never gotten the chance to tell him how much he meant to her.

C ass and Bee walked barefoot along the surf. Unlike the gentle bay waves that caressed the shore, the ocean waves pounded against the sand, ripping it out from beneath their feet as they receded. If they stood still for a few minutes, they'd begin to sink into the sand.

Cass slid her hand into Bee's.

"Are you okay, sweetie? You've been quiet since you came out of Sophie's. Did everything go okay?"

She'd been upset when she'd gotten back into the car, but she hadn't wanted to talk about the reading. It wouldn't be fair to Estelle to share her grief with anyone else. Even though Cass was no longer bound by doctor-patient confidentiality, she still respected her clients' privacy. Always. Without exception. Unless they told her something she thought might put someone in danger, like Artie Becker had. Bee respected that, and she loved him for it.

She laid her head against his arm. "I love you, Bee. You're my best friend. And I'm so sorry you got hurt because of me."

He stopped walking and turned to face her. He wiped a tear from her cheek and tucked the hair that was blowing across her face behind her ear. "I love you, too. You are the best friend I've ever had. Heck, if I wasn't gay, I'd have asked you to marry me long ago."

Cass laughed with him. "I don't deserve you."

"Oh, trust me, honey, you deserve me." He wrapped his arms around her and pulled her close, resting his chin on her head.

Hugging him back, she rested against his chest as they looked out over the seemingly endless expanse of ocean. The sheer power and enormity of it usually made Cass's problems seem insignificant. This time, not so much.

"And I didn't get hurt because of you. I got hurt because I was standing in the wrong place at the wrong time."

Cass couldn't hold back the tears.

He hugged her closer and rubbed circles on her back.

"Do you remember when I was going through that tough time, back in the fall?"

She nodded and sniffed.

He stepped back, reached into his pocket, and pulled out a black tourmaline. He turned the stone over in his hand, then smoothed his thumb over its surface. "You gave this to me at a time when I desperately needed help. When I really needed a friend, you were there. You told me it would protect against negative energy." He placed the stone in her hand and closed her fingers over it, then cradled her hand in both of his. "It comforted me, if for no other reason, because it reminded me of a friend's love."

"Oh, Bee."

"Keep it for now." He wiped her face and kissed her cheek. "You can give it back to me when things get better. In the meantime, who knows? Maybe it'll help."

"Thank you."

"You're welcome." He grabbed her hand and started up the beach. "Now come on, let's get ice cream."

Cass tucked the stone into her pocket, her mood lightening more than it had in a while. "I want chocolate . . ."

"With hot fudge . . ."

"And whipped cream." She laughed, enjoying the feel of the cool sea breeze and the warm sand between her toes. The salty, briny scent of the sea had always brought her comfort. It would forever be the scent of home.

They got into the car, and Cass rolled down the windows.

Bee turned on the radio, a soft rock station rather than the upbeat dance music he usually favored.

They drove in silence, each lost in their own thoughts.

Mansions lined the stretch of road, contemporary designs of all shapes and sizes, alongside older, more traditional homes. All of them with the enormous expanse of ocean in their backyards.

As they headed toward town, they left the stretch of beach road behind, but not the mansions. Walls of shrubs with large gates in their centers blocked many of the homes from view, although an occasional dormer or rooftop peeked over the tops.

Bee pointed out an empty parking spot beside a small park, and Cass pulled in.

"Do you want to walk in the park while we eat our ice cream?" she asked.

"Sure, if you want." Bee stared out the window, seemingly distracted.

"Is something wrong?"

"No, I just . . . That's him."

Cass leaned across the car to look out Bee's window into the park. "What are you talking ab—"

"I'll kill him." Bee's face turned beet red, and he reached for the handle and started to open the door.

Cass grabbed his arm. "Kill who? Bee, what are you talking about?"

"Look."

She twisted and leaned across Bee for a closer look.

"There. By the fountain."

Someone who looked an awful lot like Tank stood in front of the fountain talking to an attractive woman with long, black hair. "Is that Tank?"

"Yeah. The creep. And just when I was starting to like him." Bee got out of the car and started across the grass.

Cass jumped out and ran after him. By the time she caught up, she was out of breath. "Bee. Stop right now." She yanked his arm. "I'm not kidding, Bee. You have to stop."

Keeping his gaze locked on Tank and the woman, he stopped.

She had no idea what he was so worked up about, but she didn't need to be psychic to know if she couldn't calm him down, this encounter was not going to end well. "What's the problem?"

"Before you saw him, he hugged that woman."

"So?"

"It was a big hug, Cass. And he and Stephanie have seemed . . . I don't know . . . off, lately."

Stephanie had definitely been off. Cass had no doubt something was bothering her, and something between her and Tank was definitely not right. But Tank cheating on her? Cass found it hard to believe. She wasn't a naïve woman, nor was she trusting, and yet, she just didn't buy that Tank would be unfaithful. And she was a great judge of character. Usually. Except when it came to husbands. And maybe friends. Well, some friends. Bee and Stephanie had turned out okay. An image of Luke, his lips hovering over hers a moment before kissing her came to mind. Heat flared in her cheeks. Hmm . . . maybe her judgment was improving.

Bee started moving again, jerking Cass back to reality. "Calm down, Bee. You can't just go storming over there making accusations. At least watch them for a few minutes and see what's going on."

The woman threw her arms around Tank's neck, and he lifted her off the ground in a big bear hug.

Oh, boy. "Okay, that doesn't prove anything."

Bee stared at her, mouth agape.

"I'm serious."

"Sorry, Cass, no one cheats on my friends." He strode toward Tank once more.

There was no stopping him this time, so Cass settled for running beside him, trying to keep up and concentrating on breathing. How in the world he stayed in such good shape with the amount of fast food he ate, she'd never know.

The woman walked away, and Tank looked after her, smiling and shaking his head.

When he finally turned to walk away, he spotted Bee and frowned. After one quick glance in the woman's direction, he started toward Bee and Cass.

As soon as he got close enough, Bee plowed a finger into Tank's chest. "What do you think you're doing?"

Tank backpedaled. He opened his mouth, but snapped it closed again just as quickly. He clenched his teeth and fisted his hands at his sides.

Bee didn't give him a chance to say anything, even if he'd wanted to. "Stephanie is the best thing that ever happened to you, and this is how you repay her? I don't think so, mister. Now, you can just break it off with that hussy, and go home and apologize and beg for Stephanie's forgiveness, or you can stand here with that stupid grin on your face, and you and me are going to go at it." Bee lifted his fists and crouched in a not-half-bad fighter's stance he must have seen on TV.

Cass had been so busy watching Bee that she hadn't even noticed the ear-to-ear grin Tank wore before Bee pointed it out.

Bee's face reddened, and a vein in his forehead throbbed.

She'd never seen him so angry. She thought about stepping in, but she was afraid he'd take a swing at any moment and she'd get decked.

"Look, Bee . . ." Tank lifted his hands. "I apologize."

"Not to me, you jerk, to Stephanie."

"No, I apologize to you." He dropped one hand to his hip and rubbed the other over his hair, his gaze focused on Bee's platform shoes, then he sighed and lifted his gaze. "I apologize for judging you without getting to know you, for not seeing what a good friend you are."

Bee lowered his hands but still stood his ground. He'd waited a long time for Tank's acceptance.

"This is not what you think, but you are an amazing and loyal friend to Stephanie, and to me, and that means a lot." He studied Bee for another moment. "And now I have to ask you a favor."

26

Cass walked along the beach toward Mystical Musings. She'd had to leave Beast home so he wouldn't step on any broken glass. Hopefully, he'd behave.

The insurance company had already assessed the damage, and Tank had called and said she could go back in and start to clean up. And she only had four days to do it if she was going to pull off the party she was planning for Saturday night. She smiled to herself. That was just what she needed, a night spent with friends and no worries. And they had plenty to celebrate, starting with Cass's vow to stay out of police investigations.

A piece of driftwood caught her eye, and she picked it up and ran her finger along its smooth surface.

She felt bad about not spending more time with Luke over the weekend, but once again, life had interfered. Oh, well, nothing to be done about that. Maybe Stephanie or Bee could be talked into watching Beast for a weekend and she could take the ferry over and visit him. Then she'd get a chance to wear the little black dress that now hung in her closet.

Thankfully, no more visions had plagued her since Kelly had appeared to Artie Becker. Maybe his apology had satisfied her. A memory of the overwhelming sense of fear she'd experienced during the reading came back in full force. Or maybe Kelly was too terrified to return.

Cass tossed the driftwood aside and brushed off her hands.

The art gallery's back door stood open, so she headed up the beach. She'd invite Leighton to the party, then head to Mystical Musings. Tank had said the damage was confined to the window, which was boarded up and would be replaced the next day, and one wall of shelves. The insurance company would pay for someone to come in and clean up the glass, but she wanted to see if anything could be salvaged first.

She lifted her hand to knock on the open door.

A man's angry voice made her pause. ". . . had it last, Leighton."

"You were sleeping with her." Leighton's voice was calm and ice-cold. "That wasn't part of the deal."

"I told you, I had no choice."

She snorted. Very unladylike, though Cass couldn't blame her if that was her fiancé she was arguing with and he'd cheated on her.

Cass started to back away. She'd just leave them to their argument and come back later.

"That's it, Leighton. I've had it." Something shattered.

Leighton screamed.

Cass's insides tightened up, and she froze, then crept back to the gallery. No way could she leave a woman in danger. She would not get involved, but she could just sneak a peek and make sure Leighton was okay, then back out and call the police if she needed help.

"I want it, and I want it now."

Cass peeked through the back door. The door to the gallery stood partway open, but she couldn't see past it. She ducked behind the center island and crept closer.

"Oh, please. How can you be so sure she was even wearing it?" Leighton sounded a little more frazzled than she had before.

"Because she never took it off!"

"Whatever. I don't have time for this, Vincent. I don't know where the necklace is, and the engagement is off. And you are not getting the ring back."

"That necklace is worth a fortune. I don't care about the ring."

"Nice. Glad our engagement meant so much to you."

Cass peered around the corner, getting a good view of the gallery's interior and Vincent DiSilva's rigid posture as he confronted Leighton.

"I have asked you repeatedly, and every time you either blow me off or come up with another excuse. I tolerated it, because I figured I could find the necklace on my own. But I am about out of patience. There's nowhere left to look, and you were the only other person who knew about it." He pointed his finger an inch from her face and started moving forward. "This is the last time I'm going to ask, Leighton, and then you're going to wind up right next to Kelly. She never took that necklace off, said her father gave it to her, and it was special. He told her to keep it hidden so her mother wouldn't hock it for drug money. She wore it tucked beneath her shirt. Always. Other than when you were painting that portrait, which took me forever to talk her into posing with the necklace for, and even then she only agreed because that stupid old-fashioned getup she wore made the necklace look like a prop."

Leighton backpedaled until she hit the counter. "Then she was probably buried with it."

"She wasn't. I just spoke to my brother. That stupid reporter he cozied up to told him there was no jewelry found with the body."

"Oh, please. How would she know?"

"She talked to a cop, Leighton. Now, this is your last chance. This is the last place Kelly was, and she was wearing the necklace. Somewhere between here and her sandy grave, that necklace disappeared."

"Maybe it fell off. Have you searched the beach?"

He stared at her, but didn't say anything.

"I suggest you get yourself a metal detector and go search the beach between here and there before you come back in here making accusations." Leighton shoved him back and shouldered past him, then rounded the counter and stood behind the register. "Now get out of my shop before I call the police."

"Yeah, right." His cruel laughter made Cass's skin crawl. "I'll be back tomorrow, after I search the beach, and you'd better hope I find that necklace."

She waved him off, and he stormed out of the shop.

Leighton watched him go, then slumped onto the counter. Her shoulders shook as she cried.

Cass resisted the urge to go to her and offer comfort. She obviously knew her fiancé had killed Kelly, yet she hadn't reported it, even when questioned by the police. Cass wasn't excusing what Leighton had done, but Leighton was clearly afraid of him. If she came forward now and told the police what she knew, maybe they'd go easy on her.

Cass backed around the island. She had to get out of there. She'd call Tank and let him decide how to handle it. When she reached the back door, she held her breath and peeked around the corner to make sure Vincent was gone. Running into him on the deserted beach was the last thing she needed.

"Cass?"

She jumped and spun toward Leighton's voice. "Uh . . ."

"What are you doing here?"

Guilt had to be written all over her face. "I . . . uh . . ."

Leighton frowned and started toward her.

Cass hesitated. Confront her, or let it go? "I came to invite you to Harry's retirement party. I'm having it at Mystical Musings on Saturday night." She smiled, she hoped warmly, though her insides quivered. "Everyone will be there, so I figured you might like to come."

Leighton studied her a moment longer, then smiled. "Sure. I'd love to come, but will you have the shop cleaned up in time?"

Cool as could be. Either she didn't realize Cass had overheard her argument, or she was a much better liar than Cass.

"I hope so. I'm headed over there now to see how much damage there is."

"Oh." She eyed Cass for a second longer, then stepped

back. "Come on in for a minute and let me lock up. Then I'll take a walk over with you."

Indecision beat at her, but in the end she followed Leighton into the shop. "I don't think there's much damage, just a lot of cleanup."

"That shouldn't be too hard then. Will you have time to get everything ready?"

Cass shrugged. Sweat trickled down her back, and she kept her distance as Leighton grabbed her keys from her bag and locked the front door. "I think so. I already spoke to Isabella Trapani, and she'll cater it. Gina, from Tony's Bakery, will make the desserts. So all I really have to do is set up and make coffee, which I do for the group readings every month, anyway."

When Leighton turned and started for the back, Cass cut in front of her. As uncomfortable as she felt having Leighton at her back, she didn't want her to make it to the door first. Then Cass would be trapped between the locked front door and Leighton.

She didn't dare ignore the apprehension gnawing at her gut. She preceded Leighton out the back door and started down the walkway to the beach while Leighton locked up.

"Wait up." Leighton hurried to her side, and they headed down the beach together.

She had to get help.

The air in front of Cass shimmered, and she slowed down. Great. Just what she needed.

A hazy figure of a man appeared down the beach, just before Mystical Musings.

Cass stopped and stared at the unexpected visitor.

"Cass? Are you okay?"

The figure held up a hand in a stop gesture.

"Cass?"

"Oh, uh . . . sorry. My mind wandered."

Leighton frowned at her but resumed walking when Cass did.

The man winked out of existence.

"So, who else will be at the party?"

"Bee and Stephanie, Tank . . ." She'd called Luke and asked him to come, but he already had plans for the weekend. Something important, though he'd been in a hurry and hadn't told her what. "Emmett and Sara. Have you met Emmett?"

"No. I haven't had the pleasure yet."

They had almost reached Mystical Musings when the figure appeared again. An older man with a full white beard and a fisherman's cap, the brim pulled low over his eyes. Tattered clothing hung from his robust frame. He held up his hand again as if holding her back, or warning her away.

Sweat soaked her shirt and dripped down the sides of her face. Her heart hammered painfully against her ribs, and she could barely suck in a breath with the pressure on her chest.

She stood on the beach staring at the man, then let her gaze play over the back of the shop. The door was closed, but she couldn't see in with the boards over the back window.

"Is something wrong?" A note of impatience had crept into Leighton's tone.

"No, I . . . ummm . . . We should go around the front. There's a ton of glass all over in the back."

"Oh, right. You never said, did they catch whoever did it yet?"

She shook her head and rounded the shop, then pulled

her cell phone out of her pocket. "I just have to call Bee and let him know I'm here. He was going to meet me here when I was ready."

When Leighton didn't protest, Cass dialed. No way would she put Bee in danger again.

Tank answered on the second ring. "Hey, Cass. What's up?"

Her voice shook, but she couldn't help it. "Hey, Bee. I just wanted to let you know I'm at the shop and ready to start cleaning up now if you want to come over."

Leighton narrowed her eyes as she watched Cass.

Tank didn't say anything at first. Had he understood? "Sorry, Cass, you got me, not Bee."

"Yes, thanks. I'll be waiting for you."

"Is something wrong?"

"Yes."

"I'm on my way."

Her hand shook as she disconnected, and she dropped the phone in the sand. "Great," she muttered.

Leighton bent to retrieve the phone for her, and a heavy opal fell out from beneath her shirt and swung from the silver chain around her neck. She pulled a small gun from a holster on her ankle beneath her wide pant leg, then tossed the phone aside and looked around the deserted beach.

The shops hadn't opened yet, and tourist season hadn't started. Unless a jogger or a dog walker happened by, she and Leighton were alone.

"I'm sorry, Cass. I really am."

"I don't understand." But she was terrified she actually did.

"Walk." Leighton gestured ahead of her. "Around the shop and straight to the front door."

Cass nodded and started walking. "Why are you doing this?"

"There's no way you missed my conversation with Vincent."

Probably best to just fess up. "No, I didn't."

"Then you understand why I can't let you live. If it makes you feel any better, though, you were going to die, anyway. At first, I thought you were nothing more than a nuisance, that I could just scare you off. You actually proved to be a little more . . . adept than I gave you credit for. Couldn't have dear, sweet Kelly giving you any tips that would lead you to her killer, now, could we? Now start walking. And don't bother stalling. Bee can either get here in time to find your body, or he can get here early and join you. I don't care either way."

"Did you kill Kelly because Vincent was sleeping with her?"

"Stupid . . ." They reached the front steps and Leighton shoved her toward them.

Tank wasn't going to make it in time.

"He actually thought I wouldn't figure it out. He left her alone with me while I painted her portrait so he'd have a picture of that stupid necklace, wanted to show it to someone who'd know for sure how much it was worth. He was obsessed with that stupid thing. Did he really think she wouldn't talk about her lover?"

The old fisherman appeared again, this time on the boardwalk to her left.

Cass started to reach into her pocket.

Leighton pressed the gun against the small of her back. "What are you doing?"

"I-I-I . . ." She took a deep breath. "The key."

Leighton stepped back. "Go ahead."

Cass stuck her hand in her pocket. She gripped the small ring with the keys to her house and the shop, positioning the two keys between her fingers. She closed her fist over them, with the pointy ends sticking out, and watched Leighton's reflection in the front window. She'd only have one chance—

Ice-cold wind whipped across the decking from her left.

Cass swung around, knocking the gun away with her left hand and plowing her fist and the keys into Leighton's face. Without waiting for Leighton to recover, she dove over the deck railing and rolled underneath.

Tank's car barreled around the corner into the parking lot and skidded to a stop in the gravel. He flung the door open and crouched behind it, gun aimed at Leighton. "Drop the gun. Now."

Harry jumped out of the other side, gun drawn.

Cass crawled beneath the boardwalk decking. When she reached the edge closest to the parking lot, she stopped and tried to signal to Tank.

Leighton fired. A small spray of gravel in front of Tank's car shot up.

"This is your last chance, Leighton. Drop the weapon."

Cass held her breath. She could see Leighton's feet in the spaces between the boards above her, but she couldn't see what she was doing.

A police cruiser slammed on its brakes in the middle of the street, screeching to a stop before two officers jumped out, weapons drawn.

Leighton's gun landed in the sand in front of Cass with a small thud.

Cass sat in the sand, her back pressed against the cool,

concrete foundation of Mystical Musings. She pulled her knees up to her chest, lowered her head, and cried.

Footsteps pounded above her as the officers arrested Leighton.

Tank crawled under the decking and sat beside her. "Are you hurt?"

She shook her head.

"You really need to stop doing this to me, you know." He put his arm around her and pulled her close.

She buried her face against him and kept crying.

Tank just held her and let her cry until she regained her composure. "You okay, now?"

She sniffed and nodded.

"Good. Now, come on. Let's get out of here before Bee sees us and thinks something's going on. I wouldn't want to get shot at and get my butt kicked all in the same day."

27

Cass moved through the upstairs room, greeting everyone she'd missed on their way in. The cleanup hadn't been nearly as bad as she'd expected, and she'd been able to open the shop by Friday. Business had been booming ever since.

She laid a hand on Beast's head. "You behave now, boy."

He barked once.

Yeah right. She'd already lost a tray of cheese and crackers, but she didn't have the heart to lock him up. It was a party for all of her closest friends, after all, and who was a closer friend than Beast?

"Thank you so much for everything, Cass. I can't tell you what it means to me having everyone with me to celebrate." Harry hugged her.

"You're welcome, Harry."

He stepped back and smiled, his eyes twinkling. "And

LENA GREGORY

thanks for making my last week so memorable." His boisterous laughter followed him into the crowd as he walked away.

"Come on." Bee grabbed her arm. "It's time."

"Oh, wow." She hurried down the stairs behind him.

Stephanie sat at the table in the back corner of the shop. Alone.

Cass and Bee slid chairs on either side of her and sat.

"Hey. You okay?" Cass asked.

She offered a sad smile and nodded. "Yeah. I am."

Bee squeezed her hand. "What are you doing sitting here all alone?"

She shrugged. "I don't know. Tank told me to wait here. Said he'd be right back."

The back door opened, and Tank walked in, a huge bouquet in his hand. He handed Stephanie the flowers.

Bee got up and turned his chair to face Stephanie so Tank could sit with her. He took the flowers and put them on the table, then moved behind Cass's chair, tears in his eyes.

Tank sat and held both of Stephanie's hands in his. He glanced at Cass and Bee, then took a deep breath. "At first, I thought this should be a private conversation, but since Bee and Cass are our best friends, and they already know, well . . . I wanted them to be here with us."

Stephanie frowned. "Already know what?"

"I've been talking to a woman, and . . . Look, Stephanie, we've been trying for a while now to have a baby, and it hasn't been working." He shook his head and looked into her eyes. "The disappointment in your eyes when the doctor said it probably wasn't going to happen broke my heart. And I never wanted you to go through that pain again if I could help it. So, I didn't want to say anything to you until I knew more. I spoke to a woman I know who runs a program for unwed mothers."

Stephanie's breathing hitched.

"She called me last week, and I met her in Southampton. A young girl she knows is pregnant and would like to put the baby up for adoption. I've already filled out all the paperwork, and . . . well . . . she's considering our application. She'd like to meet with us next week."

"Oh, Tank." She flung herself into his arms and cried.

Tank ran a hand over her hair and held her close, eyes closed as tears flowed down his cheeks.

Bee sniffed and grabbed a box of tissues. He took a handful, then handed some to Cass and left the box on the table.

Stephanie turned to Bee and Cass. "And you guys knew?"

They nodded.

She threw her arms around them. "I love you guys."

"We love you, too."

Bee and Cass left them to share a private moment. When they reached the top of the stairs, Chief Rawlins stopped her.

"Do you have a minute, Cass?"

"Sure. I'll catch up in a couple of minutes, Bee."

"Sure thing. I'll go check on Beast."

"Thanks." Not wanting to interrupt Stephanie and Tank, Cass led the way to her new office. "We can talk in here."

Chief Rawlins preceded her into the room, and Cass closed the door behind them.

The chief got right to the point. "I'm impressed with you, Cass. And I just wanted to take a moment to let you know my door is always open."

"Thank you."

"And I'm sure Tank already told you, but we were able

to arrest Vincent DiSilva for breaking into your shop. And for throwing the brick through your window. Apparently you were starting to make Leighton nervous, so he tried to get you to back off." She pursed her lips. "Though I haven't yet figured out how to get him as an accessory in Kelly's murder."

"So Leighton killed her alone?"

Chief Rawlins shrugged. "It looks like it, probably in a fit of jealous rage."

Cass nodded. That was pretty much what she figured. "Oh, by the way, did you ever find out what she and Artie Becker were arguing about?"

"Yes. We brought Mr. Becker in for questioning again, and he admitted to confronting her about the painting. He thought he recognized the woman in the portrait as Kelly, but the necklace he'd given her was a dead giveaway. He also admitted to confronting Kelly and Vincent, but after Kelly disappeared, he was afraid to come forward. Too much similarity to his wife's fate."

Cass could see why he might have been reluctant to get involved, but still, Kelly was his daughter. She shrugged it off. In the end, it probably wouldn't have mattered. In his own way, he'd at least tried to find her.

"The only thing left to wrap up is who the skeleton you found belongs to, but we don't think it's related to this case."

"I have a sneaking suspicion it's going to turn out to be an old fisherman." Cass smiled at a fond memory of the vision she'd seen when she was on the beach with Leighton. She kept that to herself, for now anyway. Cass extended her hand to the chief. "Thank you."

She smiled as she shook hands. "And thank you."

Cass started to pull away.

Chief Rawlins gripped her hand tighter and held her gaze. "But one of these days, I want to hear the story about that fisherman's ghost."

Cass grinned and promised to fill her in, then sent her off to get something to eat and went in search of her friends. It was time to enjoy the party.

She found Bee guarding the food table. "Should I even ask?"

"One piece of sandwich someone left a little too close to the edge."

Cass laughed. "Okay, so not a complete catastrophe."

"Not yet, anyway." Bee winked. "You know, I was thinking about something."

"Oh?" Cass popped a piece of cheese into her mouth.

"Do you think they'll let Leighton paint my sunset while she's in prison?"

Cass choked down the cheese and took a mouthful of water.

"What? I already put a deposit on it, and I really wanted that painting."

"I don't think so, Bee."

He sulked. "Just because she's a killer doesn't make her any less talented, you know."

"You're right." She squeezed his arm. "I'll find out who we can ask."

He grinned. "It's going to look great on that wall."

Stephanie came up beside them and hooked her arm through Bee's. "Tank told me what you did, Bee. Thank you."

He kissed her cheek. "You know I'd never let anyone hurt my girls. I don't care who it is."

Tank stood in front of the room and called for everyone's attention.

Cass leaned forward past Bee to look at Stephanie. "I thought you weren't going to share it with everyone until you were sure things would work out."

She grinned. "We're not."

Tank held up his hands for quiet. "First, I'd like to congratulate Harry on his retirement."

Applause thundered through the room.

He lifted his glass. "And offer a toast to the greatest partner I could have asked for."

Everyone lifted their glasses in honor of Harry's service.

Harry's cheeks flushed purple with all the attention as he thanked them.

"And I figured now was as good a time as any to introduce my new partner." Tank gestured toward the stairway. "Luke Morgan."

Luke leaned against the railing. His gaze collided with Cass's, and that slow, sexy smile that made her heart stutter spread across his face. He waved an acknowledgment to the crowd of onlookers, then headed straight for Cass.

He took her in his arms and brushed a light kiss along her lips, but this time, he didn't stop. He deepened the kiss until Cass's knees went weak, then pulled back and looked at her. "I wanted it to be a surprise."

Her heart fluttered. "It definitely was."

He glanced over her head. "We had concerns Bee would spill the beans."

She whirled around to face Bee. "You knew?"

"Of course, I did, dear. He wanted to surprise you, but

he also wanted to make sure you'd be happy about it. Who better to ask than your best friends?"

Cass threw her arms around Bee and Stephanie. She couldn't think of a better way to spend a peaceful summer on Bay Island than with her best friends. And, hopefully, no bodies.

Ready to find
your next great read?

Let us help.

Visit prh.com/nextread

Penguin
Random
House